MARSHAL

BOOK 3 ~ TIN STAR K9 SERIES

JODI BURNETT

❀ Created with Vellum

United States Marshals Service
~ Justice, Integrity, Service ~

PROLOGUE

Ray straightened the tie on his rented tux and pulled open the front door of Kaysville Gems, a jewelry store in an up-scale suburb on the outskirts of Salt Lake City. He held the seemingly ordinary glass door for an elegantly dressed middle-aged couple, allowing them to enter before him. The woman, wearing a full-length, black evening gown offered him a faint wispy smile. "Thank you," she murmured.

He looked her directly in the eye and nodded, forcing himself not to stare at the intricate alarm system that ran through the doorframe where it attached invisibly to the thick glass. He smiled at the guard surveilling the guests as they filtered through the security portal. Ray's gut tightened as he stepped through the metal detector, even though he wasn't carrying anything that could set off the alarm. It was a natural response born from living under the constant eye of suspicion.

The glitzy event hosted by the jewelry store was a fundraiser for a local charity supported by the Junior League. Men boasting expensive watches and cufflinks escorted women who wore their most exquisite jewels. The festivity served as a backdrop for the guests to show off their wealth and get them to outdo each other in donations. It was everything Ray had hoped for.

He lifted a Baccarat crystal flute filled with golden champagne and pretended to sip, not wanting alcohol to dull his focus. Ray had grown his dark wavy hair long and let his beard fill in thick and full before he went to the barber and had both impeccably groomed. On this night, he was every inch the wealthy business executive. His green contact lenses seemed to attract several feminine glances, which was fine because tomorrow he'd look completely different.

One of his partners, Jason, headed toward him carrying a tray of canapes. Jason had applied for a job with the event's caterer six months ago and was now a trusted employee, one of the few who was asked to work this gig.

Ray tilted his head close to an elderly woman standing next to him. "May I compliment you on your earrings? They are spectacular."

Her veined hand reached up to touch the gems matching the collar of diamonds and emeralds draped around her crepey neck. "Thank you," she warbled. "The set was an anniversary gift."

Jason approached and offered them a selection of hors d'oeuvres. Ray waited politely for the woman to choose one before he did, ignoring Jason entirely. While the woman prattled on about her fifty-eight years of marriage, Ray watched his partner in his periphery. Jason moved around the room, eventually producing a bottle of green sports drink, which he kindly handed to the guard at the front door. The uniformed man accepted it gratefully, thirsty from standing under the bright lights beaming down on him in his heavy protective gear.

Reggie, their third partner, waited outside in a blue

Sprinter van. He was the team's tech expert, general hacker, and Ray's younger brother. Reggie was an electronic magician accomplishing feats Ray had no hope of ever understanding. The kid had discovered a way to override the jewelry store's security cameras and alarm system, but Ray and Jason would have only seconds to get what they came for and get out.

An abundance of precious gems was on display, along with enough gleaming ice to freeze the city. Ray tamped down a desire to second-guess himself about the timing. If only they had an extra five minutes. He made his way around the room, nodding to other guests, but avoiding any conversation someone might remember later. The social hour was in full swing, and it was mere seconds until go-time. He wended through the affluent crowd and got into position.

With his platter empty of food, Jason silently moved around the jewelry counters collecting discarded glasses and trash. On the edge of his tray was a crumpled black cloth disguised as an ordinary napkin, and its sight caused Ray's pulse to race. Sweat dampened the back of his neck and gathered along his hairline. Hopefully, no one noticed. He couldn't afford to stand out in any way.

The noise of the room echoed inside Ray's head, but he forced his breath to remain steady. Any minute now. He edged closer to the statuesque woman in the black gown he had held the door for earlier. He didn't make direct eye contact but admired her heavy diamond necklace with its ruby pendant from the corner of his eye. This was his primary target. He also wanted the emerald cuff bracelet that hung from the old woman's wrist.

Jason set his tray down on a tripod holder at the edge of the room. His gaze clashed with Ray's the instant before the lights went out. Surprised murmurs rumbled through the gallery, and all movement stilled. The manager of the jewelry store spoke above the din. "Don't worry folks. We've experienced minor electrical outages before. Our generators will come on in just a few seconds."

Ten seconds, in fact. Ray grinned to himself as he bumped into the woman who wore his prize. With his left hand, he gripped her elbow to steady her. "Excuse me, I'm terribly sorry. Are you alright?" he apologized while unclasping her necklace with his right hand. He jostled her again as he removed the gems while laughing with her at his clumsiness. He had three seconds to get to the tray without bumping into anyone else. The lights flickered as he slid the necklace into the sack doubling as a napkin. Its weight told him Jason had beaten him to it with the cuff.

Ray lifted the bag, tucked it into an inner pocket in his suit coat, and slid through the door to the back room where the catering was staged. The lights flickered, which he took as his signal to get out *fast.* Ray was out of time. He pushed through the emergency exit, praying the alarm remained disconnected. The door closed behind him, latching in the same second as the lights glared back on with blinding illumination.

"Hey—you! Don't move! What are you doing out here?" a gravelly voice shouted from the dark shadows of the alley, and Ray's blood turned to ice. This was not part of the plan.

Ray squeezed a chuckle from his throat. "Oh, man. You scared me."

The dark figure he hadn't anticipated stepped into the glow of the streetlight. "Slowly raise your hands so I can see them."

"What's the problem?" Ray asked as he complied with the order.

"Why are you sneaking out the back door? No one is allowed to come in or out of this door tonight."

Ray shrugged. "Sorry. The lights went out inside, and I'm claustrophobic."

"Face the wall and place your palms against the bricks above your head."

This guy was no push-over. The guard inside should be incapacitated—vomiting all over himself by now, if not dead already—but they hadn't planned on a back-door guard hiding in the alley. Ray had no time for even the slightest delay if he hoped to get away with his prize. Blood pounded in his head as he raced to think of a way to avoid being frisked. "Why? Are you a cop or something? Can I see some ID?" Ray's chest tightened, and his throat constricted. This chump was going to bust him with close to a million dollars' worth of stolen jewelry.

"Turn around." The guard's gun flashed in the beam of a streetlight as he reached to turn Ray toward the wall.

A whoosh of fabric whispered in the dark before a loud crack sounded behind him. The guard collapsed to the pavement, and Ray spun around, coming face to face with the third member of their gang.

"Thank God, Reggie! Where did you come from?" Ray stared down at the man's crushed skull.

Reggie held a bloody tire-iron in his fist, raising it again for a second blow. With the second club, blood and brain splattered on their pants and shoes.

"That's enough. You can't make him more dead than he is. Let's go!" Ray grabbed his brother's arm and turned away. Together, they raced toward the open side door of the van and dove in. Reggie clambered into the driver's seat. Without waiting for Ray to shut the door or hold on, he floored the vehicle and sped out into the night. Ray fought to yank the door closed and collapsed against the seat when the handle finally latched.

Jason remained inside the jewelry store where he would

face long hours of police searches and interrogation—but that was part of the plan. Jason was their eyes and ears. In one month, they'd all meet at the designated spot before making their way to a remote hideout, where they'd stay and wait for things to cool down.

Reggie sped across town to a grocery store parking lot where a second getaway car waited. As they sailed through the dark streets, Ray slid the gems out of the bag and stared at the diamonds glittering in the passing lights. He thumbed the ruby and pictured the elegant stones gracing the neck and wrist of the woman he loved before he gently wrapped each piece of jewelry in bubble wrap and slid them into separate pre-addressed boxes.

He removed his colored contacts. Tomorrow, he'd shave his face and head, making himself unrecognizable in black jeans, t-shirt, and a black leather jacket. Meanwhile, Reggie would take the jewelry to two different packaging stores and ship them to a motel room rented by a false company in Idaho.

Ray conjured an image of his lady wearing the ruby necklace. He thought back the day they met, years ago, in Denver. He'd been standing on the sidewalk, casing a bank across the street, when a beautiful woman backed out of the store behind him and bumped into him. The collision caused her to drop her shopping bag and a cheap piece of costume jewelry fell out and broke. The plastic gems scattered across the sidewalk and heavy trembling tears filled her eyes.

Ray had helped her gather the fake rubies and then took her out for a cup of coffee. She shared how she had never owned any jewelry—or anything nice, for that matter. And even though she had no place to wear anything like that, she wanted it. She said it made her feel like a princess. Growing up she never had any fancy things and the wistfulness in her eyes as she spoke made Ray want to give her the world.

There were a few roadblocks standing in his way, but he'd take care of those.

It was love at first sight for him on that blustery afternoon, and the more Ray heard about her difficult life, the more he wanted to take care of the beautiful creature sitting across from him. Over the past several years, even though he never stayed anywhere for long, they'd found ways to be together. They were in love and now it was finally time to do something about it. She had finally agreed to leave with him.

She would get to wear this ruby and know what the real thing felt like, but she couldn't keep it. He wished she could, but they had to sell the necklace to build their future. The emerald cuff, however, was meant for her, and one day, he'd get her another diamond encrusted ruby of her own.

1

Deputy Caitlyn Reed sat with her boots propped up on the corner of her desk in the Moose Creek County Sheriff's Office. Her dog, Renegade, dozed on his bed next to her while she read the morning paper. The entire front page of the Moose Bugle featured articles about the recent Russo murder trial. A color photo of Caitlyn and her Belgian Malinois escorting a hand-cuffed Stephano Russo into the courthouse was splashed across the page. Talk about incredible campaign promo! She couldn't have asked for anything better—and it was free. Caitlyn smiled to herself and settled back to read the headline article. Colt Branson had been there too, but the photographer didn't catch him in the image. How would he feel about that? Caitlyn was running against him for Moose Creek Sheriff, and there was only one more day before the election.

For the millionth time, Caitlyn second-guessed her decision to stay in the race for Sheriff. She loved police work, and she was naturally good at it. Renegade was the perfect K9 partner, too. It made absolute sense until she considered the Colt factor. She and Colt were finally working things out between them, and it seemed that their relationship was going well. What would happen to all of that if she won? Hell, what would happen if *he* won? Colt had wanted to be a sheriff since he was a kid, but could she be genuinely happy for him if the people elected him instead of her?

Colt pushed through the office door, balancing two cups of coffee in a cardboard carrier, and holding a folded newspaper. Renegade jumped up to greet him, and after Colt handed Caitlyn her coffee, he took a minute to stroke her dog's red-gold fur. The paper rattled when he unfolded it to study the front-page article she'd been looking at. "Nice shot of you and Ren." He grinned at her, seemingly unbothered by her free publicity. His lack of concern surprised her.

"Thanks. It was a shocker to see us on the front page."

"It's big news around here. Too bad there isn't a picture of us driving behind the US Marshal's Suburban to the airport." Colt set his steaming cup on his desk and sat on the edge. "That was kinda cool, don't you think? It sort of felt like we were playing in the big leagues. Can you imagine having a Learjet at your disposal?"

"Nope, I can't. I'll tell ya, it sure stunned me when Marshal Williams called to ask us to accompany her men." Caitlyn turned back to the paper and sipped her creamy coffee.

"Still, I'm glad the anonymous tip of a possible ambush ended up being a false alarm. Russo is now the NYPD's problem and is safely locked up awaiting his court date. I wonder if they'll make him spend time in prison before they enter him into the witness program?"

"Depends on how valuable the information he provides is, I suppose."

"Yeah." Colt twirled his coffee cup in circles on his desk. "It was amazing to be part of a federal operation, but I would have rather been out to dinner with you. Seems like we never can make our fancy night out happen."

Caitlyn peered at him over the top of her cup as she sipped and smiled. "True. And now, I suppose we should wait till after the election. You know—let the dust from the trial settle and all."

"Why? I still want to celebrate your graduation from the academy."

"We're way past that by now, don't you think? That was months ago, and besides, I already had a party and everything." She winked at him, only half teasing.

"Well, we could always celebrate the successful murder investigation and trial." Colt's brows dipped.

"We don't need an excuse, you know." Caitlyn laughed. "I want to go out, but I think we should keep our relationship low-key until after the election. Let's not go public until after that. We don't want the gossip mill churning overtime. After the votes come in, we can go all out and celebrate everything: my graduation, the investigation, and the winner of the election."

Colt pushed himself up from the desk and walked across the office to her—his hazel eyes sparkling. "Okay, fine. But I'm not going to wait that long to kiss you." He tilted her chin upward and held her gaze as he bent down and pressed his lips against hers.

Caitlyn's pulse quickened as her body responded to him. She sat up and slid her hand to the back of his head to pull him closer. After a minute, she leaned back, smirking. "This is completely inappropriate office behavior, Sheriff."

"File a formal complaint with your boss." He kissed her forehead.

Caitlyn stood and gently pushed Colt's chest with her hands. "Let's continue this discussion after work tonight. Right now, I need to go on my rounds."

Colt brushed his fingers over her cheek. "Your place, or mine?"

"Yours. Unless you want to have dinner with Dylan and McKenzie." She gave him a final peck before heading to the door. "See you in a bit. Ren, *kemne*."

Caitlyn patted her leg, and her tawny Belgian Malinois sprang to his feet and rushed to her side. She shut the door behind them and turning left, started their morning rounds. They walked up toward the vet's office and waved at Doctor Moore, who was getting out of his car.

"Good morning, you two. I saw your picture on the front page. Impressive," the vet called across the lot.

Caitlyn flushed. "Thanks. I've never had my picture in the paper before."

"Congratulations on catching the killer. We're all very proud of you and Renegade."

"It wasn't just us."

"And Colt too, of course." He waved a second time and disappeared inside his office.

Caitlyn and Renegade continued their walk along Main Street, passing several storefronts. As she peered into the shops, many folks inside waved. *People are awfully friendly now that they're no longer worried about a killer in their midst. They act like we're heroes or something.* Uncomfortable with that thought, she hesitantly raised her hand in response.

At the end of town, Caitlyn and Ren turned into the parking lot of the feed store. Her brother Dylan's F350 was there, parked alongside several other trucks, so Caitlyn led her dog inside. She nodded to Jim Miller, the owner, who stood behind the counter helping his customers. He waved and then started clapping. Others in the store joined him.

"Congratulations on catching the murderer, Deputy! You and Renegade made the front page!"

"Thanks, Jim." Caitlyn's neck heated, and blood rushed to her cheeks.

Dylan rounded the corner from the cattle-care aisle and beamed when he saw her. "There she is! My little sister—woman of the hour."

"Oh, come on, you guys. You're embarrassing me." Caitlyn regretted coming in and wanted to escape the attention. "I'm just making my rounds." She raised her hand in farewell and headed back toward the door.

Dylan followed her. "Has mom called you yet?"

"She tried, but I missed her call. I still need to listen to her message. Why?"

"She wants us all to be there for dinner on election night so we can watch the results on the news together. Think Colt will be up for it?"

"I'm sure he will. I'll ask him." Caitlyn pushed through the door. "See you later?"

Dylan nodded and Caitlyn left with Ren, hoping to avoid any more embarrassment. They crossed the street and made their way back down the other side. People passing in their cars honked and waved. Caitlyn waved back. She hadn't realized how relieved the townspeople were to have Russo behind bars. From her perspective, she was grateful they caught the killer and that it wasn't anyone she knew. Maybe now things could settle down.

Stephanie, the manager of the Moose Creek Café, parked on the street in front of the restaurant. She rounded her car and called out, "Hey, Caitlyn! You're a regular celebrity in town, what with your picture in the paper and all."

Caitlyn stifled an eye-roll. "Thanks."

"Folks are saying you're going to be the new sheriff." The woman gripped her hands together under her chin and offered a big toothy smile. "It's all so exciting!"

"It is, but honestly, I'll be glad when the election is over. I can't wait for things to get back to normal."

"That won't happen anytime soon. Not if you're elected."

"Whether I am, or not, I suppose things will change. But I'm looking forward to some quieter days either way." Caitlyn smiled through the lurking guilt swirling in the pit of her belly. If she won the election, it would force Colt to find another job. He'd be stepping down from Sheriff to a deputy position somewhere else. If Colt won, the same would be true for her. Only it would be a lateral move—not a demotion.

Stephanie patted Renegade's head. "Well, by the way folks are talking, looks like we'll be calling you Sheriff Reed in no time."

Caitlyn nodded and waved. "We'll see. Talk to you later, Steph."

"Bye." Stephanie ran up the wooden steps to the café, and the tantalizing scent of fresh-baked cinnamon rolls billowed out the door as she disappeared inside. Caitlyn's stomach rumbled with desire for one of the gooey buns.

"Come on, Ren." Caitlyn stepped away to finish her rounds. They walked several blocks to the other end of town where her friend and part-time dog trainer, McKenzie Torrington, was coming out of the Mercantile. "Hi, Kenz. Grocery shopping?"

"Yep. Saw your picture." She grinned and crouched down for a slobbery dog kiss. "Good morning, Renegade."

"I know. I know. It's like the whole town has gone crazy. I feel like a movie star or something. Everybody is waving and honking. It's weird."

McKenzie pushed the cart toward her car, and Caitlyn fell in step with her. "You can't blame them. I'm sure everyone feels safer knowing the murderer is behind bars."

"I know it's big news for this little corner of the world, but it wasn't just me who caught Russo."

"Of course not."

"But the way everyone is behaving, you'd think Ren and I solved the crime all by ourselves. I suppose it's because of the photo. I feel bad for Colt."

McKenzie lifted her bags into her back seat and side-eyed Caitlyn. "Bad enough to step out of the running for Sheriff?"

Caitlyn scrunched her lips to the side. "No..."

"Okay then. Enjoy the ride. If the article in the paper helps you win, then it's a great thing."

"I know, but I still feel bad for Colt."

"Cross that bridge when it comes." McKenzie closed the door and leaned against it. "By the way, have you talked to Dylan lately?"

"I just saw him at the feed store. Why?"

"No reason. It's just that he hasn't been returning my texts, and it seems like we haven't spoken much lately."

Caitlyn tilted her head and considered her friend. "Have you asked him about it?"

"Not really. I don't want to come across as pushy or needy. What if he's realizing he's not all that interested in me?"

"Yeah, right." Caitlyn smirked. "*That's* not it. But you know, fall is a really busy time on the ranch. I bet he's just bogged down with all the chores, and then by evening, he's exhausted. It's a good thing my mom cooks him dinner, or he'd probably be too tired to eat."

"You really think that's all it is?"

"Absolutely."

"Does your dad still work the ranch with him? I imagine Dylan needs help."

"I'd be surprised if Dylan doesn't hire a hand or two. My dad has been slowing down lately. Mom's been after him to see the doctor. Which is another reason Dylan could be preoccupied. I wouldn't worry about it." A sharp dart of concern pricked Caitlyn's heart. She looked forward to seeing her dad in person tomorrow night so she could see for herself how he was feeling. "Are you going to the ranch tomorrow to watch the election results?"

McKenzie gave her a blank look.

"My mom wants us all there for dinner and to watch the results together."

"Dylan hasn't said anything."

"I'm sure he will, but either way, I'm inviting you. So, can you come?"

"Yes—but only if Dylan wants me there."

"Don't read too much into his lack of communication. Truly."

McKenzie sighed and opened the driver's side door. "How do people make relationships work around their jobs?"

"I guess if they care about each other, they figure it out." Again, Caitlyn silently wondered if she and Colt could get past the election outcome. No matter what, one of them was going to be hurt. It was easy to say that loving couples worked everything out, but the reality of mixing career ambitions with love was nowhere near as simple as that.

McKenzie broke into her thoughts. "Speaking of figuring it out… whatever happened between you and Doctor Kennedy?"

"Blake?"

"Yeah. How did he take it when you told him you and Colt were getting together?"

The memory made Caitlyn's stomach feel oily. "He seemed to take in stride. After all, he might have been interested in me, but he hadn't developed any serious feelings, or anything."

"Is he staying in Moose Creek?"

"He said he'll give it a full year before he decides for sure, but I think he'll stay."

McKenzie tossed her purse inside the car, and her keys spilled out, jangling to the floor. "Didn't he buy a house?"

"Yes—up on the golf course. But if he decides to move, he can always use it as a weekend getaway or rent it out."

"I figured he was pretty serious about you when he made the purchase."

"Maybe, but much of what Blake says is just charm for charm's sake." Caitlyn stirred her fingers in the fur on top of Renegade's head. He sniffed her hand and licked her. "His uncle's practice is a mighty powerful incentive too."

"What do you think about him staying here? Any leftover feelings?"

Caitlyn shrugged. "I don't think I ever had any actual feelings for him other than attraction. I mean - those eyes!" She laughed.

"Don't forget his dimples." McKenzie grinned. "It's good you don't have any residual feelings because the gossip is he's been seen around town with Stephanie's friend, Kayla."

"Kayla Irwin?" Caitlyn's eyebrow quirked. The last time she'd seen Kayla was at her academy graduation party when she was hot after Colt. "I think she and Blake would make a nice couple."

McKenzie laughed at that. "I'm sure you do."

Caitlyn sent her a pretend glare. "Changing the subject—want to practice some tracking and attack drills with Ren and me later? I need someone to dress up in the padded suit." She grinned mischievously.

RAY SCROLLED through the Salt Lake City news on his phone and read all he could find about the jewelry store robbery while watching the local news on an old boxy TV. Their small gang's achievement was pasted in bright color across the news outlets. Reports of their incredible heist were touted across the nation with awe.

The robbery portion had gone smoothly, and so Ray's greater concern was the pending homicide investigation involving the two guards. His team had carefully planned for the demise of the inside guard. Prior to the event, Jason had mixed anti-freeze together with a green, lemon-lime sports drink, the flavor of which disguised the taste of the poison and made the guard's sudden death look like a heart attack. Of course, an autopsy would reveal the truth, but not until they were all long gone.

The second guard, who Reggie bludgeoned to death, had surprised them. When they left the man dead in the alley, they had kept the tire-iron his brother used to kill him, so unless there were hidden cameras from other local businesses that captured the scene, they should be scot-free. He considered the second guard a bonus unless they got caught. Then, they'd all be going away for the rest of their lives. The idea of such dangerous consequences thrilled him and lit sparklers in his brain.

Killing the guard in the alley had been necessary, but Ray had to admit that Reggie was becoming impulsively violent and getting harder to handle. He'd had to stop his brother from smashing the guy's scull in beyond recognition and costing them precious seconds they didn't have. The longer they spent at the scene, the more potential evidence they might leave behind, and the greater the chance of being caught.

Ray glanced at Reggie to see if he was working on his laptop or watching the news, but instead, his brother was wiping salt from the inside of a potato chip bag and licking his fingers. "Hey, Reg, are you paying attention? The cops suspect a man with long dark hair, green eyes, and a beard of robbing the jewelry and killing the guards." His laugh was low and gruff. "They think only one man stole the jewels before disappearing from the gala, and they have no other leads."

"Eventually, they'll watch the security video and see Jason hand the guard a drink." Reggie rattled the foil-lined bag. "Then they'll connect the dots."

"Yeah, but by then, Jason will be gone and will have a completely new look. Then, after a month of zigzagging around to a bunch of cities across the country, he'll finally join up with us."

While hiding out in a run-down motel on the outskirts of Rexburg, Idaho, the brothers waited for the two boxes of jewels addressed to the name on Ray's fake driver's license to arrive in the mail. They shared a dumpy, pay-by-the-week room with a tiny kitchenette doing their best not to attract any attention. Every few days, Ray asked the nicotine saturated man at the front desk if he'd gotten any packages.

Two weeks into their stay, the clerk shoved two small boxes across the counter with a grunt. Ray's pulse kicked, but before he snatched up his mail, he casually leafed through an old hunting magazine. He thanked the man but needn't have bothered since the guy had gone back to his TV program, ignoring him. Ray shrugged and left, forced himself to saunter back to the room. As soon as he entered, he locked the door and closed the drapes.

"Reggie! Wake up. They're here. Our packages are here." Ray tore into the cardboard and dumped the glittering jewelry on top of the 1970s brown and orange bedspread. The contrast was jarring. "Jason will be here in just a few weeks, and then we can go to our winter hideout."

"Why do we have to hide up in the wilderness?"

"Because, if we stay out of sight long enough, they'll forget about us. After that, we can really live."

During those long weeks, the brothers watched gameshows and reality TV to pass the time. The day Jason texted he'd be there the following day, Ray and Reggie went to the Army Surplus store to gather supplies. They ate steamed burgers on wilted buns from a nearby fast-food joint to celebrate. When they returned to their room, Ray packed their new survival purchases into three back-packs, while Reggie lay on the bed fiddling with a gallon-sized Ziplock bag filled with small packets.

"Leave that alone, Reg. We need it to start our empire."

"I'm just looking."

Yeah, right. "It won't be much longer. Just a few months, and we'll be able to set ourselves up real pretty. Then you can do what you want, but for now, stay out of that shit."

2

The night of the election, Colt stood in the great room of the Reeds' log cabin home. He'd practically grown up at Reed Ranch, running wild with Dylan, Logan, and Caitlyn through the mountains and pastures of the property. He couldn't remember a time before he knew the Reeds, and until he was about thirteen, he'd always thought of Caitlyn as one of the gang. She had no problem keeping up and was as tough as any of them until one day, Colt looked at her and a jolt of awareness caught him off guard. Suddenly, she was no longer one of the boys. But when he started treating her like she needed protection or when he attempted to help her do something her brothers did on their own, it earned him a painful punch in the arm and Caitlyn yelling, "What's wrong with you, Branson? I can do it myself. Get out of my way." He chuckled to himself, remembering those days years ago. He'd had no inkling how clearly that declaration defined the girl then, and the woman now.

Colt always felt at home at the Reed Ranch. Mr. and Mrs.

Reed—John and Stella—treated him like one of their own, and he thought of them in the same way. As an only child, Colt regarded the Reed kids as surrogate siblings who filled out what otherwise would have been a lonely life. His parents were good people, just poor. His dad worked two jobs and was too tired to care much about what went on in Colt's life. He was closer to his mother, but she too worked hard to put food on the table. When the time came to learn about life or receive a well-deserved talking-to, most often it was John Reed who was there for him.

Tonight was the first time he could think of when he felt uncomfortable in the midst of this family. They'd had dinner and were now waiting for the local news broadcast to inform them of the election results. John and Stella sat together on the sofa, holding hands, and Caitlyn was with McKenzie at the back of the room playing with Renegade and discussing dog training techniques. Colt accepted a bourbon from Dylan and stifled the urge to down it in one shot. He was sure Caitlyn was going to win the sheriff's badge away from him, and he was mostly okay with that. She deserved it. But it meant a lot of big changes in his life, like a new job and possibly even a new town.

"Nervous?" Dylan came around the bar and stood next to him. They sipped their drinks side-by-side and stared at the TV as they talked.

"Not really. Not about the election, anyway." Colt twisted the gold band he wore on his right pinky finger. "Maybe a little about how everyone is going to feel awkward afterwards."

"It'll be interesting, for sure." Dylan lifted his glass to Colt and then took a sip of the deep amber liquid. "If you don't win, I'd love to hire you to help me out here on the ranch until another law enforcement job opens up nearby."

"Thanks, Dylan. I might need to take you up on that." Colt welcomed the fortifying heat of the whiskey as it slid down his throat. "I've touched base with the sheriff over in Gillette and he said he'd hire me as soon as he could, but it may be a while before there are any openings."

"You'll never have any trouble finding work in law enforcement, but my offer is there if you need something between jobs."

"That means a lot. Thanks."

At the top of the hour, the newscast theme-music played, and everyone in the room stopped talking and turned to face the screen. Caitlyn crossed the room to stand next to him, her shoulder rubbing against his arm.

"In headline news tonight, we are bringing you the election results for the office of Moose Creek Sheriff." The news anchor gave a brief background on both candidates and concluded with a re-cap of the Stefano Russo murder case that they had recently solved. "Now, for the results of this very close vote." The pretty blonde announcer unfolded a sheet of paper on her desk. A glimmer passed through her eyes, and Colt accepted his fate. Women cheered other women on in the workforce. "The new Moose Creek County Sheriff is..."

He turned and held his hand out to Caitlyn, "Con—"

"Colt Branson!"

Colt's heart stuttered, and his mouth dropped open. Caitlyn's hands flew up to cover her mouth. She stared at the screen for a few seconds and blinked as her eyes moistened. She drew a deep breath in through her nose and flung her arms around his neck.

"Congratulations, Colt! I'm so happy for you." She buried her face in his shoulder and though there was truth in her words, Colt also heard her profound disappointment. If they were alone, they could talk this out, but Dylan was slapping him on his back and Stella filled glasses with champagne. During the celebratory well wishing, Caitlyn moved off to the side and kneeling, she busied herself with Renegade.

Colt wanted to go to her, but John called to him. The older man pushed himself up from the couch. He took a moment to steady himself before he reached his hand out in congratulations. "Well done, Colt. I'm proud of you, son."

This man calling him son meant more than any election. "Catie should have won," Colt murmured. "She's a better investigator."

John pulled him closer and gripped his shoulders. "Caitlyn is suited for this work, but her path will take her in another direction, one unique to her. This one is yours. You've earned it."

Colt clamped his teeth together to stave off tears of emotion mixed with the love he had for this man. John's body wavered, and Colt held him fast. "Are you feeling okay? Why don't you sit back down?"

John let Colt help him return to the couch. "I'm fine. Go get me a glass of that champagne, will you?"

"Sure." Colt glanced around the room to see if anyone else witnessed what just happened. He met Stella's concerned gaze before she lifted a flute and brought it to her husband.

When everyone had a glass, Stella asked Dylan to make the toast. His brows furrowed, and confusion washed through his eyes. "Toasts are Dad's forte."

"Of course, they are," Stella stared at her son, communicating something silently that Colt couldn't read. "But tonight, let's hear from you."

Dylan's gaze panned to his father, who was the only one in the room still sitting. A little furrow appeared between his dark brows before he cleared his throat and lifted his champagne. "Here's to the two best law enforcement officers Moose Creek has ever seen, and to Colt our official Sheriff. Congratulations. We'll all sleep safe knowing you're at the helm."

Colt sipped his champagne but sought Caitlyn out over the rim of his glass. She smiled at him and raised her drink before her eyes flicked away. He had no idea what to say to her, but he moved across the room to her, anyway. He leaned close to her ear. "This job should be yours. I'm sorry."

"No, Colt. You have far more experience than I do. The vote went the way it should. I want you to know I'm truly happy for you." She hugged him with her free arm. "But I would like to have tomorrow off if you don't mind. I need some time to myself."

A heaviness pressed against his chest. "Catie…"

"Really, Colt. I promise. I'm thrilled for you. I won't deny that I'm also disappointed, but it isn't the end of the world. I just need a little while to reflect on my next steps. Okay?"

"Of course. I wish—"

"Don't you dare wish that you didn't win. This is your dream, Colt. I'm so proud of you." Caitlyn wrapped her arms around his neck, rose onto her toes, and kissed him on the mouth. The conversation in the room stilled, and when Colt looked up, he saw John smile and nod. Caitlyn had never openly shown her feelings for him in front of her family before. That moment alone merited the champagne.

Caitlyn's throat had tightened when the newscaster announced Colt's election victory. She kept her face passive until she could manage a smile. She was excited and happy for Colt. He'd always wanted to be Moose Creek's Sheriff, and even though he'd held the position for several months already, it was only because the previous sheriff had been convicted of accessory to murder after the fact, along with a host of other criminal acts. When Sheriff Tackett was sent to prison, Colt, who had been the deputy at the time, stepped in. Now, the town had officially elected him for the job.

Though it pleased her that Colt wouldn't have to change jobs and could live his dream, Caitlyn also was disappointed. With the way folks in town had treated her the past week, she'd allowed herself to believe she would win the election. In her imagination, she had even practiced what she'd say to Colt. Now, her face heated at the arrogance of her thoughts.

She wanted to escape with Renegade and go out to the barn, but she stayed put. The right thing to do was celebrate Colt's victory. She truly was proud of him, and in a moment of clarity, she knew Colt was the wise choice. His investigative skills had increased, and he was already amazing at connecting with the people in town. Colt took the time to know them; to understand their lives and personal situations. In fact, she bet Colt knew whether Blake was dating Kayla, or not. Those were the kind of details she never focused on, though she admired that quality in Colt. Caitlyn was impulsive, often jumping in and grilling witnesses before creating rapport. Where could her crime fighting skills and her desire for justice be utilized in combination with her more direct approach? Was there a career in law enforcement that would encompass her style?

Caitlyn smirked at the memory of Colt teasing her about sounding like Joe Friday from the old black-and-white TV show *Dragnet*. "Just the facts, ma'am." It was true, she didn't have the patience or time to ask about someone's cousin or their grand-aunt's health.

"What's funny?" Colt searched her eyes.

"I'm thinking about how perfect you are for the Sheriff of Moose Creek. The voters know what they want."

Dylan flung an arm over her shoulder and side-hugged her. "I think the voters would love to keep both of you, but after that kiss, I'm guessing that's not possible." He chuckled. "It's about time."

Caitlyn pulled away and playfully slugged her brother's shoulder. "Shut up, Dylan. You have no room to talk."

"What do you mean?"

She lowered her voice. "Your single-mindedness about the ranch has McKenzie feeling like you might be having second thoughts about her." Dylan's baffled expression made her snort. "Go pay the woman some attention, you idiot." Caitlyn and Colt watched him wander over to McKenzie, who was chatting with Stella.

Colt rested his hand on the small of her back. "What are you going to do on your day off tomorrow?"

"I'll probably take Whiskey out for a long ride. I always think best when I'm up in the hills."

"Sure you don't want some company? I could meet you around four."

She touched his cheek, enjoying the rough feel of his evening whiskers. "I'm fine. Stop worrying about me. I think I'll head up past the ridge to the BLM space. I need some time to consider my options. That's all."

JASON ARRIVED on the evening bus from Boise. When his eyes met Ray's a wise-ass grin spread over his face. "We did it!"

"We sure as hell did." Ray grabbed his friend by the neck and pulled him into a hug. "I thought you'd never get here."

"You don't think I'd miss out on all the fun, do you?"

Ray chuckled and slapped Jason on the back. "Now that you're here, we can make our way to Wyoming."

"Do you have a car?"

Ray glanced at Jason from the side of his eye and grinned. "Not yet."

Later, while Ray waited at the streetlight with a sign pleading for money. Reggie and Jason hid on the backside of a dumpster in the alley behind an abandoned store. The old, pitted street was one that people drove on but never parked. The dead strip of empty shops served as a barrier between the worn-out town and its suburb. After an hour of loitering, an old Dodge Dart finally stopped at the traffic light on Ray's corner.

A frail looking old man rolled down his car window. "Having a rough time, son?" He nodded to Ray's sign.

Ray approached the car with his most charming smile. "Yes, sir. I just got back from Afghanistan and can't find a job."

"Well, that's a downright shame." The old man reached for his wallet. "Let me—"

Before the man could finish his sentence, Ray reached through the window and clamped his hand over the old man's mouth. He yanked open the door, pulling the elderly driver off his seat and then dropped him in a heap on the pavement.

"Come on, guys!" Ray called out. Reggie and Jason raced to the car and jumped in.

Ray kicked the old man who curled up and tried to roll away. "That's right, you old fart, get out of the way unless you want to get run over." He jumped into the driver's seat and peeled out. "Wyoming here we come!"

. . .

THEY DUMPED the old man's car on a gravel road in on the northern border of Wyoming where his lady waited for them. She agreed to drive them as close to their mountain hideout as she could.

Ray pulled her into his arms and kissed her hard. Gesturing to his brother and Jason, he said, "You two sit up front. We have some reacquainting to do." He opened her door and followed her onto the back seat. During the drive, Ray showed his woman the jewels and she gasped with delight. "Take these with you for safe keeping."

She nodded and after smoothing the large ruby over her cheek, she tucked the gems into her purse. Two hours later, Jason had driven as close as a car could get and pulled off to the edge of the two-track road.

"Let's get going. We still have a long trek ahead of us. We'll hike until dusk and then set up camp. We won't get to the cabin until tomorrow." Ray stared into his love's eyes. "It won't be long now, and we'll be together forever."

THE BEAMS from Caitlyn's headlights washed over the wood panels of the old red barn as she pulled into her parents' barnyard early the next morning. Renegade yawned, his pink tongue curling as he stretched his powerful jaws wide. Together, they slid open the tall doors. Enveloped with the comforting green scent of stacked hay, they padded inside to feed the horses. Caitlyn had brushed and saddled Whiskey before the moon and stars relinquished the dawn. She ran her hand down her horse's sleek neck, and he nickered at her.

"Good morning, fella. I need your grounded spirit today." It had been a hell of a night during which sleep was nowhere to be found. Riding in the mountains had always been her way of dealing with disappointment. Caitlyn was honestly happy for Colt, but his success left her without a clear direction. Growing up, she wasn't like the other girls she knew who spent hours on the phone with their girlfriends, giggling and hashing things out. Caitlyn looked to her animals and the land for comfort and clarity. With them, words were unnecessary.

The sky brightened as the trio followed the path along the far side of the arena toward the mountains, making their way past Lobo's memorial marker. Lobo had been her brother Logan's Army K9, and Caitlyn recalled how hard it had been for Logan to say goodbye. Her eyes flitted down to Renegade —her heart full of love for him. Moved by her sudden emotions, her eyes pricked, and a sob crept up her throat. As they took their first steps up the face of the ridge, Caitlyn let herself feel the weight of her disappointment and the apprehension of her uncertain future. Unchecked tears bathed her cold cheeks.

By the time they reached the summit, she'd spent her sorrow. Caitlyn hopped down to unlatch the gate at the edge of the Reed land and cross through to the Bureau of Land Management property. Silently she acknowledged the woman who had been murdered near that spot last spring. It was that crime that had nudged her into law enforcement in the first place.

Renegade, ever sensitive to her moods, bumped her hand with his muzzle. "Thanks, Ren. I love you too." She knelt and embraced him. He responded by licking her neck, ear, and cheek until she laughed. "Okay, okay, come on, silly boy. Let's go." She climbed back up onto Whiskey's saddle, and they trekked deep into the woods for the next couple of hours. Caitlyn's mind filtered through her prospects. Of course, she'd call Sheriff Harding up in Gillette to ask him about working over there, though she doubted he'd be as enthusiastic about her as he was about Colt who had more experience as a deputy than she did. Either way, she was going to have to look elsewhere for work.

If her new job required her to move, maybe McKenzie would want to rent her cabin long term. Kenzie had been looking for her own place to live anyway. That thought led Caitlyn straight back to Colt. Would she and Colt be able to maintain a long-distance relationship if she moved? She chuffed at herself. They'd loved each other since they were kids. Distance and misunderstandings—even red-hot fury—never fully kept them apart. They'd figure it out. She was sure of that, at least.

Renegade stopped several yards in front of her horse. He sniffed and pawed at the ground. "What'd you find, Ren?" He glanced up at her, but then continued digging.

Caitlyn slid down from the saddle to see what had intrigued Renegade. Chunks of black, fully burnt pieces of wood lay scattered across a ten-foot area. She squatted down next to her dog and surveyed the immediate location for other signs of recent humanity. Someone had covered the burn scar on the earth well with pine-mulch, cones, and small rocks. Whoever had been here took care to hide their campfire. This pleased her, as her dad had always taught her to leave no trace of herself behind when she visited the mountains.

Renegade uncovered a tiny piece of wax paper stuck under a moss rock and she reached to retrieve it. *So much for not leaving a trace.* The paper appeared to be a candy wrapper with a logo that said, "rockeT." Caitlyn waved the paper in the air for an indirect whiff. It still held a vague scent she couldn't place—maybe salt-water-taffy. Meanwhile, Renegade unearthed several small bones that likely came from a rabbit or squirrel. Whoever camped here had buried the evidence, except for the wrapper. She tucked the trash into her saddlebag and pulled out her lunch.

Caitlyn and Renegade sat under a tall pine with a thick vanilla-scented trunk. Renegade rested his chin on her thigh as she shoved her fingers under the pine-straw and into the soft, dark soil underneath it. And breathed. Caitlyn drew strength from the earth as she gripped the cool dirt in her fist. By the time she and Renegade returned to her family's ranch that evening, she would be ready to face whatever came next.

3

The next morning, on her way to work, Caitlyn stopped by the liquor store and asked the proprietor for his best bottle of bourbon. The whiskey would serve as both a gift of congratulations for Colt and as a token of apology for abandoning him yesterday—though he seemed to understand her need to regroup.

After she made her purchase, she and Renegade crossed the street and entered the Sheriff's Office. "Good morning, Sheriff Branson." She walked in on Colt talking to a young man she thought she'd seen around town before.

Colt stood up from behind his desk when she came in. He stuffed his hands into his pockets. "Hi, Catie. I didn't think you'd be here this early."

Caitlyn tilted her head, trying to make sense of the scene and Colt's nervousness when it dawned on her, and heat crawled up her neck. "Sorry to interrupt."

"No problem." Colt pulled his hands from his pants pockets and held one out toward the seated man. "This is Wesley Cooper. I'm interviewing him... actually, this is his second interview... for the deputy position." Colt's cheeks flamed. "In fact, I… uh.. was just offering him the position." Colt rubbed the back of his neck. But in her discomfort, Caitlyn couldn't empathize with his. She figured Colt was trying to spare her the pain of him interviewing someone for her job, but it would have been better if he warned her. She could have come in later.

"Oh. Well. Nice to meet you, Wesley." She eyed her replacement as he stood to shake her hand. He was tall and lean and seemed to have a keen awareness about him. His grip was firm, and his palm carried the callouses of hard work. She figured he came from a nearby ranch. Caitlyn nodded at him and then held up the bottle of Buffalo Trace. "Here Colt. This is for you. Congratulations, again."

Colt reached for the bourbon. "Thanks. Wow!" He bent toward her as though to kiss her cheek and then bolted upright again. His eyes shifted to his new deputy.

Caitlyn's pride stung at seeing Colt moving on so quickly, even as she told herself this was a necessary step. "So, Wesley, when was your first interview?" She failed at keeping the incredulousness out of her tone.

Colt answered for him. "I started interviewing when you were still in the hospital recovering from your stab wound. At the time I thought I was looking for a new deputy for you," his voice trailed off.

At the mention of her wound, the scar on Caitlyn's back seemed to tighten. Stefano Russo had left her with a lifelong reminder of his attempt to kill her—and her victory over him. "That seems like a long time ago."

"A lot has happened since then." Colt's eyes bored into hers, but what he was searching for she didn't know.

"Well, I'll let you two get to it. I'm going to pack up my desk." Caitlyn strode to the back room. As soon as she was through the door, she leaned against it and took a deep breath. *Keep breathing. Put one foot in front of the other.*

The office phone rang, and she heard Colt answer it before he called out her name. "You have a phone call from Marshal Williams."

Caitlyn pulled open the door. "Who?"

Colt shrugged and handed her the receiver.

"Deputy Reed?" A sharp female voice barked over the line. "This is US Marshal Laila Williams of the Wyoming Region. You were recommended to me by Deputy Marshal Dirk Sterling. He said you might be interested in the US Marshal's K9 service."

"He did?"

"Yes, and I'd like to speak with you about an eminent opportunity." Without waiting for Caitlyn to respond, the woman pressed on. "There's a new class starting up at the Marshals Academy in Glynco, Georgia, next week and one of the candidates has backed out at the last minute. I'd like to know if you are interested and available to fill that spot? I realize I haven't given you any notice and that my proposition is a long shot, but I'd love to have a K9 Marshal team in my unit, and this is my chance. What do you think?"

A bubble of excitement burst in Caitlyn's chest at the idea and pulsed through her veins. She bit down on her lower lip and as she listened, Colt shook Cooper's hand, and walked him to the door. The grinning young man had obviously accepted the job. She swallowed against a sore ball forming in her throat and said, "I am available, and I'd love to take you up on this incredible opportunity. Is there a K9 kennel at the academy?"

"No, unfortunately. Your dog will have to stay behind. We've already run a background check on you, but you'll also have to pass a polygraph, along with written and physical exams before you'd be eligible. That means accomplishing all those tests in the next couple of days. Is that going to be a problem?"

Caitlyn hated the idea of leaving Renegade, but if she could convince McKenzie to keep up with his training while she was gone, she could make it work. "No, ma'am."

"Good. I'll send you all the pertinent information. As soon as you pass your exams, we'll get you booked on a flight to Georgia."

"I'll make it happen. Thank you for the opportunity."

COLT CLOSED the door behind Wesley and turned to Caitlyn. "You'll make what happen? What opportunity?"

"The US Marshal for the District of Wyoming just asked me to fill a last-minute spot at the US Marshals Academy. Dirk Sterling, the Deputy US Marshal we met at the Russo trial, recommended me to her. She wants to add a K9 team to her unit, so she offered me the slot." Caitlyn stared at him with uncertainty in her eyes.

"Wow! That's incredible, Catie. When does the class start?" This was a tremendous opportunity for her, but it had come out of the blue.

Caitlyn rolled her lips between her teeth and let her breath out through her nose. "Next week."

"What?" Colt drew his chin back and furrowed his brows. "This coming week? Where?"

Caitlyn nodded. "Glynco, Georgia." She winced. "I'll be gone until March."

"They train K9 teams there, too?" he blurted in his shock. *March?*

"No." Caitlyn avoided looking Colt in the eye. "Ren will have to stay home. I'll be going through regular Marshal training."

He blinked and shook his head as he took in her news. He mentally forced his lungs to keep breathing. "But you never mentioned wanting to go into the US Marshal Service. And that's a long time to spend away from Renegade." *From me.* "This is a big decision." *Not to mention impulsive.* "You can't make a life decision like this from a place of disappointment."

Caitlyn's eyes narrowed, and she stood tall, squaring her shoulders. Clearly, he'd said the wrong thing. "I'm not making the decision because I'm disappointed. I'm honored to be invited. Proud that someone believes Renegade and I would be an asset to the US Marshals." She crossed her arms over her chest. "I needed a new direction, and I won't turn it away when it rings my doorbell."

"I don't mean to come across like this isn't an amazing opportunity, or that I don't think you and Renegade would make an incredible team for the Marshals. It's just sudden, so I'm a bit stunned. That's all." He approached her and pulled her to his chest. "You'll be gone a long time. I can't help it if I don't like the idea of being without you."

"I'm sure I can come home during the holidays. I mean I don't know, but..." Caitlyn laughed then. "I don't know anything. Marshal Williams is emailing me all the details."

Colt kissed her forehead and leaned back so he could see into her eyes. "Someday we'll look back on this and think it didn't seem like an eternity... right? When you find out the details, let me know what I can do to help you get ready."

"Will you come with me to my parents' house tonight? It won't be easy to tell them I'm leaving."

Ignoring the vice grip on his heart, he nodded. "Absolutely."

THE WAY her mother bustled about and grinned at Colt every time she looked his way, Caitlyn realized, belatedly, that when she called to tell her parents she had an announcement, she should have made it clear it was not an engagement. By equal measure, her dad sent dagger glances at the man he thought should have asked first before trying to steal his daughter away.

Caitlyn's dad excused himself to use the bathroom for the third time since they arrived, and Renegade followed him down the hallway. Colt made a wide-eyed, grimacing face at her. "What is going on with your parents?" he whispered when she passed by him on her way to set the table.

"Maybe they already know." Not wanting Colt to feel pressure, she said nothing about her true suspicions. "Did you tell anyone?"

"Who would I tell?"

"Dylan?" As though her words were magic, her brother entered the room. He'd come in through the kitchen in muddy clothes with dirt smudged across his face.

"You two talking about me?" He winked at Caitlyn and shook Colt's hand. "Be right down—soon as I shower." The stairs creaked as he climbed them.

Caitlyn's dad stopped and leaned against the wall on his way back to the great room. "Dad? Are you alright?"

He brushed her away. "Just tired. Let's sit down for dinner so you two can tell us what you came to say? I want to head up to bed."

She studied his face. "Are you sick?"

"Just tired, like I said."

Caitlyn glanced at her mother and caught a look of concern before she covered it over with a smile. "Dinner's ready. Dylan told me not to wait. He'll be right down. Would you rather I bring you up a plate, John?"

"No, I'll go up after we eat." Her dad's usually robust voice sounded fatigued.

They each found a place at the table, and after John murmured a grace, they passed the serving dishes and loaded their plates. Renegade sniffed at her dad and, sitting next to him, rested his chin on John's lap.

"Mom, Dad..." Caitlyn felt suddenly leery about sharing her news.

"Spit it out, Caitlyn." Her dad snapped, and she raised her brows. He never snapped at anyone—something was definitely wrong.

Her mom reached across the corner of the table and took her hand. "What's your news, honey?"

Colt held her other hand under the table, and Caitlyn breathed in. "I've been offered a slot at the US Marshal Service Academy. The US Marshal of the Wyoming region personally invited me to go because she's interested in acquiring a K9 team." Caitlyn's pulse thudded as she shifted her gaze between her parents. Her mom's buoyancy flagged, and she sat back in her chair.

"I didn't see that coming." John glanced at Colt with an apologetic half-smile. He refilled his water glass. "When will you go?"

Caitlyn squeezed Colt's hand for reassurance. "That's the thing. I have to leave on Sunday."

"Excuse me." Her mom pressed a napkin to her mouth, pushed back her chair, and escaped to the kitchen. Caitlyn bit down on her lip, awaiting her dad's response.

Dylan entered the room. His hair, still wet from his shower, dripped water down his neck and dampened his collar. He slid into his chair and, panning his gaze back-and-forth, asked, "What'd I miss?"

No one said a word, so finally Caitlyn broke the silence. "I'm leaving on Sunday to go to the US Marshals Service Academy. Mom's upset because she was hoping for different news, and I don't know yet how Dad feels about it."

Her dad sent an accusatory glance in Colt's direction. "I'd better be consulted first if the news your mother was hoping for ever surfaces." Then he relaxed back in his chair and ran a weathered hand over his face. "As far as the announcement you've shared, Caitlyn, I'm happy for you. I think you and Renegade will make a fine K9 team for the US Marshals." He stroked the sleek head resting in his lap. "But it's a dangerous job. Don't expect your mother to be overjoyed about it."

Dylan stared at her before he shifted his gaze to Colt for a time. "How long will you be gone?"

"Until March." Caitlyn took a long drink from her water glass. "Do you think McKenzie would be interested in house-sitting my cabin?"

Dylan jumped like she'd jabbed him with a hot poker and reached for his phone. "I forgot to text her back. I can ask her though. Hold on." His thumbs tapped frantically on his screen.

Caitlyn pursed her lips. "If you know what's good for you, Dyl, you'll start doing a better job of staying in touch with her."

"I know, but I've been swamped." Dylan's phone buzzed with a response, and he smiled. It vibrated again, and after reading the message, he looked up at Caitlyn. "She says she'd love to house and dog sit. You can work out the details tonight." He tapped his screen again. "She can bring Ren out here any time she wants. Mom would love her company with you out of town."

"Good thinking." Caitlyn grinned at her brother.

Her dad pointed across the table. "Pass me the water, will you?"

Colt handed him the pitcher, and he refilled his glass. "You must be thirsty, Dad. That's your fourth glass of water."

"Am I on rations?"

"No..." Caitlyn glanced at Colt to see if he thought her dad's behavior seemed odd to him, too. His eyebrow lifted as he gave her a slight shrug.

. . .

CAITLYN AND COLT left when her dad went upstairs to bed. "Sorry to eat and run, Mom, but I have a lot of studying and packing to do."

Her mom joined them at the front door. "I just wish I had some time to prepare for you being gone so long. I'm going to miss you." Her mom's blue eyes clouded over.

"I'll miss you, too, Mom. But it will go by fast. I'll call you whenever I can, and I'll be home for Christmas. Besides, Dylan is going to invite McKenzie to come out here with Ren as often as she likes." She leaned close to her mom's ear and whispered. "He's using the fact that you're going to miss me as an excuse to get McKenzie to come out here." Caitlyn laughed. "I imagine they'll have an announcement of their own before too long." She kissed her mother's cheek and so did Colt before they said goodbye and took Renegade out to Caitlyn's truck.

Colt drove and Renegade rode between them on the bench seat as they bounced down the gravel drive. Caitlyn looped her fingers through her dog's collar. "I'm having second thoughts. I think there's something wrong with my dad, and I don't want to be away from you and Ren for so long. I really should have thought this through more than I did."

Colt stopped the truck and turned on the seat to face her. "It's sudden, that's true. But one of your strengths is your ability to make quick decisions and act on them. I wish you didn't have to be gone so long. Ren and I are going to miss you like crazy, but this is a step you need to take to become a US Marshal, and frankly, I can't think of a job better suited for you. We'll all be here when you get back."

Caitlyn smiled at him and reached over Renegade to kiss him. "Thanks, Colt."

He pulled her closer and deepened the kiss, squishing Renegade in the process. The dog wiggled his way out and licked their faces, bringing their kiss to a laughing end.

"Ren! We've got to work on your timing!" Caitlyn held her dog's face and kissed his cold, black nose.

DYLAN WENT DOWN the hall to the office for privacy to call McKenzie. He'd rather hear her warm voice than read the print version in a text. Caitlyn's announcement had shocked him and their parents, and he wondered if his sister had confided in McKenzie before she said anything to them.

"No. It's news to me, but I can't say that Caitlyn making this kind of snap decision surprises me. Besides, she told me one of the Deputy Marshals she met during the Russo trial suggested she should consider applying to the Marshals Service. Caitlyn's had that thought bouncing around in her head since then."

"My mom isn't too happy about it." Dylan slid onto the soft leather chair behind the heavy hand-carved desk.

"She's going to miss Caitlyn."

"For sure. On that note, I wondered if you wouldn't mind bringing Renegade out to play as often as possible. I think seeing you will help my mom cope. She really likes you." Dylan rolled his eyes at his own obvious ploy.

But it didn't seem like McKenzie noticed when she answered, "That's a good idea. Ren and I can help distract her, and before we know it, Caitlyn will be back home."

"That'd be great." Dylan leaned his elbows on the desk and lowered his voice. "My mom's been on edge lately. There's something going on with my dad. I think he's sick or something. Tonight, he went up to bed even before Caitlyn and Colt left."

"That doesn't sound like your dad."

"No, it doesn't. He hasn't been himself for a couple of weeks. My mom has been bugging him about going to the doctor, but he won't do it."

"I'm sorry. I'll bring Renegade out on Monday. Maybe we can cheer your mom up, at least."

"That's perfect. I hope you'll still be here when I get home from the range—maybe stay for supper? That'd cheer me up, too." Dylan smiled at the thought. McKenzie giggled, sending tendrils of heat through his chest. He imagined holding her in his arms and breathing in the sunny scent of her hair. "Maybe we could go out this weekend?"

"Maybe. Let me see what Caitlyn needs first. I'll text you."

"HOW LONG DO we have to stay in this drafty little shithole?" Reggie stuffed toilet paper in the cracks around the single window of their little one-room cabin where they would be hiding out for several months. "It's freezing in here."

Ray sighed. Even with all the right winter gear, it was bitter cold in the Wyoming high country. "Put more wood on the fire."

"Why do *I* have to do it?"

"Because you're the one bitching about being cold. When did you get so whiny?" Ray glared at his brother.

Before Reggie could answer, Jason hoisted himself up to get the wood. A surge of icy wind blasted its way inside when Jason opened the front door. Reggie wrapped his skinny arms around himself. Ray estimated his brother had dropped twenty pounds since they'd been on the lam, but it wasn't for lack of food.

"Shut the damn door!" Reggie turned on Ray. "Seriously, how long do we have to stay up here? It's been plenty of time.

If we break the necklace into chunks, it will be easy to fence by now."

"It's only been a little over a month. Impatience gets you thrown in jail. You think you're miserable here? Try prison."

"Stop being so dramatic. I'm gonna go insane living in this shack with you two."

"Well, you better get used to it. We're staying here until spring. Once the weather breaks, we can go hunting and fishing. It'll be like an outdoor vacation."

"Shoot me, now." Reggie flopped onto the couch with a huff.

Jason banged on the door with the toe of his boot and Ray opened it for him. Without any comment to either of the brothers, he dropped the stack next to the small fireplace and bolstered the fire with two small logs. The flame grew and he rubbed his hands near the heat. "We *are* getting low on food, Ray. We'll need to get more, soon."

4

The following day, Caitlyn sat in the middle of a pile of clothes on her bedroom floor, choosing what to pack for the next few months. She was alone in the cabin because McKenzie had left early that morning to interview for a job at the café. McKenzie already had a job with Caitlyn, who had hired her to help finish Renegade's police training. But he didn't need her as much anymore, and the pay, which included room and board, didn't afford McKenzie a place of her own. Of course, now that Caitlyn was leaving for the US Marshals Academy, McKenzie's housing wouldn't be a problem until spring, when Caitlyn returned from Georgia permanently. Still, McKenzie said she wanted a job to help her meet more people and establish some roots in Moose Creek.

Caitlyn sighed as she sifted through her wardrobe, trying to decide what to take with her. She wouldn't need much, because they'd have uniforms and work-out gear provided for them at the academy, and she wouldn't be going out very often. Mostly, she'd need travel clothes for when she flew home for the holidays. Caitlyn picked up a sweatshirt she'd borrowed from Colt and buried her face in it, drawing in his scent. How was she going to survive the next months without him and Renegade? At least Ren would have someone who loved him taking care of him and keeping up with his training.

Though she'd miss everyone, thinking about the academy sent excited chills zipping across her skin. This surprising new step in her career as a law enforcement professional was one she certainly hadn't seen coming. But at the same time, a deep ache filled her chest and throat at the thought of leaving Colt right when they were reestablishing their romantic relationship. Caitlyn let out a tremendous sigh to relieve the pressure. At least they could visit over FaceTime, and even though Renegade didn't understand the technology, she'd talk to him anyway whenever she called McKenzie.

Caitlyn leaned back against her bed and looked at the yellow dress hanging on her closet door for later. She and Colt were finally going on their celebration date that he'd been planning for months. But if she was honest, she didn't feel like going out for dinner tonight. She'd much prefer to spend a cozy night at home with Colt in front of the fire. Just them, alone together. She hated to disappoint him, and he'd be hurt if she postponed the date once again. But the truth was, she didn't want to get all dressed up and have to look at him across an elegant table. She'd rather snuggle up close to him on the couch. *Damn, I'm going to miss him.* If she was going to ask Colt to cancel their reservations, she should do it now. She'd tell him the fancy dinner was something they could look forward to when she came home. Caitlyn reached for her phone.

McKenzie skidded her car to a stop in front of Caitlyn's cabin. She hurried inside, eager to tell Caitlyn her great news. She ran in through the door and into Caitlyn's room, where she found her friend sitting in the middle of a mess of clothes. "What are you doing?"

Caitlyn looked up at her and frowned. "I can't decide what to take. I feel as though I made this massive, life-changing decision without stopping to think about it. And now I have all these other stupid decisions to make, and I can't seem to focus. Not even on the simple ones, like what clothes to choose." She tossed a shirt into a pile on her right. "You look excited, though. Did you get the job?"

McKenzie bounced on the balls of her feet. "I did! Stephanie hired me on the spot as a second server at the café." Now she'd have a little extra money and a lot more freedom. "It's been a long time since I've been a server, but it should be fun. I'll earn a little cash and be able to meet more people around town."

"Congratulations! That's outstanding. Stephanie is great to work for."

"She seems nice."

"When do you start?"

McKenzie sat on the edge of Caitlyn's bed. "On Wednesday. What time is Colt picking you up tonight?"

Caitlyn drew the side of her lower lip between her teeth. "I postponed the date—again."

"What? You're not having second thoughts about him, are you?"

"No way. I just don't want to go out. I'd rather stay in." Caitlyn grinned.

McKenzie laughed. "Oh. I get it. Do you need me to make myself scarce?"

"No, Colt's cooking dinner for me at his place."

"Can he cook?"

"Who cares?" Caitlyn giggled, and her cheeks flushed a pretty pink. "Thanks again for agreeing to stay here with Renegade. I'm taking him with me to the airport tomorrow. Colt will drive him back here after he drops me off."

"Sounds good. I was going to see what Dylan's up to tonight. Maybe I can get him to go out for dinner or something." McKenzie reached into her pocket for her phone and sent Dylan a text.

BY LUNCH TIME, Dylan still hadn't responded, and what was becoming a familiar sense of letdown weighed upon McKenzie's shoulders. She poked her head into Caitlyn's bedroom. If possible, the woman looked even less packed than she had been before. "Still having a hard time in here?"

"I'm getting there. Did you hear from Dylan?"

McKenzie shook her head and frowned. "No. It's becoming the norm for him not to respond to my texts. Or my phone calls, for that matter." The ache of rejection squeezed her chest. "I really thought we were getting along well. I mean, it seemed like we had something together." She dropped her chin. "Maybe I misread the situation. You know him—what do you think?"

"I don't think you misread him, Kenz. Like I said, it's a super busy time on the ranch right now. Dylan is probably out with the herd and doesn't have cell coverage. It'd be better if he'd hire some hands to help, but I know he feels like he can't afford it. So, he's trying to do all the work on his own." Caitlyn stood and stretched. "Usually my dad helps, but he still isn't feeling up to it."

"I'm sorry to hear that. Is it the crud that's going around?"

"Probably." A furrow formed between her friend's eyes. "Whatever it is, he's having a hard time kicking it. Will you keep an eye on him while I'm gone, too?"

"I'm sure he'll be better soon."

"I hope so." Caitlyn sighed. "Either way, I'll call my mom. She'll have an idea of what's going on with Dylan."

McKenzie went into the kitchen to make sandwiches for lunch while Caitlyn finished packing. It was weird having Caitlyn ask her mom about Dylan—they weren't in middle school, after all. But on the other hand, how else was she going to find out? Dylan didn't seem to want to talk to her lately. She understood he had a lot of work to do during the day, but couldn't he call her at night? McKenzie shrugged to herself. She didn't really know much about the work that had to happen on a ranch. It was possible he was flat out exhausted at the end of the day. Still, it didn't take much energy to just reach out in a text. She let out a long, discouraged breath as she slathered mayonnaise on slices of bread. After piling on ham, cheese, lettuce, and tomato, McKenzie grabbed a bag of jalapeño potato chips and set their plates on the kitchen bar. "Caitlyn, lunch is ready."

Caitlyn came out of her room, holding up her phone and wiggling it. "I just got off a call with my mom. She said Dylan was up in the mountains bringing the herd down to the winter pastures. That's a tough job by himself. It could take all day, for sure. In fact, I should be out there helping him. Maybe Colt will lend him a hand on his days off."

"I wish there was some way I could help." McKenzie tucked a length of hair behind her ear.

Caitlyn smiled. "Well, I told my mom that I was having dinner with Colt, so she invited you for supper. Which is perfect. You'll be able to see Dylan and ask him to his face why he hasn't returned your calls."

"No way. I'd die first."

Caitlyn laughed. "Why? He's the one being a jerk. You have a right to know."

"Not everyone is as direct as you."

Caitlyn shrugged. "It's the fastest way to find things out. But if you want to be less forthright, that's up to you. Either way, you'll get to see him. Maybe he'll just tell you why he hasn't called."

"Maybe. It's nice of your mom to invite me for dinner. What time did she say I should be there?"

"She said dinner would be at six, but you could come around five, if you want to. Or she also offered to have you come out this afternoon, if you're interested in learning how to can green beans." Caitlyn smirked. "I love how she poses that as a favor to you."

"I've never canned anything before. It might be fun to learn."

"Sure. But don't let her fool you. Canning is hard work—it's probably why she invited you to help."

"I'll head over after lunch. Will I see you tomorrow or will I be saying goodbye to you today?"

"I've already said goodbye to my parents and Dylan. I'm taking Ren with me to Colt's tonight and we're leaving for the airport around four in the morning. So, unless you want to get up that early, I guess I won't see you before I leave. Colt will need to drop Ren off with you when he gets back to town, though. Will that work?"

"Sure, and I promise to take great care of him. We'll both miss you a ton."

"Me too. I hate that part."

STELLA OPENED the door and welcomed McKenzie inside with a warm smile. "Thank you for coming. It's always much more fun to can vegetables with a friend. You said you've never done any canning?"

"No, ma'am." McKenzie followed the older woman through the great room, back to the kitchen. John was snoozing on the sofa as they passed by. When the kitchen door swung closed, she asked, "How's John feeling? Caitlyn said she thought he had come down with something?"

"He's been feeling run down lately. Hopefully, the daily napping will have him back on his feet again soon."

An enormous covered stainless-steel pot bubbled away on the stovetop and glistening glass canning jars filled the counter next to it. Inside the sink, a colander overflowed with freshly washed green beans.

"First, we need to trim off the ends of the green beans, cut them into pieces, and then blanch them."

"Blanch them?" McKenzie was out of her depth.

A gentle smile graced Stella's face, and she patted McKenzie on the shoulder. "You haven't spent much time in the kitchen. Have you, dear?"

"Not really. But I'm willing to learn."

Stella held her hands together in front of her chest and beamed. "That's all that's necessary. A willing heart, and a can-do attitude."

"Pun intended?" McKenzie asked, and both women laughed.

"I'll teach you everything you need to know."

McKenzie spent the afternoon in Stella's kitchen canning her first green beans—learning the entire process before switching over to raspberry jam. Caitlyn was right: a ton of work went into canning food. But McKenzie had enjoyed herself, too. Coming from the competitive K9 training world, she hadn't experienced a lot of feminine camaraderie before, but Stella drew her in and made her feel at home. By four o'clock they had finished, and taking a coffee break, they shared a plate of crisp peanut butter cookies before starting on dinner. McKenzie found that even though it was hard work, she truly enjoyed being in the kitchen. Funny—she had no idea.

"Caitlyn told me she was going to Colt's house for dinner tonight." Stella's eyes sparkled. "It's about time those two figured things out, don't you think?"

McKenzie laughed. "I'm new to the scene. But even *I* can tell they're meant to be together. Electricity crackles between them every time they're in the same room."

Stella reached over and squeezed McKenzie's arm. "It's been like that between them since they were in high school. John and I always thought they'd end up together, but something happened between them before Caitlyn went off to college. I'm just glad to hear they're working things out. Colt is like a son to us."

McKenzie sipped her coffee and thought about the words she wanted to use to bring up the next topic. "Caitlyn tells me there's a lot of work to do on the ranch in the fall. Dylan must be very busy."

"Yes. Spring and fall are both hectic times around here. We've had a few lean years, so Dylan doesn't feel he can hire any help right now. Consequently, he's up trying to bring the herd down by himself. Colt and Caitlyn usually help him, but obviously they can't this weekend. John rides too when he's feeling up to it." Stella's gaze dropped to her hands. Her knuckles whitened as she tightened her grip on her coffee mug.

"Is he doing all right? Caitlyn seemed to think he might be sick."

Stella's eyes shot to McKenzie's. She studied her for a few seconds before saying, "To be honest, I'm not sure. He's not feeling well, but I don't know why, and I can't convince him to see the doctor."

"Has he had a fever or any other symptoms?"

"No fever." Stella's eyes focused on her hands. "He just doesn't have any energy, and that makes him grouchy." Stella stood and collected their dishes. "I'm sure it will all blow over. Do you mind helping me get dinner going? Dylan will be back in a couple of hours, and he'll be roaring hungry." She laughed as she stacked the cups and plates in the dishwasher. "You've heard the term 'hangry' before, haven't you?" McKenzie nodded. "Well, that's mild compared to how Dylan can be when he comes off the range, especially when he's working out there on his own. Of course, I imagine with you here, he'll be on his best behavior."

We'll see. My being here may irritate him even more.

Stella walked McKenzie through the steps of preparing beef stroganoff with a thick creamy gravy that they would spoon over butter noodles. They cooked fresh green beans with bacon, and McKenzie put together a salad. Stella shared the secret recipe that made her biscuits as fluffy as clouds. For dessert, they would serve left-over cherry pie that Stella had baked the day before.

At five-thirty, McKenzie thought she heard horse's hooves trotting on the gravel drive near the house. Stella confirmed this as she peered out the window toward the barn. McKenzie's pulse quickened in anticipation. She truly wasn't sure how Dylan was going to feel about her being there, but she couldn't wait to see him. Would he think her being in his house when he got home was overstepping? What if he was too tired to talk with her about where they stood? Would he withdraw even farther?

"Dylan will be in just as soon as he puts his horse away and feeds the animals. Let's set the table." McKenzie followed Stella into the dining room with four place settings. John was still dozing on the couch, and Stella touched his shoulder to wake him. "Dinner's just about ready, John. Are you hungry?"

He grumbled something that McKenzie couldn't hear and slowly got to his feet. He gripped the back of the sofa for balance and nodded to her. "Sorry, I didn't realize we had company."

McKenzie held up a hand as if to stop him from apologizing. "I'm not company today. Just a helping hand here to learn how to can green beans."

John smiled, but his eyes were drained of energy. "Sounds like you earned your supper, then. Glad to have you." His voice trailed off as he shuffled down the hallway toward the bathroom. The back door in the kitchen creaked open and then slammed shut. "I'm home, Mom, and hungry as a bear. Something smells good in here. What's for dinner?"

A dirt covered cowboy that vaguely resembled Dylan strode through the kitchen door into the great room, wiping his face on a blue bandanna. As he rubbed the cloth down below his eyes, he caught sight of McKenzie. She held her breath.

Raw hunger radiated from his gaze as he took her in. His eyes flitted quickly over her frame and back up before a half smile stretched one side of his mouth. "I didn't know you were here, McKenzie."

"I, uh, I..."

Stella moved to his side and pushed him gently back toward the kitchen. "McKenzie is my guest today. She helped me can beans and put-up raspberry jam. She also helped make dinner. So, you better go get cleaned up. You're not coming to my table looking like a giant tar-baby. Go on, go up and shower. Dinner will be ready when you come back down."

Dylan let his mother usher him through the kitchen to the back stairs, but at the last minute turned to look over his shoulder at McKenzie. "You cook?"

Stella gave him a final shove toward the steps. "Of course, she cooks, at least better than you." The swinging kitchen door closed behind them.

McKenzie couldn't tell if Dylan was happy to see her or not. Was the look in his eyes one of pleasure, or was that wishful thinking on her part? He seemed more surprised than anything, but surprised wasn't necessarily happy. This could turn out to be a long dinner.

In the end, dinnertime was short. Dylan hardly said anything between bites, though he made many appreciative noises. In contrast, John hardly ate. He seemed more thirsty than hungry, and Stella kept a sharp eye on him. McKenzie picked at her food, eating only to be polite. She was too nervous about talking to Dylan after dinner. When they finished their meal, Dylan stood to help collect the plates, but Stella shooed him away. "You don't need to help tonight, Dylan. You've had a long day. Why don't you relax on the couch with your father? McKenzie and I will make quick work of the dishes and bring out some pie for dessert."

"Are you sure, Ma? I don't mind helping. McKenzie and I —"

"I'm sure. Go relax. We'll be out in just a few minutes."

McKenzie loaded her arms with plates and followed Stella to the kitchen. While she rinsed and filled the dishwasher, Stella cut slices of cherry pie. They carried dessert out to the great room, only to find both John and Dylan sound asleep on the couch in front of a crackling fire.

Stella set the plates on the dining table and took the ones McKenzie held back into the kitchen. When she returned, she gestured for McKenzie to take a seat. "Many of my nights are like this during the busy seasons."

"It's okay. I've had a wonderful time with you today, Stella. And I must admit, I'm a bit tired myself. I think I'll head home right after dessert."

"I sure appreciated all your help. I hope you'll come back again, soon."

"Thank you, and thanks for teaching me. I had fun."

Dylan was still sound asleep and snoring softly when it was time for McKenzie to leave. She may not have had a chance to talk to Dylan privately, but at least she saw the truth of what Caitlyn suspected. Dylan certainly was working extremely hard during the day and exhausted at night. Unfortunately, she still didn't know how he felt about her. On a whim, she turned back to Stella. "How much longer will Dylan be working this hard?"

Stella gave her a knowing gaze. "Ranching is a tough occupation. It's hard work, day in and day out. But there's a beautiful closeness that comes from building a life together through the struggle, and a lot of joy. This ranch is Dylan's life. I think it might be a good thing for you to learn about ranch life from the inside out. It surely would help you understand *all* of my children."

Stella's kindness overshadowed any embarrassment McKenzie felt at the woman coming directly to her point. "Well, you certainly have a beautiful home and a wonderful family. This life seems to suit you. Thanks again for sharing it with me." McKenzie opened the front door and stepped out onto the porch. Before Stella closed the door, she poked her head out and said, "I'll tell Dylan you said goodbye."

McKenzie nodded her head and went to her car. She sat in the seat for a minute, thinking about all Stella had said. Was the woman trying to warn her off the hard life of ranching? McKenzie didn't think so, because the one thing she knew for sure about the Reed family was they were utterly direct. Stella had gone out of her way to make the work of canning beans a fun experience—but she was right—it would be a good idea to see the full picture of what Dylan's life looked like before she got too heavily invested.

RAY STOMPED the snow off his boots outside the front door before ducking inside the cabin. "I swear, I thought the hunting would be easier than this." Ray cursed himself for not stocking more food. But how could he know wild game would be so hard to find? He'd counted on hunting for food, but so far, they'd only been able to get one skinny rabbit, and canned beans only stretched so far. "I've been thinking about our best options. I don't like the idea of going to any of these little mountain towns where everybody knows everyone else. We'd stick out. I'll ask my lady to get us more food and supplies, but I think we need to plan a bigger grab far away—maybe a town up in Montana."

5

To Caitlyn's surprise, Colt hadn't been disappointed about the date at all. He agreed he'd rather spend the evening with her alone and invited her to his house for dinner. At six o'clock, she pulled her truck into his driveway. Night darkened the sky early, and he had all the lights on in his house. A welcoming glow shone from his front window.

"Come on, Ren." She knocked on the door. An unusual case of nerves trotted around in her belly, and she pressed a flat hand against her stomach, attempting to settle them. As Colt opened the door, the light from the kitchen backlit his frame in a halo and cast shadows on his face emphasizing his strong cheekbones and square jaw. Caitlyn sucked in her breath.

A slow smile spread across Colt's mouth. "Hey. You're right on time. Come on in."

"Thanks for this." Caitlyn stood on her toes to give him a kiss. She stepped into the living room, her shoulder brushing against his hard chest as she walked by. Tantalizing aromas wafted from the kitchen, but Caitlyn wasn't hungry. It didn't seem like she had any room for food next to all the weighty emotions crowding inside. The heaviest of all were her feelings about leaving Colt.

Renegade bumped her hand with his muzzle. When she didn't immediately reach down and scratch his ears, he nudged her fingers with his cold nose once again and let out a little whine. He was sensitive to her distress. How could she explain to her sweet pup that she was leaving for a long time, but that she'd be back? Would he still feel as close to her when she returned? Would Colt? Was this the best decision of her life—or the worst?

Colt came up behind her and gripped her shoulders. He pressed his cheek against the side of her head and asked, "What's going through your mind? You look upset."

Caitlyn turned within his grasp to face him, and she peered up. "Am I doing the right thing, Colt? Leaving you—leaving Ren?"

Colt took his time answering. "You're doing the right thing, Catie. Though I have to admit, I wish you didn't have to go. But don't worry, Renegade and I will be here waiting for you when you get home. And remember, it's only a handful of weeks until Thanksgiving. Let's take this in bite-size chunks. How does that sound?"

"Thanks for your support, Colt. It means everything to me. I feel bad because we've started something together, and now I'm leaving."

Colt brushed his thumb across her cheekbone, and staring into her eyes, he smiled. "We're not starting something, Catie. What's happening between us began back when we were kids. And I know it will last all our days. If you look at it like that, the time you'll be away is just a breath." His eyes were full of unspoken emotion, and he blinked at the sudden moisture in them. He pressed his mouth against her forehead in a lingering kiss, and then, with his hands on her shoulders, he stepped back to arm's length. "We better have dinner before we forget to eat." He chuckled and moved past her to the kitchen. She followed him, leaning on the door-frame to watch him put the finishing touches on their meal.

"What did you cook?"

"My specialty." Colt wiped his hands on a kitchen towel and set it on the counter. He turned off the gas stove top before brushing by her. He went out the back door, pulled two steaks off the grill, and returned to fill their plates.

After dinner, Colt lit a fire in the fireplace, and they sat together on the couch. Caitlyn snuggled up under his arm and leaned against his chest, fitting perfectly in that space. She stared at the golden yellow flames and watched them reflect in her wineglass. "I'm really going to miss you, Colt. More than I expected, I think."

He kissed the top of her head. She sipped her dry wine and placed her glass on the table. Rolling to her side, she faced him and stretched up to kiss his mouth. He set his wineglass on the end table and pulled her onto his lap. A long-ignored pilot-light ignited with a searing blue flame somewhere deep inside her belly, and she pressed herself into him. Colt's arms tightened around her. His mouth left hers and trailed fervent kisses along her jawline and down her throat.

"I love you more than life, Catie." He murmured. "I always have."

Caitlyn pressed a kiss against his temple, then holding his face between her hands, she looked deep into his eyes. "You're the only one I've ever loved. The only man that's held my heart."

Colt's gaze bore into her eyes as though trying to find an answer to an unasked question in their depths. A slight smile formed itself on her lips, and she nodded. Colt slid his arm under her knees and lifted her. Pivoting, he laid her on the black bear rug in front of the fireplace and stretched out next to her. His fingers brushed gently over the planes of her face. His eyes followed his touch as though he were memorizing her. Caitlyn pulled him down so she could kiss him again. The sensation of his body against hers was the memory she wanted to carry with her when she left.

AT SOME POINT in the middle of the night, after the fire died down, Colt and Caitlyn had made their way to his bedroom. Renegade followed and slept curled up at the foot of the bed. Sharp prickles in Colt's hand and arm woke him in the gray dawn. Caitlyn's silky, chestnut hair draped across his chest, and he kissed the top of her head while she slept nestled in the crook of his shoulder. As quietly as he could, not wanting to wake her, he slid his numb arm from underneath her, and padded out to the kitchen to make coffee. Renegade trotted after him, and Colt opened the back door to let him out.

When the coffee was ready, Colt filled two steaming mugs and turned to find Caitlyn leaning against his bedroom door frame. She wore one of his shirts, and with her hair mussed from love and sleep, she was the most beautiful creature he'd ever seen. If he could, he'd live frozen in this moment for the rest of his life and die a satisfied man. In that second, the thought of her leaving hit him like a cannonball blast to the center of his chest. He cleared his throat. "Good morning, gorgeous." She smiled sleepily at him. "Ready for coffee?"

"Always." She crossed the room in bare feet, took both mugs from his hands, and set them on the counter. Reaching up, she slid her arms around his neck and pulled him close. She smiled lazily. "Last night was —"

Colt pressed a finger to her lips to quiet her. "Just the beginning."

IT SEEMED HE BLINKED, and it was already time to drive Caitlyn to the airport. Sipping their coffee, they put off dressing, trying to slow the minutes down. Still the clock ticked on, regardless of love—heedless of heartache.

Colt transferred Caitlyn's bags from her truck to his Jeep, and before long, they were on their way to Rapid City. Two and a half hours later, they stood in the airport parking lot where they shared a lingering, teary farewell. Eventually, Colt nudged Caitlyn toward the automatic doors outside of airport security, and he and Renegade stood watching Caitlyn until they couldn't see her anymore.

"Well Ren, I guess it's just us guys for a while." Renegade looked up at him and cocked his head. He barked twice and then pulled against his lead toward the door. "Not this time, buddy. You're coming with me. How does some leftover steak sound before I take you home to McKenzie?" Renegade sat by the glass doors and whined. "Come on, Ren."

Renegade laid down on the cement, and Colt's stomach churned. The dog sensed Caitlyn's absence, but he couldn't understand. The best thing to do was give Renegade a job. Colt tugged on the leash and asked Renegade to heel. Eventually, the dog relented and left with him. On the way to the Jeep, Colt texted McKenzie. **Just leaving the airport now. Can you meet me at Reed Ranch?**

6

McKenzie was glad for an opportunity to drive out to Reed Ranch again. She might run into Dylan under the guise of meeting Colt and working with Renegade. Colt was probably heart-sick after dropping Caitlyn off for her flight to Georgia, knowing he wouldn't see her until Thanksgiving. He could probably use some company, too.

She parked by the arena, figuring the location offered her the best chance of seeing Dylan. She left her engine running and bumped up the heat. A definite fall chill had seeped into the air overnight. It would probably snow soon. Coming from Florida, she had no winter weight clothes and with her uncertain relationship status—she didn't think it would be wise to buy any right now. Besides, with Caitlyn in Georgia, McKenzie could borrow one of her coats.

The barnyard was quiet. Dylan was nowhere to be seen, though that wasn't surprising. It was near lunchtime, and he had probably been out on the range since before dawn. She grudgingly admired how hard the man worked to keep his family ranch going.

A knock on her car door window catapulted McKenzie's heart rate to the stars. She clapped her hands to her cheeks and spun to see Stella waving from outside. McKenzie pressed the window button and rolled it down.

"Stella! You scared the jeepers out of me."

"Sorry, dear. What are you doing sitting out here by yourself?"

"I'm waiting for Colt. I'm supposed to meet him here. He's dropping Renegade off with me before he goes to work."

"Well, come inside. It's cold out here. Colt will know where you are."

McKenzie forced a smile onto her heated face. If she was in the house, she'd miss Dylan if he happened to ride by. But not wanting to admit to her semi-stalking behavior, she rolled up her window and opened the door.

Stella slid her arm around McKenzie's waist as they walked toward the house. "It's just about lunchtime. Why don't we make some sandwiches? Colt will be hungry, and if we don't feed him, he'll eat some horrible thing from the convenience store."

"Will Dylan be coming home for lunch?" McKenzie did her best to sound casual, but the smile on Stella's face told her she'd missed the mark.

"No. I'm sorry. He packed a few sandwiches before he left. He's riding the fence today and coming all the way back to the house for lunch would waste a couple of hours."

Pushing aside her disappointment, McKenzie asked, "Riding the fence about what?"

Stella laughed. "No—he's not *on the fence about anything.* He's riding the fence line. A rancher has to ride along all the fences on the property and mend any breaks or fallen posts."

"Oh." She was so far out of her element—the language was even different. "I see. What causes a fence to break?"

"Mostly those silly cows. They rub on the posts and lean

through the fence to get grass on the other side. They're so big and thick-hided, they can snap right through the wire."

"I get it. The grass is greener on the other side." McKenzie grinned, realizing where the saying came from.

"They seem to think so. No matter how many acres they have to graze, they always want what's on the opposite side of the fence."

"How long does it take Dylan to ride the entire perimeter?"

"Well, he also has to check all the interior pasture fences. It takes at least two days. More if there are a lot of repairs."

"But he comes home in time for dinner?

"He tries." Stella paused and studied McKenzie's face. "Ranching is not a nine-to-five, Monday-through-Friday job. It's a solid seven days a week, twenty-four hours a day type of life. Sure, he has time off, but he's always on call. You never know when he'll have to ride out to fix something or care for an injured animal."

Stella's words stung, and McKenzie turned away. Her gaze floated over the golden pastures to the mulberry mountains beyond. "Are you trying to warn me off, Stella?"

Dylan's mother took McKenzie's hand in hers. "No. Nothing would make me happier than to see you and my son together. But I'd hate to see you two make any rash decisions. You should have a full understanding of the type of lifestyle you could expect if you and Dylan choose to move forward together." She continued toward the house, keeping hold of McKenzie's hand. "Wyoming is an entirely different part of the world than Florida. I just want you to know how life is here. It's better to know all of this up front than to choose it and regret it later. That would hurt worse, don't you think?"

"You're a wise woman, Stella, but I don't even know if Dylan is all that interested in me. I think that should come first. Don't you?"

Stella squeezed her hand. "Let's get some lunch."

McKenzie heard Colt's jeep coming up the road, and she and Stella waited for him to park. He opened the door, and Renegade bound out across his lap. The exuberant dog ran straight to McKenzie, his energy crackling in the noontime breeze. After a quick greeting, Renegade raced toward the barn. He darted inside and back out before running around the entire building. He barked and sprinted off, racing past the arena rail to the path leading out to the tree swing and Lobo's memorial.

"I don't know how you and Catie deal with all that energy." Colt scratched his chin while he watched the dog run.

McKenzie held her hand up to shade her eyes. "He's looking for Caitlyn. I imagine he'll be hard to live with for a couple of days until he realizes she's not playing hide and seek."

"Poor guy. He already misses her."

McKenzie bumped his shoulder with hers. "I'm sure he's not the only one."

"Yeah, well." Colt pressed his cowboy hat further down. "Guess we both better get used to it."

"Let him run." Stella mounted the porch steps. "Come on in for lunch before you go to work, Colt. McKenzie and I were just about to make some sandwiches."

McKenzie and Colt followed Stella like wayward children. "Where's John?" McKenzie asked when she didn't see him on the sofa.

"He's still in bed. I'll take him up a tray."

Colt removed his hat and hung it on the rack by the door. "Have you heard from Doctor Kennedy?"

"No. Besides, it's Sunday. I imagine he has the day off."

McKenzie raised her eyebrows. *Apparently, Sundays are days off for everyone besides ranchers.*

"I suppose." Colt followed Stella into the kitchen and

opened a cupboard for a glass. "I'm surprised you're not at church."

Stella pulled sliced ham and cheddar cheese from the refrigerator. "I don't want to leave John right now."

McKenzie found a loaf of yeasty smelling homemade bread in the breadbox and reached for a knife to cut slices. "Next time, give me a call. I'd be happy to hang out here with John if you want to go to church or anywhere else."

"That's so sweet. I'm hoping we'll have John on the mend soon, though."

"Of course."

"McKenzie, would you have time today to help me with some household chores? Renegade can stay in the yard and play."

Bless this woman. Here was McKenzie's excuse to stick around until Dylan came home. Otherwise, there was no telling when she'd see him next. "Of course. Whatever you need."

AFTER LUNCH, Colt ran upstairs to say hello to John before leaving for work. Stella and McKenzie tidied up the kitchen. "What do you want help with Stella?"

"I'm going through all the books in the office. Moose Creek library is holding a book drive and I'm sure we have plenty to donate. Besides, the shelves could use a good dusting." Stella led the way down the hall. "I have some boxes we can pack the donations in."

McKenzie had never been into John's office before and noticed how perfectly it reflected the man's personality. Burgundy leather wingbacks nestled near a small plaid sofa which sat before a cheery fire glowing against the honey toned log walls. Floor to ceiling bookcases lined two sides of the room and a heavy rustic desk rested in courtly silence by the window. Gun racks stood sentinel on either side of the double doors.

"You have quite a collection of books here, Stella." McKenzie trailed her fingers over a row of embossed cloth spines. "How many are you going to donate?"

"We'll keep the leather-bound books and all the sets. Everything else is up for debate on a book-by-book basis." Stella reached for a banker's box and set it on top of the desk.

It was past six when they reshelved the last book on the freshly polished shelves. "Oh, my." Stella stared at her watch. "I didn't realize how late it was. You must be starving. And I need a cup of tea."

"I'd love a cup, too."

"I'll just run up and check on John. Why don't you turn the kettle on?"

"Is he still in bed?"

Stella climbed the stairs. "I hope not. He's probably reading or something." Her worried eyes said more than she did.

The kettle whistled, and McKenzie dropped tea bags into two mugs. She poured the boiling water over them to steep. It was dark outside, and the clock said it was time for supper, but there were no lights on in the barn. McKenzie opened the back door and let Renegade inside. "Are you ready for your dinner, Ren?" He bounced on his paws, scampered to his dish by the pantry door, and sat next to his bowl, waiting. She filled his dish with a high-protein food and went back to preparing the tea.

Stella pushed through the swinging door. "John was sleeping. He said he had a headache."

"I hope Blake can figure out what is going on so John can get some relief."

Stella rolled her lips between her teeth and nodded. She looked just like Caitlyn when she was deep in thought.

McKenzie gave her a hug and Stella said, "Dylan left a message on my phone. He said he'd be home late. He came across an injured calf."

"Oh, no! What happened?"

"Dylan thinks a pack of coyotes or wolves attacked it. He isn't sure, but he has to doctor the poor thing."

McKenzie's heart swelled at the thought of Dylan out in the cold darkness, caring for a wounded animal by moonlight. She loved his dedication and work ethic, but on the other hand, she realized that a life with him meant spending long days with his mother and precious little time with him. Time when exhaustion precluded anything but food and sleep.

"Well, I better get Renegade home. Tell Dylan I said hello and that I hope the calf is going to be okay."

"Won't you stay till he comes home?"

McKenzie sighed and dropped her shoulders. "No. I don't think so. It's time for us to get home."

Stella's steady gaze told her the woman understood not only that she wanted to go home, but why. "I'll tell him you were here and have him call you if it's not too late."

"Thanks." The women embraced, and McKenzie called Renegade. They drove home in silence while McKenzie thought long and hard about her future.

Later, when McKenzie was brushing her teeth, her phone rang. She spit the minty foam into the sink and ran to the living room to answer. But the name on her screen was not Dylan. It said Tony Cross - Escambia County Police K9.

"Tony?"

"Hey, McKenzie. Long time no talk to. Where are you?"

"I've been in Wyoming for about six months. I have a training job up here."

"Well, when are you coming home? The team needs you."

"Why? What's going on?"

"We've hired two new K9 handlers, and they need to select dogs and learn to train with them. Of course, we want only the best to teach them, and that's you."

"Wow. Uh… When would you need me there?"

"Yesterday. How soon can you come back?"

McKenzie's gut seized and hardened like she'd swallowed ten pounds of kibble. "I'm committed to train the K9 I'm working with now until March, while his handler is away at the US Marshal's training center."

"March? Damn. Well, we can get these guys started, but I'd do anything to get you back here to tighten up the whole team when you're finished with your job up there. What do you say?"

"I'm going to have to think about it. Can I let you know?"

"Sure, but don't take too long. We need you… and some of us miss you. Just saying."

THEY'D LONG since blown through what cash they had, and the food Ray's lady re-stocked them with was dwindling again. The robbery-homicide continued to be in the news which kept the gems too hot to sell. "We're going to have to get ahold of some money for more supplies," Ray told his partners as he stirred the fire warming their hideout. "We're short on food, again."

Jason poured himself a cup of coffee from the pot near the flames. "How much longer before we can move the diamonds?"

"It's still too soon. I'm guessing another couple of months."

Reggie jumped up and paced the floor behind them. "This is chicken-shit. We're sitting on a million bucks while we freeze to death out here. Come on, Ray." He scratched at a sore on his cheek and in his loose-jointed walk ambled to the window and peered out. "You never said we'd have to be up here all winter. It's ass-biting cold. We should have just stayed at the hotel we were at." Reggie kicked a cupboard door closed and it bounced back open. "I gotta get outa here, man."

"What you *gotta* do is stay out of our investment stash. You're bouncing all over the cabin like a ping-pong ball." Ray glared over his shoulder at his kid brother. He hadn't thought it would hurt if he let Reggie try some of the candy-like pills, but now the kid was hooked. "It would have been too risky to stay in Idaho under a false ID. They'll never find us up here and we need to lie low for a little longer before it'll be safe to make our next move. We'll leave as soon as I think it's safe, and when you're on a beach sipping colorful umbrella drinks, you'll see all this was worth it, I promise."

Reggie opened the door and winter swept in. "But *you* get to go out, Ray. And you tell me to stay out of the speed, but *you* took the gems and gave them to that woman!"

"I only went out a couple of times to check on the news and charge our batteries. We need to know what's going on and I can't get anything on my phone up here without any cell coverage. I left the jewels with my lady for safe keeping, and I needed to check in on her and get more food, so you'd stop complaining." Ray walked to the window and stared out at the snow. "Besides, you should be grateful. She's the one who gave us the Jim Beam."

Jason reached for the empty bottle on the mantle. "That's long gone, now."

7

Caitlyn asked the Uber driver to stop at the gate and she stared at the Federal Law Enforcement Training Center sign. From what she understood, the first ten weeks of training at FLETCE was Criminal Investigation School. It hadn't been that long ago that she'd gone through the Wyoming Law Enforcement Academy, and she figured this would be more of the same. Still her nerves jangled inside causing shallow breaths. She felt utterly alone. Caitlyn sucked in a deep gulp of air and let it out slowly.

"Nervous?" the driver asked as he peered at her in his mirror.

"A bit, yeah. I feel fairly confident about the CI School. I learned about surveillance, search and seizure, firearms, and the law at the academy last spring, but I confess I'm a little scared about the second half of the training."

"Ah, the actual marshal's training." The driver chuckled.

"Yeah. That's when the rubber hits the road, I hear. I hope I can cut the defensive tactics course."

"You look pretty scrappy to me. I'm sure you'll do fine. Are you ready to go in?"

Caitlyn swallowed her nerves and nodded. "Let's do it."

Caitlyn had accurately placed her confidence in the book learning section of training. She'd studied criminal justice in college and then went to the law enforcement academy after that, so much of the teaching was review. Now that she was back from the holiday break, she faced the increased physical training and teaching specific to US Deputy Marshals. Caitlyn would have to force her mind away from her concerns about her dad's degrading energy. She tucked her worry deep in a locked compartment in her mind. Her mom and Dylan would take good care of her dad. She had to trust that.

Caitlyn took an extra minute to look at Colt's picture that she had taped to her mirror. She touched his face with her finger and a painful grip squeezed her heart. "I'm almost done." She smiled at his image before heading out to meet her team at the flagpole.

Today the full class was divided into male and female exclusive groups to learn and experience strip searching. She'd be glad when that was over with. Tomorrow they'd practice safe hand-cuffing procedures, fugitive transport, and learn the ins and outs of the Witness Protection Program, or Witsec.

With the first half of training behind her, Caitlyn was in the best physical shape she'd ever been in. So, though she still dreaded the long grueling hours of running, weight training and defensive tactics training, she was ready to meet the challenge.

WITH ONLY ONE more week to go, Caitlyn would soon be a full-fledged US Deputy Marshal and would get to go home. She couldn't wait, but she couldn't afford to lose the bubble now, either. Today, her class would face the first of three major rites of passage: Marshal's Beach. The instructors watched as the students were pitted against each other in a grueling physical event.

First thing in the morning, all the would-be marshals and their instructors met at the edge of a fifty-meter pit of deep sand. The students were divided into two teams. Caitlyn was on the silver team. She and her teammates would battle against her roommate and others on the gold team. The instructors wiped white zinc oxide on their noses and sat in camp chairs in their swim trunks at the edge of the pit.

The chief instructor paced before them, shouting, "The object of this event is to outlast the opposing team. You will all begin on the starting line. First, you will run down to the other side of the pit and back for a total of one hundred meters. Then comes ten sets each of pushups, jumping jacks, sit-ups, burpees, and mountain climbers. All in the depth of the sand pit. And that my baby marshals will complete round one. You will continue for a minimum of ten rounds. After that, if anyone's left, we'll continue until the last iron man is standing." He slowly panned his gaze over the group of students. "Who are we?"

"Marshals!" everyone at the event shouted.

"Who are we?"

"Marshals!" they shouted again.

"Who?"

"Marshals!" the students screamed as loud as they could.

"Then show me! Ready… Go!" The chief instructor blew his whistle.

Caitlyn took off and the sand under her foot gave away. She fell forward, face first into the deep sand. She pushed herself up and spit sand as she raced after the group of students clambering to the far side of the pit. This event was pure hell, but she wouldn't miss it for the world.

In the end, the gold team won giving their instructors bragging rights for the rest of the week. Purely happy to have survived, Caitlyn took an extra-long shower and skipping dinner, went straight to bed. The next day held the second milestone: Kumite, a free-style martial arts competition. The students were allowed boxing head gear and gloves, but other than that, pretty much anything was fair play. Caitlyn worked harder on this section of training than on anything else. She hoped she was ready. The rest of the week held final testing and paperwork. It wouldn't be long now until graduation day.

United States Marshals Service Academy Graduation
FLETCE ~ Glynco, GA

The morning of graduation, Caitlyn woke before her alarm. It was still dark out when she dressed in her PT gear and slid on the thirty-pound ballistic vest over her Marshal Trainee T-shirt. She gathered with the rest of her class and prepared for the traditional ten-mile run referred to as the Marshal Mile that ended at a memorial for fallen US Deputy Marshals.

Their instructors said a few moving and motivational words to the class and Caitlyn, trying to keep her emotions in check, bit the inside of her cheek so hard she tasted blood. She was overcome with a deep sense of accomplishment and the pride that came with belonging to this elite group of warriors.

When they returned from the run, a kilt-clad bagpiper led the class up the circle drive toward the headquarters building where family members waited to cheer them on. Caitlyn searched for Colt, and once she saw him in the crowd, all other faces blurred as if he were the only one there. Her pace increased until she stood before him radiating with pride.

The next step in the ceremonious day was receiving her Velcro Marshals badge. Family members pressed the badges onto the newly minted Deputy US Marshals' ballistic vests. That moment, and the look in Colt's eyes as he honored her with her badge, would live in Caitlyn's heart and memory forever. It was by far the proudest moment of her life.

Before the new deputy marshals had any real time to connect with family, the class jogged back to their barracks to shower and change for the graduation ceremony. The lapel of Caitlyn's brand-new navy-blue pantsuit displayed a shiny US Deputy Marshal pin—a miniature version of the badge she had earned through sheer grit and perseverance.

Inside the auditorium, Caitlyn sat in her assigned seat and stared at the table on the stage that held a stack of badges. She thought back over the long months of grueling work she'd gone through at the US Marshals Service Basic Training Academy at FLETC. The past several months had been the hardest of Caitlyn's life, physically, academically, and psychologically. Memories of her training played across her mind. She'd always been a runner, but running in formation while singing a cadence and never knowing if the run would be five or fifteen miles almost did her in. Two members of her class had dropped out after failing to keep up with all the physical training.

Her time at Glynco certainly was physically demanding, but it was hardest on her emotionally. Caitlyn's heart was sore from missing Renegade, Colt, and her family. Not being with them affected her far more than she had expected. Homesickness often distracted her from her academic work. Her feelings for Colt hadn't diminished in any way. In fact, if at all possible, they had deepened.

For Caitlyn, the best part of the training was the self-defense and firearms portions. She had learned a lot in the Wyoming Law Enforcement Academy, and she further honed those skills at FLETC. But after all her training, she came to understand that her greatest strength came from her relationships, and she couldn't wait to get home. She had spoken with her parents last night, and Caitlyn understood that they couldn't attend her graduation because her dad was still feeling weak. She wished they could be with her but having some alone time with Colt was a fantastic consolation.

Caitlyn found it hard to sit still during the commencement, even after the exhausting early-morning run. She was graduating with honors, and so she listened for her name to be called among the first. She was proud of herself and the entire class of new Deputy Marshals. But in truth, she was eager for the ceremony to end. She was obligated to attend the following reception, at least for a little while, but what she really wanted was to spend time in Colt's arms and get home to Renegade.

Colt had come to Georgia without her dog which was disappointing for sure, but she understood. Though he had told her he wasn't bringing Ren she had still secretly hoped he'd be there. Traveling with a high energy police K9 was a challenge, even for her, and after all, she'd be seeing him as soon as she got home. McKenzie had been faithful about FaceTiming with Renegade, and that helped Caitlyn cope during their separation.

With a jolt, Caitlyn realized she hadn't been listening to

the commencement speech. She forced her mind back to the graduation, though her arms itched to encircle Colt and feel his body close to hers. She had seen him and Renegade over the holidays, and she and Colt had talked every weekend on FaceTime while she was in Georgia—except for the times she had training exercises or dispatch had called him out on a disturbance of some kind. She was grateful for the technology that allowed her to see his face while they were apart, but now she was impatient to touch the real thing.

Before Caitlyn left Moose Creek last fall, Colt had hired Wesley Cooper to replace her as his deputy. Eventually, he'd need to hire a second deputy so that all involved could have full shift coverage and backup if they ever needed it. Memories of Colt and her working six-day work weeks and constantly being on call made her smile. It had been quite an experience, being Moose Creek's solitary deputy, but she was ready now to move on into what she hoped would be a more exciting job chasing fugitives.

Starting next Monday, she'd be officially attached to the US Marshals Wyoming Office. It was difficult to get her mind around the idea of this new life. She would also directly support the Billings field office where Dirk Sterling and Sam Dillinger worked, and anywhere else the Marshals Service called her. Because of the vast amount of barren land to cover in their part of the country, Caitlyn and Renegade would remain posted in Moose Creek. While constantly on call, she'd be able to work from home doing computer search and case work, hunting down leads, and primarily keeping her K9 partner's sniffing, tracking, and attack skills sharp. She and Renegade would deploy whenever and wherever her unique team was needed. Sterling promised to keep her busy, and she figured she'd enjoy the diverse work of a Deputy US Marshal.

Loud applause snapped her attention, once again, back to

the room, and Caitlyn glanced at the USMS Director to see if he had concluded his commencement address while she'd been daydreaming about the next chapter in her life. The speaker made a few final congratulatory statements and took his spot next to the badges at the center of the stage. The academy's Assistant Director stood before the graduates and asked them to rise. The Director raised his right hand and after asking them to recite their pledge of duty, he officially swore Caitlyn's class in as Deputy United States Marshals. Pride and a deep sense of honor swelled in her chest, and her eyes pricked with unshed tears.

The Assistant Director read the names of each new deputy in the class. When Caitlyn heard her name, she went up on the stage, accepted her new circle-star Deputy US Marshals badge and credentials, and shook the Director's hand. She bit down hard against a sudden rush of emotion as she walked across the platform.

Following the ceremony and a resounding standing ovation with shouts of approval from the audience, the Assistant Director invited everyone to attend the reception in the next room. Colt made a beeline straight for her, but classmates and friends drew her into embraces, high-fives, and handshakes, and she temporarily lost sight of him. She sensed instantly when Colt's hand claimed the small of her back, and she turned to face him. He pulled her to his chest, wrapping his arms possessively around her. And she was home.

Caitlyn felt the vibration of his voice more than she heard it. "Congratulations, Catie. I'm about to burst with pride for you. Everyone at home is, too."

"Thanks. I wish my mom and dad could have been here, though."

"They do too."

"Mom said Dad hasn't gotten any better since Christmas."

"No, he hasn't." Colt swept his hand over her cheek to her hair that was pulled back into a French-twist. "Logan wanted to come with me to surprise you, but he was called in on a case and couldn't get away."

"He called me last night to congratulate me."

"What did he say when you told him you were graduating with honors?"

Caitlyn laughed. "That he expected no less." Her middle brother, Logan, had graduated from the FBI Academy at the top of his class as well and told her he was tremendously proud of her. She rose on her tiptoes and spoke into Colt's ear. "Honestly, I don't care about any of that. I have to grab a cookie and at least one glass of punch for appearance's sake, but then let's get out of here."

Colt stepped back, his gaze reading her intent. A slow smile spread across his mouth. "I should have gotten a hotel room."

Caitlyn giggled. "Surprised you didn't. We could have flown home tomorrow." Colt's expression grew serious, and a cold pall settled over Caitlyn's shoulders. "What's wrong?"

"It would've been selfish of me to keep you to myself." He hesitated. "Your dad's taken a turn for the worse, and I knew you'd want to get home as soon as you could."

It was Caitlyn's turn to search his eyes for answers. "What are you saying, Colt? I talked to him last night. I know he's been feeling worse, but he's going to be okay, right? What does Blake say?"

Colt glanced away from her, lowering his gaze to the floor before looking at her again. He shook his head. "Your dad still refuses to see the doctor. He insists he only needs a little rest. Your mom is hoping—we're all hoping—that you'll be able to convince him to get checked out. Maybe he'll listen to you."

Caitlyn stood tall and took a step back, taking a firm

grasp on her fear and frustration. "I don't care if he listens or not. Why hasn't someone called Blake out to the house? That's what I'll do if Dad still refuses to go in."

"Your mom tried that, but your dad locked himself in the bedroom and refused to let Doctor Kennedy in." Colt scanned the crowd before his eyes met hers again. "It was just a few days ago, and everyone involved agreed that it might be more upsetting to John to bust down the door. Dylan insisted you'd be able to convince him to see the doctor once you got home."

"Damn straight. When is our flight?"

"We have two hours before we have to be at the airport. Any longer and we won't have enough time to get through security and still make our flight."

"I have to go to the armory to pick up my government issued Glock .40, but then we can leave." She flashed him a grin. "Today will be the first time I've ever flown armed." Caitlyn turned around and searched the crowd for the Assistant Director. When she saw him, she marched up and explained that she had to leave early to make her flight home.

"I understand, Deputy Marshal Reed. It has been my great pleasure to supervise your class during this year's course. I look forward to hearing great things about your future career, and someday I hope to meet that K9 partner of yours."

"You know where to find us, sir. Thank you for everything." She shook the Assistant Director's hand, turned on her heel. She took Colt's hand and they walked together to the armory to pick up her officially issued handgun. Caitlyn held up her new Glock and Colt took pictures of her with his phone. She laughed and packed the weapon back in its case before they made their way to the holding room where her other bags were waiting. Colt followed her and helped carry her things to the rental car.

"I have something for you." Colt reached into the trunk and pulled out a large, sturdy gray box with a silver bow taped to the top.

Caitlyn grinned. "What is this?"

Colt chuckled. "Open it and find out."

The box was heavy, and she slid the lid off to find two more boxes inside. One was a locked black case, and the other was wrapped in blue paper. "Colt!"

He punched a code on the lock and the case opened. Inside, resting in a felt-lined tray, was her personal Glock 43, only now the handgrip was engraved with the US Marshals circle star badge. Caitlyn brushed the emblem with her fingertip and looked up at Colt blinking back tears. She lifted the flat-black weapon and wrapped her hand around the grip, feeling the etching against her palm. After checking to see that the magazine was empty, she cocked the slide and held the weapon out to look down the sights. "It's beautiful!" She reseated her newly emblazoned gun in its case and unwrapped the second gift, which she knew by its weight was a box of 9mm ammo.

"This is the most thoughtful gift I've ever received." She realized then that this man truly knew her better than anyone else in the world. Caitlyn set her gift down and threw her arms around Colt. "I love it!"

"You certainly earned it." He brushed a loose strand of hair from her face and kissed her. "I'm proud of you, Catie."

ONE CONNECTION and six hours later, Caitlyn and Colt stepped through the doors into the parking lot of the Rapid City airport. Dusk had already settled over the cool spring sky. Renegade, who had been sitting politely next to McKenzie, tore his leash from her hand as he bolted toward Caitlyn. She fell to her knees and embraced her dog, who nearly toppled her over backwards with his exuberance. Elated, he licked her face and neck. Caitlyn laughed, trying to escape his robust welcome.

"Easy, Ren. I'm happy to see you too, buddy. I'm home for good now, sweet boy." She laughed and pushed against his chest, allowing the slathered greeting for another minute before she firmly commanded, "*Sedni*, Renegade. *Sedni*."

Her dog obediently sat down next to her, but there was no stilling his tail as it brushed back-and-forth over the concrete. He occasionally lapped at the drool escaping his broad K9 smile. Before she rose from the ground, Caitlyn leaned forward and held his head to her chest. One of the best things about dogs was no matter how disciplined they were, they never held back on the honesty of their emotions. She nuzzled his ear. "I missed you, buddy. I love you." She squeezed him tighter, and he licked the nape of her neck.

Eventually, Caitlyn stood and faced Dylan. Without preamble, she asked, "What's going on with Dad?"

Dylan towered over her, but anyone watching could tell he felt cowed by Caitlyn in that moment. He shrugged and bent to embrace her. "He's not doing well. He's constantly tired, can't seem to get enough to drink, and is so cranky, he's hard to be around. Mom's the one who has to deal with him all the time, and he hasn't been very nice to her. I've never seen him treat her like this. McKenzie's been trying to give Mom a break when she can, but you know Mom. Between our two parents, I don't know which one's more stubborn."

Caitlyn sighed and hugged her brother. "Thanks for coming to get me. I'm sorry I haven't been here to help with Dad." She shifted her gaze to McKenzie, and reaching forward, Caitlyn slung her arm around her shoulders. "Hey, Kenz. Thanks again for taking such good care of Renegade and for helping to take care of our mom and dad." She stepped back and addressed them both. "Did either of you talk with Blake?" Dylan scratched his chin and nodded.

"Well, what does he think?"

His dark piercing eyes, ones that matched her own, didn't flinch. "Blake thinks it could be Dad's heart. But it might also be diabetes, or any number of things. But with Dad refusing to allow him to do any tests, the doc is only guessing."

"Dad." Caitlyn groaned to herself. "Ren, *kemne*." She strode off, leaving the others to follow. "Where's your truck?" she called over her shoulder to her brother.

IN HIS BOREDOM, Ray's stomach gnawed on itself. His hunger put him in a wicked mood. They'd been hiding out for several months now and begging for a few bags of groceries at a time or driving hours away to hit random convenience stores for small amounts of cash, was no longer viable. Not to mention, it put their whole venture at risk. Ray figured their trail was cold enough now that they could move to another out-of-the-way motel. One with heat and a TV. But they needed cash to rent a room, and they were flat out. Ray spent the morning staring at the fire, sifting through a series of plots and plans to get more money.

Reggie lay, stoned out of his mind, on the worn mattress of his bunk. What a disappointment he was turning out to be. That brilliant mind, rotting with crank. Ray got up and stood over his brother. A slow rage boiled in his gut. He tilted a tin cup to his lips and took a sip of water from the snow they'd melted but he turned and spit it into the fire. The resulting hiss matched his mood.

Ray kicked the bed and slapped the side of his brother's head. Reggie's glassy gaze floated up to him. "Pay attention, idiot. I have an idea, so listen up." He glanced over his shoulder to make sure Jason was listening too before he continued. "Things are about to change. We need to go to another town, and that means stealing another car. I think Sheridan is far enough away. We'll hit a bigger store for enough cash to stay at a motel. We can snag a couple of bottles of whiskey while we're at it, too. I can't drink another ounce of this melted snow."

8

Colt hurried to match Caitlyn's brisk cadence. She had always been a leader, but it seemed the Marshals Service Academy had sharpened her edges. Colt remembered back when Logan returned from the Army's Officer Candidate School. He had changed, too. Then, after he was released from the Army, Logan carried the invisible weight of grief over the loss of Lobo, his Army K9 partner. Fortunately, Logan's new FBI-K9, and his girlfriend, Addison, seemed to help lighten the darkness that had surrounded him for so long. Over time, Logan had settled into himself again. Hopefully, it wouldn't take Caitlyn as long as it did her brother.

Caitlyn didn't have to grapple with the darkness, but still she maintained a subtle separation from them. He'd noticed a slight emotional distance in her at Christmas, but it seemed more obvious now. Maybe some time at home with him and Renegade would ease her back into the Caitlyn they both knew and loved. But no matter how Caitlyn presented herself, she was in complete possession of his heart.

Dylan pointed to his dually in the second row to the right.

On their way home, Dylan and McKenzie sat in the front, while Colt and Caitlyn rode in the back with Renegade resting his head on her lap. Colt draped his arm across the back of the seat and massaged Caitlyn's neck, hoping to be a comfort and ease her tension.

McKenzie turned around in her seat to face them. "I bet you're glad to be home."

"Yes." Caitlyn's abrupt answer caused McKenzie to glance at Colt with concern and confusion in her eyes.

He tried to cover. "You guys would have been so proud to see Catie graduating at the top of her class. She'll have to show you her new badge. It's been a big day. I know *I'm* tired."

Dylan glanced at his sister in the rearview mirror. "I'm sorry we couldn't be there, Caitlyn. When do you start work?"

"Monday."

Her brother's eyebrow twitched. "Where are you stationed? What'll you be doing?"

"Casper—hunting fugitives."

McKenzie smiled and let out a laugh that sounded forced.

Dark eyes narrowed at Caitlyn in the reflection. "Come on, Caitlyn, give us a break. We want to hear about the academy and your new job. Quit with the one-word answers."

Caitlyn glared back. "I'm more interested in why you've allowed Dad to avoid seeing Blake."

During the rest of the drive, what little conversation there was seemed forced, and so did their laughter as everyone besides Caitlyn aimed for normalcy. By the time they reached Moose Creek, the tension inside the cab was thick. When Dylan turned onto the Reed Ranch Road, Caitlyn's neck muscles tightened under Colt's fingers. He understood she needed time to make the transition from basic training to coming back home, but it was unlike her to be so abrupt.

Before Dylan shifted the truck into park, Caitlyn opened her door and jumped to the ground, and Renegade sprang out with her. She ran up the porch steps and in through the front door.

As Colt hurried after her, Dylan said, "We better get in there before there's an explosion between the two of them." Dylan and McKenzie followed him into the house.

When Colt entered, John was sitting on the couch, pale and ashen, with Caitlyn standing above him, her hands curled into fists at her sides. Renegade sat at John's feet nuzzling his hand. "You don't get to make that decision, Dad! Not when so many people around here love you. If the doctor figures out what's wrong, he can treat it. I can't believe you're being so stubborn." Caitlyn's jaw clamped shut, and she pierced her mother with a fierce glare. "Mom, get Blake on the phone, right now."

John crossed his arms over his belly and huffed. "You may be a US Deputy Marshal now, young lady—" A smile glinted in John's eyes and hovered around his mouth. "Congratulations on that, by the way—" His brow scrunched back down, and he cleared his throat. "But I'm still your father. I'm the one who says what goes on around here. I'm not having that teenaged Doctor Kennedy come out here on the night we're supposed to be celebrating your accomplishments. I'll see him tomorrow."

Caitlyn jammed her hands onto her hips. "No, Dad, you'll see him tonight. And if there's still time to celebrate, he can be a part of it. But first things first." Colt had never seen anyone talk to John the way Caitlyn did and her dad's lack of anger in response surprised him.

Renegade crawled up on the couch next to John and rested his muzzle in John's lap. This position was one Caitlyn's dog had taken recently, and it seemed to calm her dad's mood. But the look on Caitlyn's face when she watched her dog climb on the furniture was priceless.

"Renegade, *knoze*." She barked out the order and pointed to the floor next to her left foot. The poor dog slunk off the couch and sat next to Caitlyn's heel. She scowled first at her father and then sent an icy glare toward McKenzie. "Have you been allowing this? Has Renegade lost all his discipline? I thought I—"

McKenzie held up her hand to stop Caitlyn. "He has lost none of his discipline, Caitlyn. I realize you must feel out of the loop since you've been gone, but everyone here has been doing the best they can. As far as Renegade goes, I'm sure you know dogs can sense illnesses. He's been showing us, like he just did, that your dad is about to have an episode." She turned to Dylan and Colt. "I suggest we get John to bed. Caitlyn, why don't you call Blake?"

Caitlyn's cheeks flushed, and she lowered her head. Colt rested his hand on her shoulder and gave her a gentle squeeze. McKenzie had knocked her down a peg, and Caitlyn looked remorseful. Colt brushed his lips across her temple and said, "I'll be right back as soon as Dylan and I get your dad upstairs."

McKenzie went to Stella and put her arm around her shoulders. Stella seemed to lean into and draw from McKenzie's strength. "Come on Stella, how about we make a pot of tea?"

Stella nodded slightly, but then turned back to Caitlyn and opened her arms. "Okay, but not before I congratulate my baby girl. Caitlyn, we're all so very proud of you." Moisture filled Stella's eyes, but she clenched her jaw, refusing to allow the tears to flow. "I had wanted to surprise you with a grand celebration—bigger than the last one." She closed her eyes briefly and then met Caitlyn's gaze directly once again. "But as you can see…"

Caitlyn rushed to her mother and threw her arms around her. "Oh Mom, I'm so glad you didn't. I know you're proud of me, and that's more than enough. I'm sorry. I didn't realize things had gotten so bad." She drew back and searched her mother's face. "He didn't seem this bad at Christmas. Why didn't you tell me? I would have come home."

A small smile formed on Stella's mouth. "That's why we didn't say anything. Your father would have been furious if you left training because of his health. I think that's why he tried to hide his symptoms. But now you've graduated, and you are home." Stella pulled her back into an embrace, then she followed McKenzie into the kitchen.

Caitlyn rounded on Colt and Dylan. The pain in her eyes burned Colt's cheeks, and her brother looked contrite as he stared at the floor. "You two heard McKenzie. Take Dad up to his room." She pulled out her phone, swiped it on, and tapped. Colt noticed Blake was clearly still on Caitlyn's speed dial, but he decided to think about that later.

"Blake? Hi, it's Caitlyn."

The guys each took one of John's arms and pulled him to his feet. They led him to the stairs and waited for him to catch his breath. Colt met Dylan's eyes behind John's head, and nodding, they both clasped John's shoulders and slid their other arms under his knees. When they lifted, John protested, but eventually he closed his eyes and sighed.

Caitlyn's voice slapped against the log walls of the living room below as Colt and Dylan made their way up the stairs. "Yeah, I just got home. My dad is not well at all. What do you think it is?" There was a pause while Caitlyn listened to Blake's response, but then she snapped, "That's no excuse, Blake. You're the doctor. You should've insisted." Colt watched her from the balcony above. "Thanks. We'll see you in thirty minutes." Caitlyn tapped her phone screen and shoved the device into her back pocket.

Colt swallowed hard, and when she peered up at him, he gave her a flat smile. Caitlyn acknowledged him with a slight bob of her chin before she turned and marched to the kitchen. Renegade, acting chastised with his head and tail down, locked his eyes on Caitlyn and responded to her movements with precision. *Poor guy. He doesn't understand.*

Colt and Dylan maneuvered John into the master bedroom. When they settled him on the bed, Dylan said, "You know, Dad, it might be better if we set up a bed for you downstairs in your office. That way, when you need to rest, you can easily lie down."

"You mean when *you* need to rest." John glared at his son, and Colt noticed the muscles in Dylan's jaw bulge. Colt remembered the last days of his mother's life when she was reeling from the horrible effects of her cancer. Sometimes, she had been mean and difficult to be around —grouchy and snapping the way John was behaving now. But Colt knew things could get worse. Like when his mother no longer had the energy to object. It had been only a few days after that when he lost her altogether. Colt tucked the blankets around John, who angrily flung them off again.

Dylan dropped into the chair next to the bedside. "Guess you'll be seeing the doctor tonight, Dad." A soft chuckle emanated from Dylan's throat. "That little wildcat you raised downstairs doesn't take no for an answer." Colt smirked to himself at the truth of Dylan's words.

John wiped his hand over his eyes. "This isn't how I wanted her homecoming to go."

"I know, Dad. It's okay. Caitlyn understands. We need to find out what is wrong with you so we can fix it. No one in this house is ready to lose you."

"I'm not going anywhere." John responded, but his voice was weak.

A hard lump formed in Colt's throat, and he turned toward the door. "I'll go see if the girls need help."

VENTING some of her helplessness on the swinging kitchen door, Caitlyn burst into the room, coming face-to-face with a bouncing black-and-white short-haired puppy with black ears and nose. She drew up short, and her eyes flew to McKenzie. "Who is this?"

McKenzie smiled as she dropped tea bags into the teapot and filled it with hot water. "This is Lariat. Larry for short. He's Dylan's new ranch hand."

"What?" Caitlyn couldn't resist the warm joy that bubbled up, and she squatted down to pet the playful puppy. "Hello, Larry. You are adorable." Renegade sat obediently next to her, but he couldn't prevent a small whine from leaking out of his throat. Caitlyn realized she'd been a little rough on him when he was only trying to help her dad, and now he was working to make up for it by being extra good. She slung an arm around his shoulders. "It's okay, Ren, my heart belongs to you, alone." The turmoil of conflicting emotions was getting the best of her. She'd been riding high on the thrill of graduation and then had plummeted at the news of her dad's poor health. She felt out of the loop and exhausted. Worried dog eyes appraised her, and she laughed. Ruffling the top of his head, Caitlyn said. "I'm sorry, boy."

Holding Renegade's shoulders, she reached with her other hand to scoop up the puppy. Renegade trembled as he sat, trying hard to stay seated until Caitlyn released him. She snickered again. "Okay, Ren. You can go play." Renegade lunged forward, and Larry scrambled out of Caitlyn's arms—

bouncing on all fours before spinning and taking off through a newly installed dog door that led out to the backyard. Renegade followed, hot on the puppy's heels.

"Last fall, when Dylan was working so hard, we all told him he needed help, but he refused to hire anyone." McKenzie placed the sugar bowl on the tray next to the teapot. "Colt came out whenever he could, but it wasn't enough. I thought long and hard about how I could help, but I knew I'd be more trouble than help if I tried to ride a horse and chase cows. One night in January, when I was watching a movie with your mom, it suddenly occurred to me that there was something I could do."

Stella took up the tale. "McKenzie found Lariat at an Australian Cow Dog rescue, and she kept him hidden over at Colt's place so Dylan wouldn't see him while she started his training. During the day, she worked with both dogs out at your place. Then she gave Larry to Dylan for Valentine's Day." Caitlyn noticed the look of love her mother sent McKenzie, and she smiled inside. Things were clearly moving along nicely between Dylan and McKenzie. She pumped her fist mentally. At least that was working out the way she had hoped.

As McKenzie set a small pitcher of cream next to the sugar bowl and lifted her tray, she said, "Larry is still just a puppy, but he's already showing signs of being very smart, and he loves to work. By this time next year, he'll be a full-on ranch hand."

"What was Dylan's response to getting a puppy for Valentine's Day?" Caitlyn asked.

McKenzie stammered, "He wasn't actually a *Valentine's* gift." Her cheeks flamed.

Caitlyn's mother mouth turned up at the corners and shook her head as she picked up a tray holding enough teacups for everyone. "If you say so." She followed McKenzie, who leaned against the swinging door, holding it open for Stella and Caitlyn. As she went through the door, her mom said, "At least Larry makes Dylan smile a lot more often."

Caitlyn followed the two other women into the living room, noticing how close they seemed, as though they'd known each other for years. But she was left to wonder about how things truly were between McKenzie and her brother. Maybe the fond relationship between the two women had nothing to do with Dylan after all.

"I can't believe you didn't tell me about Larry."

Stella answered, "We all agreed not to talk too much about home while you were gone. I remembered how hard it was for Logan to focus on training while he worried about things here, and we didn't want you to have to go through that."

Caitlyn bunched her brows together in frustration but didn't respond. Her mom obviously did what she thought was best.

Colt met Stella on the stairs and took the tray from her hands. They all climbed the steps and filed into the master bedroom.

Everyone sat or stood around the room staring at John while sipping their black currant tea. Occasionally, someone asked Caitlyn a few questions about her training. She answered, forcing cheerfulness into her voice, aware of how much her dad hated sitting in bed with all eyes on him. It was exactly why he didn't want to be stuck there. He hated being the center of everyone's doting and attention.

The dogs started barking, and a moment later the doorbell rang. Caitlyn's shoulders relaxed, and she sprang to her feet. "I'll get it." She ran to the hall and sprinted down the stairs.

COLT FOLLOWED Caitlyn from her father's room and watched her run down the curving staircase toward the front entrance. When she flung the door open, a beautiful smile lit her face, and Colt's gut tightened as he leaned against the rail to view the scene below.

"Hi, Blake. It's great to see you." She reached up to embrace him. "Thank you so much for coming out so late, but I'm extremely worried about my dad."

Blake's deep, smooth voice carried up to where Colt stood. "I'm always available to you, Caitlyn. You know that."

"I appreciate it." Caitlyn stepped back to let Doctor Kennedy enter the house. The doctor kept his hand on her shoulder. He leaned toward Caitlyn as if to brush her cheek with a kiss, but at the same time, his eyes caught Colt glowering down at him. Kennedy nodded once, acknowledging him, and pulled back without the kiss. "Where is your father?"

"He's upstairs in his room. Come on up." Caitlyn turned to mount the stairs, and when she did, she seemed to notice Colt watching them. Her gaze dropped to the tread on the steps, and she didn't meet his eye when she passed by with Blake following behind her.

When Kennedy reached the landing, he held his hand out to Colt. "Sheriff."

Colt forced his hand out to grip Blake's. "Doctor."

Blake followed Caitlyn, and Colt brought up the rear. He leaned against the doorjamb of the master suite and observed the proceedings, keeping a close eye on Caitlyn's expressions. Had he been foolish to believe Caitlyn had resolved everything between her and the doctor? Seeing them together now, he wasn't sure. *Does she have left-over feelings for him?*

Kennedy approached the bedside. "Mr. Reed, I hear you're still not feeling very well." He pressed his palm against John's forehead.

John turned his head away from the doctor's hand. "I'm fine—just getting old is all."

Kennedy responded with a comforting smile and chuckled. "Aren't we all? Do you mind if I set my medical bag on your bed?"

"Depends on what you have in there, Doc."

"Nothing ominous, I promise. All I'm going to do tonight is give you an exam and take a little blood. Other than that, you're already where I think you should be—in bed."

John pushed himself up and spread the blankets across his lap. "You drove all the way out here for that?"

Blake's friendly smirk answered him. "Well, apparently, you weren't willing to come to me for the same simple tests…"

John sighed, seeming to accept the gentle rebuff.

Kennedy opened his bag and pulled out a stethoscope and a portable blood pressure cuff. He listened to John's chest and various points on his back before he asked, "Your pulse rate is higher than I'd like to see. Have you been having any headaches?"

"Off and on."

"How often?"

"I don't count them." John's eyes hardened.

"Best guess. One or two a week? Once a day?"

"A few a week, I guess."

Blake nodded. "Has your vision been blurry at all?"

John shrugged. "A little, but that's not unusual."

"It's not? How long have you had blurry vision?"

Stella answered. "I've been on him to see the eye doctor for about a year, but you can see how stubborn he is."

"Okay, Mr. Reed, I'm guessing you're okay with needles?" John chuffed and held out his arm. A ghost of a smile crossed Blake's lips. "Good." Turning to the family, he said, "I think

John might like some privacy for the next couple of tests. Now might be a good time for more tea."

Caitlyn nodded and pushed everyone out of the room, shutting the door behind her. "Let's go downstairs. Blake will tell us what he thinks when he's done."

Stella slipped her hand under Caitlyn's elbow. "This isn't exactly how I hoped your welcome home party would go. I made you your favorite cake. I hope there'll still be time to enjoy a slice before you go home."

Colt studied the tension that stretched tight across Caitlyn's forehead and bunched her shoulders. Celebrating was obviously the last thing on her mind.

"Sure, Mom. I'd love a piece of your Death by Chocolate cake." Caitlyn walked arm-in-arm with her mother down the stairs, and her eyes met his when she walked by him, but he couldn't read her emotion.

The group congregated in the kitchen. Stella retrieved the cake from the refrigerator while McKenzie filled another kettle of water to boil, and Colt carried slices of cake out to the table.

Caitlyn sidled up to McKenzie and leaned against her shoulder. "So, things are good between you and Dylan?"

"To be honest, there's not much going on between me and Dylan. Nothing has changed. He's either working or sleeping."

"But you gave him a puppy." Caitlyn couldn't believe her brother was so dense.

"I know. And I thought we could connect over raising and training him… and we have." McKenzie sighed and turned to look Caitlyn in the eye. "Some days I think things are great, but then he becomes distant."

"Distant… how?"

"I don't know. Not distant really, but I don't think he's

interested. It's like he expects me to be here and it's no big deal whether I am or not."

"Do you mean he takes you for granted?"

"I guess, but that seems extreme. I mean, it's not like we're in enough of a relationship for me to claim that. Anyway, I have a job offer back in Florida that I'm seriously considering."

"What? McKenzie, you can't just leave. Have you talked to Dylan about this?" Caitlyn glanced at Colt, and he shrugged. None of this was his business.

"No. I don't have any ground to stand on. It's not like we have any kind of understanding or anything. I have no claim on him." McKenzie stepped away from Caitlyn when Dylan came out of the kitchen with Stella, ending their conversation.

By the time the dessert was all set up, Blake descended the steps, and Caitlyn rushed toward him. "So, what do you think? What's wrong with my dad?"

Blake met her gaze directly. "I have some thoughts, but John has asked that I keep them to myself until we get further test results. We want to be certain about what we're dealing with and how best to care for him. John's sleeping, for now, which is always the best thing." Kennedy's matinee-idol grin spread across his face, deepening the dimples all the women seemed to love, and Colt clenched his teeth, bunching his jaw muscles.

"Will you stay for a piece of cake?" Caitlyn tugged on the doctor's arm.

"Death by Chocolate? That's your favorite." Briefly his gaze flashed to Colt, then with a slight shake of his head, Kennedy turned toward the door. "Thanks, but I'd better be going. Congratulations on becoming a US Deputy Marshal, Caitlyn. The whole town is very proud of you." He chuckled. "I heard talk of folks wanting to hold a parade."

Caitlyn grinned and smacked his arm. "You did not."

Colt's fingertips whitened as he gripped his plate and watched a silent exchange pass between them.

"I'll get these samples to the lab first thing in the morning and will call John as soon as I know anything. Have a nice celebration." Kennedy raised his hand in farewell to everyone else. "If there are any changes, please feel free to call me anytime. Otherwise, I'll speak with you soon."

Stella crossed the room and, together with Caitlyn, showed Blake out before returning to their cake.

Dylan picked up the TV remote from the coffee table. "It's almost time for the ten o'clock news." The flatscreen clicked on just as the program began. "Good evening, I'm Meredith Stanwick, here with WNN. Tonight, our news correspondent in Sheridan joins us with an update on a liquor store robbery that left one man dead and one man fighting for his life in emergency surgery at the Billings Hospital, where Flight For Life took him earlier this evening. Here is the latest update."

The screen filled with the face of a young clean-cut reporter on location. "Thank you, Meredith, I am here in Sheridan, Wyoming, near First and Main Street with Sheriff Blankenship." He tilted an oversized microphone toward the sheriff. "Can you tell us what happened here tonight, Sheriff?"

The full, round face of Sheriff Blankenship took over the screen. Colt recognized the man he'd met a couple of times before. "As far as we can tell, two gunmen entered the liquor store at approximately 8:25 pm. They approached the counter and drew their guns, demanding all the cash in the register drawer. The clerk managed to step on an emergency alert button before shots were fired, but unfortunately by the time we arrived, he was shot and killed at the scene. Another man, we believe to be a customer was also shot and was flown by helicopter to a hospital in Billings for emergency surgery."

The reporter asked, "Have you had an opportunity to view the security tapes, Sheriff?"

"We've seen a small section, but the tape is currently in possession of crime investigators, who will enhance the video for a clearer image. We are hopeful to learn the identity of the shooters before long. Crime scene investigators are searching for evidence as we speak. We've enlarged a still image of the robbers taken from the video. We'd like to show it to your viewers, now."

The sheriff looked directly into the camera and held a grainy, gray-scale image up for all to see. "If anyone recognizes either of these men, please call the number at the bottom of the screen immediately. We believe they are traveling with a third person who is suspected of driving the getaway car. If you see any of them, do not approach. These men are armed and extremely dangerous. Thank you."

The camera panned back to the young reporter who signed off, and the news returned to the program in the studio. Meredith Stanwick recapped the information they'd just heard while showing the blurry image of the robbers again, then moved on to further news.

Colt realized he and Caitlyn had both moved to positions directly in front of the wall mounted TV.

He glanced at her, and she faced him. "Sheridan isn't far from here. We all need to be on alert."

Colt grabbed his cell and called Deputy Cooper. The phone rang twice before the man answered. "Wes, have you heard the news? I'm out at the Reed Ranch. I'll be back in town as soon as I can." Caitlyn nodded at his words as he spoke. He put his phone away and went to her. Sliding his hands over her shoulders, he gripped her arms. "I'm sorry,

Catie, but I need to get back to town. I should be in the office on standby."

"Of course. What can I do to help?"

"If I think of anything, I'll let you know." He slid his hand to her shoulder blade and guided her toward the door. "I hate to cut your celebration short, but are you ready to go?"

Caitlyn circled his waist with her arm as she walked him to the front of the house. "I'm going to stay at my folks' tonight to keep an eye on my dad. Call me if you need me."

Colt pulled her out through the front door and turned to her. "I understand." He closed the door behind them. "This isn't how I pictured your homecoming night going." He searched her eyes, but with the porch light off, it was too dark to gauge her emotions in their depths.

Caitlyn cupped his face in her hands and pulled his head down to her. "Me either," she whispered, her breath brushing across his lips. She kissed him, communicating all the love he had hoped to see in her eyes. His shoulders relaxed, and he met her kiss with promises that time and circumstances didn't allow for. Yet.

9

Dylan opened the front door, and light flooded over Colt and Caitlyn's embrace on the porch. The couple was obviously reluctant to part, and McKenzie, holding a sleeping Larry in one arm, tugged on Dylan with her free hand, pulling him back so Caitlyn and Colt could have some privacy.

But being the big brother that he was, Dylan barked out a laugh. "Nothing's going on out here that I would disapprove of, is there Branson?" He laughed and slapped his friend's shoulder.

The smile Colt gave him was cold, and no spark of humor glinted in his eyes. "You two heading back to Catie's place?"

"Yeah, I'm running McKenzie home." Dylan bumped his shoulder against Colt's on his way by, and then reached down to embrace Caitlyn. "Sure am proud of you, squirt." A chuckle rumbled in Dylan's chest.

McKenzie followed him. "I'm glad to have you home, Caitlyn." She gave her friend a quick hug and whispered, "Sorry for interrupting."

Caitlyn's gaze was glued to Colt, but she smiled at

McKenzie's words. "Don't worry about it. We have all the time in the world now."

McKenzie was inordinately happy for them. It had taken Caitlyn and Colt a long time to work through their issues. She skipped down the steps and hurried to catch up with Dylan, wishing things were as clear between them.

He opened the passenger's side truck door and murmured in her ear, "Let's get you home."

McKenzie climbed in and settled Larry on the middle section of the seat. Dylan closed the door behind her and jogged to the other side. She waited until they were on the Mountain Highway before she said, "This is my last night at Caitlyn's cabin. I move out tomorrow. I'm going to miss living there."

Dark eyes slid over to her. "Does your new apartment have a fireplace?"

"Unfortunately, no."

"Then, I guess we better make good use of Caitlyn's while we can." He reached over Larry's head for her hand. The little dog repositioned himself, and Dylan pressed McKenzie's palm onto his thigh.

The pulse in McKenzie's fingers thrummed, and she wondered if Dylan could feel the erratic beat. She peered at his profile. The first time she met Dylan was almost a year ago. She had thought he was attractive, but too quiet. The strong, silent type didn't usually do anything for her. But during the past year, circumstances continued to throw Dylan in her path, and they had become tentative friends. Many times, she thought their relationship was growing into something more, but then he would pull back and seem distant again.

Dylan was often frustrated by his inability to control his uncontrollable life. Last fall, after John got sick, Dylan behaved as though he was determined to work himself to death. Meanwhile, McKenzie had grown close to Stella. The poor woman needed a companion with Caitlyn gone, Dylan always busy on the ranch, and John getting sicker.

McKenzie was helpless. There was nothing she could do to help Dylan, other than keep his mother company. She had tried but failed to convince John to see the doctor. Still, McKenzie became comfortable in her daily routine of training with Renegade in the morning and spending the afternoons with him out at the ranch. Repeatedly, Dylan came in after a hard day's work on the range, hardly spoke to anyone, and after eating enough dinner for three grown men, promptly fell asleep in front of the TV on the couch with his dad.

One night, Stella had clicked through the channels on the TV, when she landed on the old movie about a pig called, "Babe." She had set down the remote and eased back into her chair. "I love this movie, but of course, John will never watch it with me."

McKenzie had sat next to Stella. "I'll watch with you. I love it too." Together they watched James Cromwell play the farmer and just as he was about to utter his famous quote, McKenzie and Stella had chimed in together with him, "That'll do, pig." They had burst into laughter, causing both John and Dylan to jerk awake. It was during that movie when McKenzie realized how she could help Dylan. The next morning, she had searched for cow dog rescues on Google.

McKenzie and Dylan bumped along in silence, enjoying the comfort of each other's company as she smoothed her hand over Larry's silken ears. She couldn't help anticipating what the rest of the evening might bring. It was late, and Dylan was usually asleep by now, but he'd taken most of the day off to drive out to Rapid City to pick up his sister at the airport. Hopefully, that meant he could stay awake a little longer, but it wouldn't be the first time he fell sound asleep in front of the fireplace.

When they got to Caitlyn's cabin, Dylan brought some logs inside while McKenzie settled Larry inside his crate. "Would you like me to open a bottle of wine?" McKenzie asked as she came out of the bedroom.

"Go ahead, if you want some." Dylan's eyes glowed in the firelight's reflection, and the intensity in his expression stopped her breath. "I don't think I'll join you for wine, though. It tends to put me to sleep. And I don't want that to happen tonight."

Suddenly shy and a little nervous, McKenzie made herself busy in the kitchen. She found an already opened bottle of wine on the counter, pulled the cork and drained the bottle into a glass. "Do you want something else? A beer, maybe?"

Dylan stood in the living room with his hands resting on his hips, and as he watched her, a slow smile curled the edges of his mouth. His eyelids lazily closed and opened again. "I think I'll just enjoy having you sit next to me on the couch. Come on in here." His low voice swirled inside her, curling around her heart like sultry smoke as she moved toward him.

She bent to sit, but before she could, Dylan reached his arm around her and pulled her to him. He flung his cowboy hat across the room. She was so caught up in the rough kiss Dylan pressed upon her; she didn't notice where his hat landed. He slid a work-worn hand down her arm until it reached the glass in her hand. He took the wine from her and placed it on the end table, his lips never leaving hers. He bracketed her face in his powerful hands and kissed her as though to devour her. McKenzie's knees dipped, and she clasped onto his shoulders to steady herself.

With one hand, Dylan reached down to her knees and scooped her up into his arms. He lowered himself onto the couch and settled her on his lap. McKenzie stared into his dark eyes, wondering if she'd ever discover the bottom of them. She envied his long, black lashes. She ran her fingertips through the thick hair of his trimmed beard. Those features were the only soft things about him… except for his heart. The tenderness of which he buried deep under a gruff and sometimes fierce exterior.

McKenzie slid her arms around Dylan's neck and returned his kiss, exploring his mouth with her tongue. She swept her fingers over his powerful jaw and corded throat, pressing herself into his broad chest.

Dylan ran his hands over her back. Bringing one hand forward, he paused and watched her face as he unbuttoned the top button of her blouse. He studied every nuance of her expression. Smiling, she kissed him, and taking that as permission, Dylan made quick work of her top. When his lips left hers, he traced hungry, wet kisses down her throat. "My goal tonight is to make you forget about that job in Florida."

Done. McKenzie smiled to herself.

One hand slid up underneath the back of her shirt to unclasp her bra. As his fingers slid around her side, loosening the lace, Dylan's phone rang. He growled, kissing the sensitive flesh swelling above the cups. The ringtone buzzed again.

"Dylan…" McKenzie breathed.

"No." He nuzzled her.

Laughing, McKenzie sat back, modestly pulling her blouse closed. "It might be your mom." She reached for his phone and peered at the screen. Icy dread splashed her in the face. "It *is* your mom." She handed the device to Dylan.

He sighed and answered the call. Closing his eyes, he lifted the phone to his ear. "Yeah, Ma. What's up?" He listened, and as he did, his lids snapped opened, and he stared at McKenzie. "I'll be there soon as I can." He crammed his phone into his pocket. "Dammit, Kenz. I have to go."

"What happened? Is your dad okay?"

"Mom says he fell and hit his head. She and Caitlyn got him up, but my mom is worried and wants me there."

McKenzie fixed her clothing and stood before him. "Do you want me to come?"

"No." He shoved his hands in his front pockets. "I don't think there's anything you can do. And it's late. I'll just see you tomorrow." Dylan retrieved his hat from the floor where it landed. "Is it okay if I leave Larry here tonight? Poor guy is wiped out."

She nodded and walked him to the door. He kissed her, but when the energy intensified, McKenzie drew back. "You better go. Call me and let me know when everything's all right." He pulled her close and pressed his lips against her forehead, murmuring against her skin, "I'm sorry."

McKenzie smiled up at him. "Don't you ever be sorry for loving your family. I'll see you tomorrow."

She watched his taillights as they disappeared down the drive and wondered when they'd have time alone together again.

"WHAT THE HELL were you thinking, Reggie?" Sizzling rage erupted inside Ray's chest. "That was supposed to be a quick liquor and cash grab. Now the cops will be searching for a killer, and they won't stop. They don't take that shit lightly, you stupid son of a bitch!" Reggie had been hopped up when he shot the two men. "You're done with that trash, too. You are out of control, and you're gonna get us caught."

"Who made you God? I'll do what I want." Reggie's glazed

eyes wavered over to Ray as he scratched his arms. "Besides, that store is over two hours away. They'll never find us here."

Jason snatched up the two bottles of bourbon they stole, along with the measly eighty-two dollars they had swiped from the till. "This haul won't last us a week. So much for moving to a motel. We'll have to go out again."

10

When Colt arrived the next day for roping practice with Dylan, Caitlyn was still at the ranch. She sat with McKenzie on the top rail of the arena, watching Dylan warm up Sampson, his roping horse, while Renegade and Larry played together on the grass below. Colt parked behind them and appreciated the view of the fancy back pockets on Caitlyn's jeans. When she turned and waved, he tore his mind away from the slope it was sailing down.

"Hey, Catie," he called as he stepped out of his Jeep and inhaled a deep breath of fresh mountain air. "How's your dad?"

The smile on Caitlyn's face deflated, and concern filled her eyes. "He fell last night when he tried to get out of bed to go to the bathroom. Other than a few bruises, he's not hurt, but I had to call Dylan home to help calm our mom."

Colt's throat constricted, and he slid off his mirrored aviator sunglasses. "You should have called me, Catie. I would have come."

"But you were working, and I didn't want to bother you."

A mischievous grin replaced her serious expression, and she nudged McKenzie. "Besides, these two were up to no good." McKenzie's color rose, but she smiled as her gaze followed Dylan's riding patterns.

Colt chuckled, but it rankled him that he and Caitlyn hadn't had the opportunity to reconnect either. "You can call me anytime—you know that."

Her eyes warmed. "I do know that. Thanks."

"Did you hear back from Kennedy?"

"I called Blake this morning, but he hadn't heard from the lab yet. He promised to call as soon as he gets the results. He wanted us to bring Dad to the clinic so he could check him after the fall, but of course, Dad refused. He said if he went to the doctor every time he had a bruise, he'd live at the clinic." Caitlyn rolled her eyes, and though she laughed it off, Colt saw the concern hovering in their depths. "Did you hear any more about the robbery-homicide last night?"

"No. Things were quiet all night. We're still on alert, but I imagine those murdering bastards are long gone by now." He climbed up on the rails next to Caitlyn and gave her a quick kiss. "I've gotta go get Whiskey ready."

Caitlyn slid her fingers to the back of his neck and pulled him close for a longer greeting. "He's already tacked and ready to go. I left him waiting for you in his stall with some hay to keep him busy."

"Thanks." Colt swallowed an invitation for her to walk with him because he was already late for practice, and if he was alone with Caitlyn in a stall, he might never make it back to the arena at all.

"Hurry up, Branson!" Dylan shouted.

Colt gave Caitlyn another quick peck before he hopped down and strode to the barn. Once in the arena, he quickly went through a few warm-ups for Whiskey's sake and then backed him into the heeler's box. A brown calf with a white face bolted from the chute and Dylan shot off after it. His lasso landed well, but the calf turned at the last minute, almost shirking the hold. Colt and Whiskey were in hot pursuit, and he threw his rope at the calf's back feet, catching them clean. Both horses backed up until the ropes were taught.

Caitlyn cheered from the rail and called out their time. Funny how a little thing like roping a steer and having his girl cheer for him could make him feel like he was king of the world.

Dylan grinned at him. "Nice work. Let's go again."

McKenzie clapped for the guys. "Who would have thought I, a devout city girl, would ever have found myself cheering for a couple of cowboys roping calves?" She smiled at Caitlyn. "You're gonna have to help me pick out a cowboy hat now, you know. I want to look like I belong when we go to the next rodeo."

"Uh-oh. Sounds like you're drinking the Dylan Reed Kool-Aid."

McKenzie smirked and rolled her eyes, but inwardly she agreed. "It's nice to see him laughing and having fun. Your brother works too hard." She glanced down at the dogs. Renegade let Lariat climb all over him. He tolerated the puppy chewing on his collar and even his paw, but when the sharp puppy teeth clamped down on his ear, Renegade yelped and jumped to his feet. But that only encouraged Larry to jump on him again, and the two wrestled, rolling over the top of each other. "Larry won't be old enough to help Dylan with the herd until next year, but he's already showing an amazing natural herding sense."

"Where did you find him? My mom said you got him at a rescue?"

"Yep, just like you did with Renegade." It had thrilled McKenzie when she found the New Hope Australian Cow Dog Rescue in Colorado. "I love giving abandoned or abused dogs another chance. So far, I haven't regretted it." She pulled out her phone and looked up the rescue's website. She held the device so Caitlyn could see, and they watched the site's video, cooing at the irresistible puppy pictures.

"Aww. They're so cute! I want one," Caitlyn crooned.

"No way. You already have your hands full with an extremely high-energy Belgian. Trust me, trying to train both of them at the same time is a full-time job in itself."

"Right. That's why I have you." Caitlyn laughed. "I should get Colt a puppy. He's never had a dog."

"No. He doesn't have time for a puppy. Not right now, anyway. You have to be realistic about the amount of time and dedication puppies take."

Caitlyn sighed and leaned against McKenzie's shoulder. "I know you're right, believe me. But those puppies are so cute!" She handed back McKenzie's phone. "Speaking of a full-time job, you mentioned something in Florida? You're not really considering taking that job, are you?"

McKenzie let her shoulders slump forward. "I don't know. If I thought that things were going somewhere solid with Dylan, I'd be happy to stay and work at the café and start a dog training business out here. But if that's not happening, the job in Florida is a sure thing with people I know and have worked with before."

"Have you talked to Dylan about it?"

"Not much. I told him there was a job, but I don't want him to feel like I'm pressuring him."

"Cowgirl up, Kenzie. Talk to him. He has a right to know

you're actually thinking of leaving, and it might get him off his ass."

As the practice continued, Caitlyn and McKenzie became distracted by something on McKenzie's phone. After an almost perfect run the women missed altogether, Colt rode up next to Dylan. "What's the point of having adoring fans if they're not paying attention?" He winked. "Watch this." Colt galloped around the arena, and when he was about thirty feet from Caitlyn, he sent his rope flying. It sailed over her head, bumped off her cowboy hat, and landed over her shoulders. He tightened the rope just enough for it to stay on as he loped toward her.

"Hey!" She laughed as he pulled her from her seat on the rail and swung her onto the back of his horse.

"Just trying to get your attention." He nudged Whiskey back into a lope and rounded the end of the arena.

"I didn't realize you were so needy." She held on around his waist as they sped up.

"Oh, you have no idea. Want to grab some dinner tonight? I'll be happy to show you just how needy I am for dessert."

Laughing, Caitlyn slapped his shoulder. "I'm sure you would."

Colt guided Whiskey to the gate. McKenzie hopped down from the fence to open it for him, and he rode from there into the barn. Without releasing his rope from around Caitlyn, he dismounted and pulled her down into his arms. "I have all sorts of thoughts about you being tied up in my rope."

"Oh, you do, do you?" her eyes sparked. "Well, don't forget, I'm pretty good with a rope too, and I just might have my own ideas."

Her words sent an electric jolt crackling through him. He couldn't wait to get this woman alone. "I look forward to a demonstration." He backed her against the stall wall and kissed her. When she tried to raise her arms, he tugged the rope, tightening it. He grinned against her mouth. "What are you going to do now?"

Caitlyn hooked her leg around the back of his knee, and he responded by pressing into her. He released the tension on the lasso as he thrust his fingers into her hair. Just then, she pushed him hard in the chest and when his weight shifted, his knee buckled, and he lost his balance. Caitlyn snorted, but as he fell backward, he held onto her bringing her down with him. Giggling, she rewarded him with a lusty kiss.

Dylan and McKenzie walked through the barn door with Sampson and the two dogs. Almost tripping over Colt and Caitlyn on the floor, he said, "For God's sake, Branson, that's my little sister you're rolling around with. Do I need to kick your ass?" He smirked. "Can't you two wait five minutes? Geeze. Get a room."

Caitlyn pushed herself up to her feet. "Maybe you could learn by example, Dyl." She smirked at her brother and offered Colt a hand. "Come on, Cowboy, I believe you said something about dessert."

RAY'S younger brother had become an addict and the truth of that crushed his heart. It was all his fault, too. He should have never let Reggie know he had the stash. His brother had become a liability in the field, and he was seriously depleting the funding for their future. He should have never brought Reggie into this scheme. If things kept going on as they were,

Ray would be forced to do something permanent about his brother. *Damn him!*

Ray had planned to set himself up with the bag of crank his brother was mowing through. He'd envisioned how he'd get some townies hooked and then force them to sell to their friends to earn their next fix. The web would grow and so would Ray's kingdom. But now there wouldn't be enough to get his network started. More importantly, how the hell was he going to explain the situation to New York when he had no money to send them for the drugs, they gave him to get started with? "Jason's right. We will have to go out again, but next time—no mistakes." He clapped his hand over the pain shooting up the back of his neck. "If things don't change, Reggie, your screw-ups are gonna get us all killed. One way or another."

11

Sunday morning, Colt and Dylan met Caitlyn and McKenzie at the cabin. McKenzie's boxes sat packed next to a few furniture items she'd been collecting for her new apartment. Caitlyn had enjoyed having McKenzie as a roommate, but now that things were heating up with Colt, she was happy to have her privacy back. She figured the same would be true for her friend if Dylan ever copped a clue. Especially since he lived with their parents. *How awkward is that?* Caitlyn snickered to herself as she carried a box out to Dylan's truck.

"Hey Dylan, how was Dad this morning?" she asked her brother as he passed her on his way back into the cabin for his next load.

"Still sleeping when I left."

Caitlyn turned and walked backward, facing him so he could hear her. "That's so weird, isn't it? All our lives, Dad was up before dawn. I'm worried. I hope Blake gets those test results first thing tomorrow morning."

Dylan stopped, and looking over his shoulder, said, "I'm worried it's something serious."

"I'm trying not to worry, but..." she released her breath without finishing her sentence.

"Yeah." Dylan's brows crunched together before he disappeared through the door.

Caitlyn's phone vibrated in her back pocket, and she set the box down on the tailgate to answer the call.

"Deputy Marshal Reed? This is Dirk Sterling from the US Marshal's office in Billings."

Caitlyn's chest puffed with pride. "Hey Dirk, you're the first person to call me by my new title."

"Right. Congratulations, by the way. Listen, I'm calling on business. I'm sure you heard about the liquor store that was robbed over in Sheridan?"

"Yes. Are the Marshals getting involved?"

"Not officially. Not yet. But we have reason to believe that robbery might have connections to a couple of fugitives who robbed a jewelry store in Utah several months ago."

"No kidding? What makes you think they're linked?"

"Images from the security tapes from each location. We're also trying to determine if there are similar connections to a bank robbery and subsequent murder in Denver over a year ago."

"Hence the Marshal's involvement."

"Exactly. If they are the same guys, we think they're hiding out in this area somewhere."

Excited nerves zipped up the back of Caitlyn's neck. "How can I help?"

"At this point, I just wanted to touch base and let you know what we're thinking. If we determine these are the guys we're hunting, we'd like you to bring your dog up here."

"If you want him for tracking, sooner is better."

"Good to know. I'll call you if we need you."

"I'll be waiting." Caitlyn ended the call and bit down on her lower lip, deep in thought. She'd forgotten to ask about how the man who had been shot was doing. Could he identify the robbers?

Colt's hand settled on her back. "Who was that?"

She bounced on her toes and smiled up at him. "That was Deputy Marshal Sterling calling to put me on alert. They may need Renegade's and my help to track some fugitives."

"Where?"

She explained the possible relation between the jewel thieves and the recent robbery in Sheridan. "They're trying to get a positive ID on the robbers in the video. If the man who was shot is conscious, he should be able to help."

"Nice."

They finished loading McKenzie's belongings into the truck bed, and Dylan secured everything. Caitlyn rode with Colt and they followed Dylan and McKenzie to town. The dogs wrestled together in the back seat of Dylan's truck; the two pups were quickly becoming best friends.

After dropping the boxes off in the middle of McKenzie's new living room, they stopped at the café for lunch. The after-church crowd was there, and all the indoor tables were full.

Stephanie waved as she zipped through the restaurant like a whirling dervish. "McKenzie!" she called from across the dining room. "Is there any way I could talk you into giving me a hand for the next hour? Lunch for all of you will be my treat. I'm dying here!"

McKenzie glanced at Dylan, who shrugged. "Sure." She handed him her purse. "Why don't you guys take a table on the patio?"

Caitlyn passed Renegade's leash to Colt. "I'll jump in too. As the saying goes: Many hands make light work." She followed McKenzie to the kitchen to get an apron and order book. Only a little over a year ago, Caitlyn had worked at the café herself. During the week, one or two servers could easily handle the patrons, but Stephanie definitely needed extra help on the weekends.

After the rush, Caitlyn and McKenzie returned to their table where they all lingered over juicy burgers and crisp fries, glad for the warmth of the sun on the chilly spring day. The weather in town hinted of the pending season change, though even in the sunshine, they kept their jackets on. The mountains remained covered in blankets of white, and the breeze that blew down off the peaks was still frosty.

Caitlyn leaned toward Colt and whispered. "I'm thinking a glass of red wine with you in front of my fireplace sounds like the perfect idea. What do you think?"

A flame ignited in Colt's eyes, causing the green-gold flecks in his hazel irises to glow. He stuck his hand into the air, signaling Stephanie. "Check, please!"

RAY FINISHED FILLING the tank on their stolen car and dashed back inside the all-night convenience store where Reggie and Jason were loading up on supplies and taking all the cash. Through the glass entrance he saw a stricken expression pasted on Jason's face. Ray yanked open the door and followed Jason's line of sight to the edge of the counter. What he saw there, on the floor, curdled his stomach. He ran to Reggie and yanked him up by the collar. "What the hell is wrong with you?"

Reggie jerked away, laughing hysterically with a feral gleam in his eyes. Blood was smeared across his cheek like war paint and dripped from his fingers. "What? A man has needs."

"Pull yourself together and get in the car! And don't touch anything on the way out!" Ray glanced back at Jason, who seemed frozen in shock. "Did you get the cash out of the register?"

Jason shook his head.

"Do it! I'll take care of this." Ray had hidden the remainder of his crank supply, but Reggie either found it, or had some stashed away, because the man was clearly out of his mind. Ray stared at the gruesome mess his brother made and pressed his hand over his mouth. After a few seconds, he asked, "Is there a key in the register drawer?"

Jason lifted the cash divider from the drawer. "Yeah, here." He tossed a small brass key to Ray.

"Wipe your prints off the register." Ray called over his shoulder as he ran to the back of the store. He jammed the key into the lock of the office door. It was stiff, but after a firm twist, it finally opened to what Ray had feared he'd find. On middle shelf of a metal rack sat three old-style video monitors. He watched black-and-white versions of Jason stuffing bills from the register into a zippered bag from three different angles. Ray searched the room and finding a push broom in the corner, he swung the long handle with all his strength, smashing the video equipment beyond repair. He hoped.

Ray locked the office door behind him and wiped his fingerprints from the key on his shirt. Stepping over a growing pool of blood, he dropped it into the register drawer as he walked by. "Come on. We gotta get out of here. Now!" Ray ran to the door with Jason on his heels.

They sprinted outside and dove into their stolen car. Ray gripped the steering wheel and fought his instinct to push the gas pedal to the floor. Instead, he eased the compact sedan out of the parking lot. Maintaining the speed limit, he followed the brown road signs that guided them to a nearby lake.

The full moon offered enough light for him to see the

gravel road without headlights, so Ray switched them off. He drove up the winding mountain road until he spotted silver glints shimmering on the water's surface. Gliding past the parking lot, he coasted to the edge of the lake.

"Get everything out. Jason, wipe down the door handles and anything else we might have touched." Ray leaned his car seat forward and yanked Reggie out of the back. His brother's body curled into itself as he came crashing down from his high. Ray slapped Reggie hard across the face. "Wake up, asshole. We're hoofing it from here."

"I can't, man. I think I'm going to be sick."

"You don't have a choice. We have to get back and clear everything out. Our timeline is moved up, thanks to your stupidity." Ray yanked Reggie from the car.

As soon as they cleared everything from the car, Ray put the vehicle in neutral and together, the three of them pushed the car into the lake.

"They're gonna find this, you know." Jason grumbled as he watched bubbles of trapped air from the sinking car pop on the water's surface.

"Yeah, but not for a while. This should buy us a few days." Ray pushed a button on his watch and waited for the compass feature to light up. "We need to head northwest from here and we have at least ten miles of rough country to cover. Let's go." He stepped off.

Reggie's breath puffed hard in white billows well before they made the first mile mark. He stumbled and cried for rest so often, Ray estimated his brother cost them over an hour of precious escape time. Reggie's idiocy was outweighing Ray's patience and pushing firmly against his loyalty.

Ray held his tongue all during the long, freezing trek back to their one-room cabin deep in the woods. They finally arrived well after dawn, and Ray threw a bag of groceries along with the canvas zipper bag full of cash onto his bunk.

"You're done, Reggie. I don't know what I'm gonna do with you yet, but you've gone too far this time."

"Come on, Ray. I was just having a little fun."

"What you did last night—that was *fun* for you?" His little brother was completely out of control.

12

A cold front blew in overnight, and Colt cranked the heat when he got to the office the next morning. Wesley arrived a few minutes behind him.

The new deputy hung his coat on the rack and rubbed his hands together, blowing on them for warmth. "I thought we were done with winter. It was so nice yesterday."

Colt poured water in the coffee machine and filled the filter with grounds while he remembered exactly how nice yesterday's cozy afternoon with Caitlyn had been. Heat flared in his belly, and grinning to himself, he added an extra scoop of the fragrant grounds for good measure. "You know how Wyoming winters can sometimes last into June."

"Yeah, but I hope it won't this year. I'm ready to be warm during my early morning ranch chores. I woke to a split pipe this morning. I'll be digging down into freezing mud after work."

"That sucks. If nothing is going on, you can take off early. It will still be cold, but at least you won't be digging in the dark."

"That'd be great. Thanks!"

The dispatch radio in the front corner of the office crackled to life. "Sheriff Branson, this is dispatch. Do you copy?"

"It's a little early for a call. I haven't even had my coffee," Colt commented as he strode across the room to answer. "This is Branson. What's the emergency?"

"Slim Dunton just dialed 911 from the convenience store. When he went inside to pay, he found Cherylynn Hill sprawled on the floor behind the counter. He said it looked like someone had attacked her."

"Did you call an ambulance?"

"Yes, but… Slim said she was already dead when he got there."

"Dead? Did you tell him to stay there?"

"Yes."

"Good. We're on our way." Colt swallowed a mixture of fury and nausea. He'd known Cherylynn most of his life. She was nice to everyone, friends, and strangers, alike. Why would someone attack her? He shoved his cowboy hat on his head and grabbed his fleece-lined coat. "Let's go."

Wesley jumped to his feet, glancing around, seemingly unsure of which direction to move or what to bring. Colt sighed. He wasn't looking forward to breaking in the new deputy in this manner. "Wes—grab your coat and follow me. We'll take my car. I think you're gonna have to put off fixing your pipe."

They pulled into the convenience store parking lot and stopped in front of the double glass doors. Slim Dunton waited for them outside, wringing his hands and pacing back and forth.

"Sheriff, thank God you're here. She's in there." He pointed a sausage shaped finger toward the back but didn't look. "Behind the counter."

Colt opened the door. One of Cherylynn's feet was visible

from where they stood. "Wes, you stay here with Slim and wait for the paramedics." Colt sucked in a deep breath and held it, bracing himself for what he might see.

Standing with Wes, Slim prattled on. "I drove up and filled my tank at the pump. See." He pointed to his truck, still parked by the filling station. "Then I came in, like I always do, for a cup of joe and a Twinkie. I didn't see her at first, so I called out. No one answered, so I went to the back counter to pour my coffee. When I came back toward the register..." Slim jammed his hands in his pants pockets. "That's when I saw her lying there."

Colt rounded the corner of the counter. Cherylynn lay on her back on the tile floor. Blood was caked on her bruised face around her nose and mouth and was matted in her graying brown hair. A broken tooth sat in the pool of dried blood encircling her head on the floor. Her blouse was torn open, and one of her legs had been pulled from her worn corduroy pants. Blood-stained underwear was wadded up next to her waist held in place by the remaining elastic waistband. Cherylynn's open eyes bulged and stared blankly at nothing. Colt covered his mouth with his hand before balling his fingers into a fist. He cleared his throat and, careful not to disturb any potential evidence, crouched down next to the body and felt her neck for a pulse—knowing he wouldn't find one.

A siren wailed in the distance, and within seconds, the volunteer firetruck screeched to a halt outside. Jeff and Dave, the town's volunteer paramedic-firemen, dashed inside. They stopped immediately when they saw Colt.

"Dead?" Jeff walked slowly toward the victim. Dave pressed his hands on his hips and looking at the floor, nodded.

Colt cleared his throat again, scraping away the ache. One of the hardest parts of being Sheriff in a small town was that he personally knew everyone. Whether there was a crime or an injury, he had some level of relationship with those involved. But this scene gutted him. Who would do something so brutal to Cherylynn? "Yes. Call Doctor Kennedy. He'll need to be here."

"Which one should I call? Young Doc? Has he taken over the coroner's duties for Old Doc?"

"Yes. Blake Kennedy. He took over all of his uncle's duties as of last January."

"On it." Dave jabbed at numbers on his phone.

Colt dialed the number for the CSI team in Gillette, then turned to Wes. "Get Slim's statement."

Slim, who was anything but, rubbed his beefy hands together. "Is there anywhere I can sit down? I'm not feeling so good."

Colt glanced around. The only place to sit other than the stool behind the counter was a bench outside in the cold. "Deputy, take Slim up to the office. You can get his statement there where it's warm. Take my Jeep. I'll walk back."

Wes nodded and led Slim to the car. Colt pulled in another fortifying breath before he reached for his phone and took photos from every angle. Jeff and Dave brought in a stretcher, and together, the three of them waited for Blake to arrive.

The now familiar black Porsche 911 glided to a stop next to the firetruck. Colt missed the days when old Doc Kennedy arrived in his ancient station wagon. It was a far more sensible vehicle for a part-time coroner. Absently, Colt wondered when Blake would realize how impractical his fancy sports car was in this part of the country.

"Sheriff." Blake nodded to him as he rushed through the doors.

"Kennedy." Colt shook the young doctor's hand. Blake wore khaki pants, with a button-down shirt and tie. *At least he's not wearing a suit.* Colt chuffed to himself. "The victim, Cherylynn Hill, is back here. It appears someone attacked her. She was beaten, strangled, and most likely raped. The man who found her this morning is at my office giving his statement to my deputy. I'm sure you'll want to speak to him, but this is exactly how she was when he came in this morning to pay for his gas. The blood on her face and the floor is mostly dry, so I imagine this happened late last night. I haven't looked for any security video footage yet, but that would give us an accurate time to help you with your autopsy report."

Blake followed Colt to Cherylynn's body. "Was it a robbery gone bad—do you think?" Blake slid on a pair of latex gloves and knelt. He attempted to lift the victim's stiff arm.

"I just got here and haven't had time to investigate anything yet." Colt stepped aside to give the doctor more room to maneuver.

Blake rested Cherylynn's arm back on the floor and looked up at Colt. "With this degree of rigor, I'd estimate her time of death somewhere between eight o'clock and midnight last night."

Colt nodded. "I need a few more pictures, but then you and the boys can take her body to the morgue."

"I need to bag her hands. Hopefully, we'll find some hair or skin particles from her attacker under her fingernails. A couple of them are broken, and there are bruises on her arms. Looks like she put up a fight." Blake directed the paramedics to help him preserve any potential evidence.

Colt's morning coffee threatened to come back up his throat. The thought of Cherylynn fighting for her life while he slept just blocks away made him sick. "I'll stop by and see you later. We can share notes."

Soon, word spread through the town, and people gathered at the edge of the parking lot. Colt called Wes. "As soon as you're done with Slim, I need you to come back down here to tape the building off and manage the crowd that's showing up."

"Yes, sir. Slim's finishing up now."

"Good. Have him sign his statement, then make a copy. Put one in my desk and the other in the evidence room, then get back here."

"On it."

Colt clicked off with Wes. CSI would have to do the deeper crime scene investigating and gather samples to take to the Wyoming State Crime Lab, but for now, he would do a preliminary study and get started hunting down whoever did this to Cherylynn.

Colt jammed his hands into a pair of thin rubber gloves and slid plastic shoe covers over his boots. Stepping over the dried blood, he went to check the register. As he expected, the drawer was open, and the only money left inside was a handful of pennies. He photographed the register, then ran the day's total report before dusting the keys and drawer for fingerprints. Lifting the cash drawer up, he saw that any large bills that might have been there were now gone. Only a single key remained. Quickly, he dusted the key, but found no fingerprints at all. Someone had wiped it clean.

Assuming the key opened the door to the back room, Colt made his way around Blake and the EMTs. As he stepped over the red stain once again, he noticed a sliver of boot tread on the upper edge of the blood, partially obscured by Cherylynn's tangled hair. He pulled a quarter from his pocket and set it next to the print for size perspective and snapped several photos before moving to the storage area at the back of the store.

The key was stiff in the lock mechanism, but with some rough jiggling it finally turned, and Colt pushed the door open. If they were lucky, the equipment would be unharmed. The owner kept his security video equipment on a shelf next to the bathroom supplies. But when Colt turned on the light, he found splintered pieces of plastic scattered across the shelf and floor. A shattered monitor screen leaned crookedly against a dented and demolished recording machine.

Shouting erupted from the parking lot, so Colt darted out to see what was happening. A crowd of people pushed against the yellow tape printed with "Sheriff's Line – Do Not Cross." Wes was doing his best to string the plastic boundary line around the parking lot.

Colt addressed the concerned townspeople. "Quiet down, everyone. Deputy Cooper is hanging up this tape to protect any evidence we may uncover that will help us find the perpetrators of this crime."

A voice shouted, "What happened, Sheriff? We heard Cherylynn was killed."

"I would like to conduct our investigation before I speak on the matter, so I'd appreciate your patience. I'll call Meredith Stanwick at the local TV station and set up a press conference as soon as I have anything definitive to share. Until then, please go back home or to work, and let us do our job."

"Do we have reason to be afraid, Sheriff?" A petite woman called out. "Should we bring our kids home from school?"

How could he answer that question? He didn't know what happened, or if the rapist-robber was a town resident or was long gone by now. But one thing he knew for sure was he wanted to avoid a town-wide panic. "We have no reason to believe you, or your children are in any immediate danger. However, if any of you remember seeing anything out of the ordinary last night, I'd appreciate it if you would go to the Sheriff's Office and fill out a statement. In the same vein, if you see anything or anyone unusual today, call me and one of us will come and check it out. Thank you all for your patience and understanding. We'll let you know everything we can as soon as possible."

The CSI team arrived, and he recognized the familiar duo. Stout, gruff, and strictly business, Maeve Dunn popped out of the driver's seat of her tan Nissan Cube. Her taller counterpart unfolded herself from the awkward vehicle and followed Maeve toward the storefront. "What do you have for us today, Sheriff?"

"Thanks for coming, Maeve." He led the pair inside and introduced them to the doctor and paramedics. "Blake is old Doc Kennedy's nephew. He's taken over Doc's practice, so he is now our local coroner." Both Maeve and her cohort smiled when they shook Blake's hand, which surprised Colt. He'd never seen Maeve smile before. *Guess it pays to look like Clark Kent.*

Doing his best not to roll his eyes, Colt continued, "I didn't find any usable fingerprints with my dusting kit, but there is a partial boot print at the edge of a pool of blood near where the victim was found. There is security tape equipment in the back room, though clearly someone tried to destroy it. We'll send that with you, and hopefully the tech guys at the lab can find something on it we can use." He led them to Cherylynn's body and then stood to the side as the women got down to business.

First, they took their own set of photos from every angle of the crime scene, measuring the broken tooth and diameter of the blood seepage. The spatter was consistent with the woman's head being slammed repeatedly against the floor, but it appeared the probable cause of Cherylynn's death was strangulation. The blood that had pooled on the floor came from her battered mouth and nose, broken teeth and the back of her head where it had been smashed into the tile. Violence of that kind in an up-close and personal murder sent an arctic chill deep into Colt's bones. This crime was pure evil.

He wished Caitlyn was in town so he could discuss the robbery-murder with her. He would have liked to hear her perspective, but she left that morning with Renegade to drive over to Sheridan to meet with Deputy US Marshal Sterling about the recent liquor store robbery. And after she finished in Sheridan, Caitlyn would head down to the US Marshal's Department in Casper and wouldn't be home until the end of the week.

Colt wondered if the robbery in Moose Creek was perpetrated by the same men who committed the crime in Sheridan. Only, as far as he knew, the trio of jewelry thieves the Marshals were hunting had never brutally raped anyone before. He would ask Caitlyn what she thought when they talked after work. It was possible their violence was escalating.

Maeve bent down and, with a pair of tweezers, plucked up the broken tooth that was stuck to the floor with blood. She dropped it into an evidence bag and labeled it. When her eyes met Colt's, shadows of sorrow lurked inside them. She'd always seemed so matter of fact—so pragmatic—it surprised him to see her guarded emotion. He nodded, acknowledging her unspoken sentiment.

The CSIs gathered all the evidence they could find, and it was well after lunchtime when they finished. "We'll personally drive all this evidence down to the lab in Cheyenne today. I don't think we have any usable fingerprints, but we'll run what we have. It's obvious, whoever did this tried to wipe everything down. We got a couple of partials though, and some hair and fibers from the victim's clothing. Hopefully, they're from the perps and not the clerk." She peered up at Blake. "You'll send the clothing to the lab as soon as you can?"

"Right away." Kennedy nodded. "As soon as we get her to the morgue."

Maeve's mouth flattened, and she sighed. "I stopped in this market last time I was here. Had a pleasant chat with the victim. It's awful what happened here."

Colt's chest ached as the reality of Cherylynn's last moments of life pressed in on him. "It makes me sick. Cherylynn didn't deserve this, and I will hunt down the scum who did this and make them pay."

Maeve nodded, and then without another word turned to leave, followed closely by her partner. After they packed their evidence in the back of Maeve's car and drove away, Blake asked the paramedics to lift Cherylynn's body into the black body-bag. He sealed it with a tamper-proof evidence tag. "Thanks, guys. I'll meet you at the morgue." He pulled off his gloves and watched them wheel the black bag out to their truck on the gurney.

Blake clapped the back of Colt's shoulder. "I'm truly sorry about this, Colt. I'll make sure to get every bit of evidence possible and let you know what I find."

Colt nodded but couldn't edge any words past the ache in his throat.

13

Caitlyn and Renegade had left early that morning before the sun stretched its first rays into the sky. Sporting a buttoned-down shirt and blue blazer, she clipped her new Deputy Marshal's badge to the belt on her dress jeans. It was nice not having to wear a uniform, but the blazer and her shoulder holster were bulky underneath her heavy Carhartt jacket. Caitlyn wore the Glock 43 Colt had engraved, as a secondary weapon in a holster at the small of her back and it was even less comfortable while driving, so for the long haul, she kept it inside her truck's gun safe.

She drove as fast as she safely could over the snow-packed roads on her way west toward Sheridan to meet up with Sterling and Dillinger at the liquor store. She pulled off the highway and turned down Main Street. Yellow crime-scene tape snapped in the breeze, making obvious which parking lot she should pull into.

Someone had recently plowed the lot, and Caitlyn pulled up behind two police cruisers and a black Suburban parked next to a great mound of snow. Renegade wore an official US Marshal K9 vest, and Caitlyn clipped his lead to the ring on the back. "It's our first official day as Deputy Marshals, Ren. You ready?" He jumped from her truck and walked by her side as she ducked under the tape. Caitlyn's heart fluttered in anticipation of her first case. She licked her lips and straightened her coat before she opened the door.

"Reed. Good to see you." Dirk Sterling broke away from a group of men and came toward her in a confident swagger. Sterling made her think of the fabled Marshals of the wild west with his swarthy complexion and sharp expression. He shook her hand. "Thanks for coming up." Dirk reached down, letting Renegade sniff his hand before rubbing the dog's head.

"Absolutely. Happy to help if we can." Caitlyn noted the blood spatter on the shelves behind the counter and the items that had been knocked to the ground before she scanned the rest of the store. More blood was smeared across the floor in front of the refrigerator section. "How is the man who was shot?"

"Flight For Life flew him to a hospital in Billings. He's stable, but still unconscious. Hard to know if he'll survive and be able to identify the thieves."

"Hopefully, he will. I saw the photo Sheriff Blankenship showed on the news, but it looked too grainy to be of much help."

Sam Dillinger joined them and raised his chin. "Hey, Reed." He gripped her hand in greeting. "I have to admit, I'm not sure how your dog is going to be much help here."

Caitlyn nodded. "Yeah, unless the robbers left something for him to smell and track, we might not be able to do much. Does the security video show the parking lot or the front doors? If we can determine where the perps parked, we could start there. Though without an original scent, it will be hard for Renegade to differentiate the thieves from other people."

Dirk scratched his chin. "We have found nothing like that so far. Come to the back and watch the video. At one point, the shooter picks up several wine bottles and smashes them on the floor. We should be able to get some prints from the necks of the bottles. Do you think your dog could pick up a scent from the glass too?" Dirk led the way to a back office.

"It's possible." Together, they watched three shadowy figures wreak havoc inside the store before one of them shot the man behind the counter, then pivoted and fired at the customer in the aisle. "It helps to know exactly where the shooters were standing. Are any of the bottle necks still intact?"

"Yes, two of them. They're in evidence bags."

"Let's have Renegade smell them and see if he can pick up the scent anywhere else."

Caitlyn and her dog followed the Billings Marshals out to the retail section of the store. Dirk lifted an evidence bag from a box of them on the counter. After making a note on the bag stating that he opened it for a police K9, he handed the bottleneck to Caitlyn. She snapped on a pair of rubber gloves before she took it from him.

Holding the green glass for Renegade to sniff, she commanded, "Renegade, *stopa.*" He smelled it and then dropped his nose to the ground. Renegade scampered in what seemed like random directions, up and down an aisle and around the floor in front of the counter. "I'm not sure he's picking up any particular scent."

"Won't the wine overpower any human scent he might smell?"

"No. Dogs can have as many as three-hundred million scent receptors in their nose. Their sense of smell is approximately ten-thousand times more sensitive than ours. Trust me, wine won't be a problem."

Her dog sniffed his way to the door and sat down. Caitlyn

tilted her head. "In the video, it looked to me like the robbers entered from the right side of the store. Presumably, they drove in and parked out of view."

"That's how I see it." Dirk stood next to her as she peered past Renegade, out the door.

She slid her teeth over her lower lip. "When was the parking lot last plowed?"

"Early this morning. The owner wanted to be sure we could get in and out easily."

Caitlyn glanced at Dirk from the corner of her eye. "That was considerate, but not helpful. It's likely the plow scraped away any scent Renegade might have followed. Of course, the scent would probably have only led to the getaway car, which wouldn't have told us much, anyway." She crossed the room and opened the door for Renegade, who trotted outside to follow the trail. Caitlyn jogged after him, buttoning her coat against the frigid morning breeze.

Renegade moved with purpose. He was onto something, and Caitlyn rushed to keep up. Her dog stopped, sniffed, padded off, then returned. He repeated the motions, only changing directions slightly each time. Caitlyn presumed that the spot he continued to return to was where the shooter stepped in and out of the getaway car. She let him wander further around the parking lot when suddenly he sprinted toward a large green trash bin on the side of the building.

With his tail wagging, he followed his nose to the base of a mound of recently plowed snow piled next to the bin. He barked and dug at the icy mass. A second later, Caitlyn was by his side and could see that Renegade was pawing at a navy-blue knit cap. "Good boy! *Sedni*, Ren." He sat down, but his tail swept the pavement, and he wiggled with excitement. His pink tongue hung over the side of his sharp Malinois fangs, and his eyes remained glued on her.

Caitlyn reached down with her gloved fingers to retrieve the cap. She had to scrape away frozen snow to pull it free and when she did, a wrapper of some kind loosened from the ice next to the hat. The printed wrapper looked vaguely familiar, and she took a picture with her phone before she tucked it inside an evidence bag along with the knit cap.

"*Stopa*, Ren," she commanded, wondering if he could find anything else. After he searched around a few more minutes but didn't come up with anything further, Caitlyn went inside to show Dirk and Sam what they found in the snow.

"Have the sheriff send this in with the rest of the evidence," she said. "Are there any fingerprints or DNA from the other crime scenes to link this robbery to your jewelry thieves?"

Dirk held up the clear bag and studied the wet cap. "We have a partial print on a champagne flute from a party held the night of the jewelry theft that matches a print found at the bank, and a couple of security tapes depicting three men whose size and movement patterns suggest they are the same trio."

"That's not much to go on." Caitlyn held a fist above Renegade's head, and he sat down in obedience to the silent command.

"No, but it's something. These guys are smart, and so far, have been able to avoid showing their faces on the videos. If they are hiding out somewhere in this area, they're probably robbing stores like this one for cash to live on until their trail goes cold. The fact that they are adding murder to their crime spree shows they, or at least one of them, is escalating. They're becoming desperate or getting bored. I don't like the implication of either scenario."

"Well, if the cap belonged to one of them, we'll have DNA." Caitlyn sifted through the box of evidence bags to see what else they had. "Knit caps are notorious for holding hair samples. Whatever is behind their elevated emotion, it's causing them to get sloppy, and in the end, that's how we'll catch them."

WHEN SHE'D FINISHED in Sheridan, Caitlyn loaded Renegade into her truck and headed south on I-25 to Casper to meet her new boss in person. She parked on the street at the side of the cream-colored brick building. With Renegade by her side, she entered the office and introduced herself to the receptionist. Soon she was standing before the US Marshal of the District of Wyoming, Laila Williams.

"It's a pleasure to meet you in the flesh, Reed." Williams stood to shake hands with Caitlyn and to introduce herself to Renegade. Her dark skin was soft and supple, but the strength of her grip could crush bones. "I see you made it through training in one piece."

"Yes ma'am, but I have to admit it was the hardest thing I've ever done."

Marshal Williams's deep brown eyes glittered. "Well, if it was easy, everyone would do it." Her laugh was deep and hearty. "So, you were up in Sheridan this morning? Were you able to find anything useful?"

Caitlyn explained the history of the case from Dirk's perspective, and then she told Williams about the knit cap and candy wrapper. "The wrapper might not be associated at all, but since they were together, I tucked it in the evidence bag as well."

"Can't hurt." Williams patted Renegade's head. "I knew having a K9 would be helpful. You two haven't even been on the job for twenty-four hours yet, and you're already making the investment worth it."

"Thank you, ma'am. I hope so."

"I have no doubt." Marshal Williams swept her hand

toward a man who stood behind the desk. "This is your direct supervisor, Chief Deputy Marshal Keith Spencer."

"Sir," Caitlyn held out her hand. "It's nice to meet you."

"Welcome aboard, Reed." He gestured for Caitlyn to follow him. "I'll introduce you to everyone, then show you where you can stow your gear. We have a room with a cot in the back." He led the way through a large office area with four desks, two on each side. "Everyone, this is Deputy Marshal Caitlyn Reed and her dog, Renegade. They're the new K9 team attached to our region."

After the introductions, Spencer continued toward the back of the building to a tiny room designed for the night shift. "You can stay here when you're in Casper, but unless there is an active need for you and Renegade, you'll be able to work remotely. A lot of the day-to-day work happens online anyway, along with making phone calls and the like. When you're up in Moose Creek, you're equally close to this office and the one in Billings. And of course, as you already know, you're on call for anywhere in the country the USMS might need you. How does that sound to you?"

"Fantastic. Will I be spending nights up in Billings as well?"

"Only if there is an active case in need of your special skills. If so, you'll need to make arrangements for your accommodations with them."

"Sounds good."

"Very well, then. If you want to get your things and get settled, we thought we'd take the full Casper team out for dinner to welcome you."

LATER, after Caitlyn settled in the bunkroom for the night, she called Colt. "I miss you already."

"Same here." His deep voice soothed the ache in her heart.

Her shoulders relaxed, and she realized how tightly she'd been strung, wanting to make a good first impression. "Especially today." Colt continued. "I could have used you at work. Training a new deputy is challenging."

"Did something happen?"

"You could say that." Colt sounded weary, and Caitlyn wished she was there to rub the tension from his shoulders. "Someone robbed the convenience store last night."

"Oh, no! Did you catch the thief?"

"No. In fact, it was more than a robbery. I hate telling you this over the phone, but Cherylynn Hill was killed... well, beaten, raped, and then killed."

"Oh, my God!" Caitlyn gripped her phone and sat up.

"Yeah, Kennedy is doing an autopsy, and the CSIs came up to get evidence for forensics. It was awful, Catie."

"I'm so sorry."

"We didn't find any prints at the site and the video equipment was destroyed, but we're still hoping the tech guys can find something."

"Did Blake find DNA evidence under her fingernails or anywhere else on Cherylynn's body?"

"I haven't heard from him yet. I hope he finds some DNA to work with."

"No kidding. Was anyone else hurt? Did anyone report seeing anything?" Caitlyn pictured the incident in her mind's eye.

"No. Cherylynn was in the store by herself."

"Did you look at the cash register log?"

"I don't think they paid, Catie. They robbed the place."

"Of course, not—that's not why I'm asking. I'm wondering why they stopped there in the first place. If it was to get gas, the gallons taken will be on record."

"Right, I see what you mean, but how will that help?"

"It'll give you a time stamp and might indicate the size of

their tank. Did the CSIs take prints from the gas pumps nozzles?"

"I honestly don't know. I'll call Maeve and ask, but to be safe, I'll run back and do that myself tonight. Good thinking. Slim Dunton is the one who found Cherylynn this morning. He said he was there getting gas, so he might have already smudged the prints."

"You never know. It's worth a try."

"I'll have him come in and give me a set of his prints to compare with."

"I can't help wondering if this is the same group of guys. The robbers of the liquor store in Sheridan killed the clerk and shot a customer. The customer is still unconscious, but hopefully he'll be able to give us a description. Either way, the robbery in Moose Creek was only two days later. These guys have killed before, but rape is new. Of course, she may have been the first woman they came across."

"Why are the Marshals involved?"

"They think these guys might be a set of fugitives they're hunting that hit a bank in Denver and a jewelry store in Utah. So, we have a violent multi-state crime spree. Renegade found a knit cap in the parking lot that hopefully belongs to one of them. If we're lucky, Blake will find matching DNA. Prints would help too. I'll talk to my chief in the morning. He'll probably ask if you guys will be a part of the joint task force he's setting up to hunt these bastards down. I'm sure we'll need all hands on deck."

"Guess maybe we'll be working together again, after all."

"Best of both worlds." Caitlyn smiled. "You might even get deputized by the US Marshals."

Colt chuckled. "When will you be home?"

"Friday night."

"Can't wait."

14

The next day, Chief Spencer approached Caitlyn's desk. "Reed, you're going to officially be part of the District of Wyoming Fugitive Task Force—a team compiled of local police and sheriff's offices, the Wyoming Highway Patrol, Division of Criminal Investigation, the FBI, DEA, ATF, ICE, and the Secret Service. Our combined mission is to track, locate, and apprehend state and federal fugitives."

Caitlyn swallowed her overwhelming sense of inadequacy. "I'm honored to be a part of such an elite law-enforcement team, and Renegade is the perfect K9 for this type of work." She only hoped she was up to the task.

Caitlyn spent the rest of the week getting to know her new co-workers and learning the way they did things in the Casper office. She shadowed the other deputies, desperate to learn the ropes.

But as thrilling as her current career was, Caitlyn missed Colt. She hadn't been home from the academy for more than a few days before she'd had to leave again, and now she was eager to drive back to Moose Creek for the weekend. She'd barely arrive home in enough time to shower and dress for a night out. Colt planned to meet her at the Tipsy Cow for drinks and some pool.

It was after dark when she got home, and after cleaning herself up and getting Renegade settled, she drove into town. McKenzie was the first person she saw in the local watering hole, standing at the bar waiting for her drink.

"Hey, girl." Caitlyn hugged her friend and scanned the crowd behind her for Colt. He was bent over a pool table preparing to take a shot. Dylan stood behind him, laughing and trying to distract him. Her brother must have mentioned her, because just as the stick slid across Colt's hand toward the cue ball, he looked up and scratched his shot. Their eyes met, and Caitlyn was home again.

Colt handed the cue stick to Dylan and headed straight for her. He didn't waste time with words. He simply slid his hands to her face and held her as he kissed her. A blue-hot flame flared to life in her core, and she wondered how long they'd have to stay at the bar to be considered friendly. Fleetingly, she considered zipping over to Colt's house with him for a quick minute or two.

When he ended the kiss, Colt touched his forehead to hers and stared into her eyes. "I missed you."

"Same here. I—"

"Don't try to skip out on this round of pool, Branson." Dylan's shout cut her off. "You're losing, and I plan on collecting. Drinks are on you—for sure."

Colt kissed the tip of her nose. "Can I get you a beer?"

"I'll get it. You better go back to the pool table and show Dylan how it's done. He's getting too cocky." She gave him a quick kiss before pushing him toward his game. "I'll be right there."

Caitlyn looped her arm through McKenzie's. "Need another?"

McKenzie held her bottle up to check the level before tipping it into her mouth to finish it off. "Yep."

"Come on, I'm buying."

"How was your first week?"

"Good. Renegade already proved his worth up in Sheridan. He found some items that we're pretty sure belonged to the robbers of the liquor store up there."

"That's our boy!"

"Right? It was slower at the office in Casper, though. I met the team, and the Marshal seems nice, but all I did was try to get up to speed on some current cases and pitch in with some computer searching. A lot of that kind of thing I can do from here, which is awesome."

"How often will you need to drive to Casper? You don't have to move down there, do you? I mean it's a hefty commute."

"It would be if I had to do it every day, but I only have to be down there once a week or so and there's a room available for me to stay in overnight, so it won't be too bad. I'll be spending some time up in Billings with the deputy marshals there too. The two offices are sharing us since Renegade and I are the only official US Marshal's K9 team in the area."

"Sounds like you'll never get bored."

Caitlyn laughed. "That's for sure." They leaned on the shellacked wooden counter while they waited for the bartender to take their order.

Caitlyn ordered a stout and McKenzie asked for an IPA before her gaze drifted beyond Caitlyn to the door. "Uh-oh."

A shiver prickled the back of Caitlyn's neck, and she reflexively squeezed the gun she wore in a shoulder holster between her ribcage and her elbow. "What's wrong?"

McKenzie gestured toward the entrance with her chin. "Blake Kennedy just came in."

"So?" Caitlyn relaxed and turned to see.

"So… is he over you?"

"Oh, brother, Kenz. Of course, he is."

McKenzie nudged her. "Colt saw him. Look at his face—he doesn't look pleased."

Caitlyn took in his scowl. "There is no reason for him to care. But just in case, I better reassure him. Come on." A nervous laugh tumbled from her chest as daggers shot from Colt's eyes toward the town's doctor. Caitlyn hurried to the pool table. "So, who's winning?"

Dylan, poised over his next shot, grinned up at her. "That would be me."

"Not for long." She slid her arm around Colt's waist and raised up on her tiptoes to kiss his cheek. "Colt is about to clean the felt with you." He gave her a half-hearted smile.

Blake approached the table. "Hey, everybody."

Caitlyn felt Colt stiffen as she turned and smiled. "Hi, Blake."

He bent down and kissed Caitlyn's cheek before pulling his date's hand and bringing her into the fold of the group. Blake placed his hands on the woman's shoulders. "Does everyone know Kayla Irwin?"

Relief broadened Caitlyn's smile, and she reached out to shake the newcomer's hand. "We haven't officially met, but you're Stephanie's friend from Arizona, right? I think you came to the party at my parents' ranch last summer. Sorry, I didn't get a chance to talk to you."

Kayla's milk-chocolate brown eyes shifted to Colt. "Yes. It was a really fun party." She paused for a second before lowering her voice. "Hello, Colt." She reached an arm around his neck for a hug.

An odd sensation stuck Caitlyn's throat, and her shoulders stiffened. She stepped aside and looked over her shoulder at Colt. "I didn't know you two were friends?"

Colt cleared his throat. "Nice to see you again, Kayla." He shifted his gaze to the doctor. "Kennedy."

"Sheriff." Blake's tone matched Colt's and Caitlyn resisted the urge to roll her eyes.

"Any useful evidence back from the autopsy, yet?"

"Still waiting on the nail scrapings, and—"

"We should discuss the details tomorrow at my office."

"Of course." Blake went on to introduce Kayla to Dylan and McKenzie before he moved to the bar to order drinks. Kayla's gaze remained on Colt, though he returned to his game with Dylan.

"So, Kayla, how long are you staying in Moose Creek before you have to head back home?" Caitlyn asked over the sound of clacking pool balls.

Kayla flushed, and Caitlyn's eyebrows edged together. "I'm not sure. Stephanie invited me to stay as long as I want."

Questions flooded Caitlyn's naturally inquisitive mind, and they carried a slight sting. *Were Colt and Kayla friends now? Did that happen while I was at training? Was it Kayla, rather than Blake, who made Colt uncomfortable? Had something happened between them?* She couldn't voice any of these questions without sounding suspicious and jealous, but she'd find out, one way or another.

McKenzie sensed the weird tension that entered the bar with Blake and Kayla. Colt should be happy that Blake had a date, but it didn't seem like he had relaxed at all since they arrived. She glanced at Caitlyn, looking for an indication of what was going on, and noticed her friend's scrunched brows. Edging up next to Caitlyn, she murmured, "What's up?"

Caitlyn shrugged and faced her. "Did something happen

between Colt and that woman, Kayla, while I was in Georgia?"

McKenzie's mouth dropped open, so she closed it quickly and swallowed. "Not that I know of. I never saw them together. Why?"

"Never mind. I'm sure it's nothing." Caitlyn turned back to the table in time to see Colt sink his last ball. He pointed to the corner pocket with the cue and set up for his final shot.

Kayla had moved to the opposite side of the table and leaned her hip against the edge near the pocket Colt aimed for. "You've got this, Colt!"

His concentration faltered, and he glanced at Caitlyn, who raised a solitary eyebrow at him. He refocused and tapped the cue ball with just the right amount of force for it to bump against the eight-ball and send it into the pocket. Kayla bounced on her toes and clapped.

McKenzie smirked to herself. *If Kayla knew anything at all about Caitlyn, she'd stop cooing at Colt. Besides, isn't she here with Blake?*

Dylan groaned at losing to Colt once again, and he sidled up next to McKenzie, pulling her close with one arm over her shoulders. He nuzzled into her hair. "Kenz, I need you to console me." The vibration of his deep voice tickled, and she giggled as she shuddered.

"Aw, you poor thing." She faced him and slid her arms around his neck.

He reached up and removed his dark felt cowboy hat before bending down to kiss her. Hoots and whistles sounded from the group of friends behind them, and he laughed against her lips. "What do you say we finish our beers and get out of here?"

15

McKenzie didn't have to be at work until 11:30 a.m. for the lunch rush, which gave her a couple of hours to spend out at the ranch. She pulled in as Dylan was riding out, with Larry scampering along behind Sampson.

Dylan trotted over to her car. "Didn't think I'd get to see you before I headed out. I'm running late." Dylan's eyes sparkled. "I hardly slept last night."

McKenzie grinned. "Me either." She got out of her car and leaned back against the door, stifling a yawn.

"Don't let my mom see you yawning like that." He snickered.

"You act as though she doesn't know why you got home so late."

Dylan winked and bent down from his saddle to kiss her good morning. His mustache and beard brushed her skin, and he tasted like coffee. "I'll be back for lunch. Will you still be here?"

"No, I have to work. How about tonight?" She squatted down to give Larry some love.

"Dinner?"

McKenzie's shoulders sagged. "I'm on the dinner shift, too. Sorry." She liked it better when her full-time job was practicing Renegade's training. She'd had a cozy cabin to live in and ran her own schedule. Now, she had to pay rent on an apartment and that meant a regular job with longer hours. "How's Larry doing with the cows?"

"Mostly good. He's easily distracted, though."

"He's still young. Keep working with him."

Dylan nodded. "I could come by later—after you get off?"

"You better." She stood on her toes and pulled his stiff canvas coat sleeve so he'd lean down for another kiss.

Dylan rode off and McKenzie climbed the porch steps. She noticed Stella watching them from the front window with a broad smile wreathing her face.

"Good morning," Stella sang. Heat flooded McKenzie's cheeks, though she didn't know why she felt embarrassed. She and Dylan were adults, after all. "Ready to learn about starting vegetables indoors?"

"Why do you plant them inside?"

"Our growing season is short up here. I'll grow them in my greenhouse in the summer too, because it gets too cool at night even then, and tomatoes and peppers love heat."

"Were all the tomatoes you canned last fall from your greenhouse?"

"They sure were." Stella took her hand and led her to the kitchen. "Coffee first?"

"Please." Once she had the hot mug in her hands, McKenzie asked, "Have you heard from the doctor about John's bloodwork yet?"

The lines on Stella's face pinched together. "Not yet. Doctor Kennedy is still waiting on the lab."

"Is John in bed?"

Stella nodded as she stared into her coffee. "It's so unlike him to sleep in, but I have to admit, I'm glad he does. I don't have to worry about him falling if he's in bed, and he can't grouse at me either."

"I imagine he's grumpy because he feels sick."

"I know, but that doesn't make it any easier to deal with." Stella reached for a basket on the counter and pulled out several packets of seeds.

A loud clunk followed by muffled swearing came from the great room. Stella dropped the envelopes and rushed toward the door. McKenzie darted out behind her. John lay sprawled out halfway down the staircase.

"Johnathan Mayberry Reed! What are you doing?" Alarm filled Stella's voice as she ran up the steps. "Are you alright?"

He brushed her aside. "I just tripped, Stella. It happens to everyone. I'm fine, dammit. Stop fussing."

"Well, you scared me to death, so I'll fuss if I want." She gripped his arm to help him up, but he jerked it away from her.

When John pulled himself up on the rail, he wavered as though he was dizzy and blinked his eyes several times. Hoping she wasn't overstepping, McKenzie joined Stella on the step below him. "Maybe you should sit down for a minute, till you gain your bearings."

John glared at her but had the good grace to keep his mouth closed. He lowered himself back down. He ran his fingers over his wrist and winced.

"Did you hurt your arm?" McKenzie reached out to feel it. The swollen tissue was red and bruising. "Looks like you might have sprained it." She actually thought he might have broken it, but she didn't want to upset Stella. "I'm calling Dylan."

John pulled his arm away from her and held it against his body. "Leave that boy alone. He has work to do. I told you, I'm fine."

Dylan's phone rang five times before it went to voicemail. She left a message for him to call and then hung up to dial Caitlyn.

CAITLYN WAS on the phone with Chief Spencer when a call from McKenzie beeped through. She sent it to voice message. "Yes, sir. We aren't sure if the robberies are related or not at this point. We're still waiting for forensics to get back with us first."

"Let me know if you find anything. Tell Sheriff Branson we're happy to come alongside his department either way. And Caitlyn, I'm sorry to hear about the woman from your town who was killed. Were you friends?"

"Not friends exactly, but it's a small town. I knew Cherylynn Hill for as long as I can remember."

"We'll get these guys," Spencer assured her.

When Caitlyn ended the call, she listened to McKenzie's message stating her dad had fallen on the steps and that McKenzie couldn't reach Dylan. Caitlyn grabbed her coat and whistled for Renegade as she sprinted for her truck. As soon as they were on the road, she returned McKenzie's call. "Does he need an ambulance?"

"No, but I think he might have broken his arm. It's definitely sprained at the very least."

"I'm on my way. Has my mom heard from Blake?"

"Not yet."

"I'll call him next. I'll be there in about forty minutes."

"Don't speed. I've got things under control here, and Dylan said he'd be back for lunch. I'm supposed to work today, but I'll phone in and explain."

"Okay, see you soon. And Kenzie—thank you." Caitlyn clicked off and called Colt. He told her he'd meet her at the ranch, which had her breathing a little easier because if Colt left town now, he'd beat her by twenty minutes. He'd know what to do and could handle her dad's bad temper.

When she reached her parents' place, Caitlyn jumped from her truck, leaving the hanging door open for Renegade to follow. She bolted up the porch steps and through the front entrance. Colt was there helping her dad to sit on the couch, and her mom stood next to them, holding a bag of ice.

"Dad! Are you okay?" Caitlyn ran to his side and studied his puffy purple wrist, tenderly pressing the joint. "You need to go to the hospital."

"Oh, for God's sake. You're worse than your mother," her dad grumbled.

Caitlyn stood tall and glowered down at him. "Look Dad, you can't intimidate me with your bad attitude. You're going to the hospital to have that arm x-rayed. Period. Now, you can come willingly, or I'll have Colt pick you up and carry you." She crossed her arms. "What's it going to be?"

Renegade had more mercy than Caitlyn and rested his chin on John's lap. He whined at the man as he peered up at him. John patted his head with his good hand. "It's okay Ren, she's been bossy since she was little."

"I don't think he's sympathizing with you for being hollered at, Dad. That's Ren's way of saying you should go to the doctor."

Caitlyn's mom draped her dad's arm with a kitchen towel and rested the ice on his wrist. "McKenzie, will you please get John's jacket from the hall closet?"

Colt squatted down and looked up at Caitlyn's dad. "I agree with the girls, John. It can't hurt to have your wrist looked at. If it's nothing, then they'll have to leave you alone." He glanced up at Caitlyn, and she rolled her eyes. But Colt's tactic worked, and John grunted in acquiescence.

"Come on. I'll drive." Colt helped her dad to his feet.

Caitlyn called Blake on the way back to town, and he promised to meet them at the clinic. McKenzie stayed at the ranch with Renegade to wait for Dylan. Colt dropped Caitlyn and her parents off at the entrance before driving off to park. The automatic doors slid open, and Blake met them with a wheelchair.

"I don't need that contraption. I'm not an invalid!" her dad barked.

Blake patted John's shoulder. "I'm sure you don't, but it's a precaution." He helped John to sit in the chair. Then he greeted Caitlyn with a kiss on her cheek and when Colt jogged in, Blake held his hand out to him.

Colt shook it. "Thanks for meeting us here."

"Of course. I was visiting a few elderly shut ins. I was close." Blake turned to Caitlyn. "What happened?"

"I wasn't there, but I guess my dad fell on the stairs."

Blake bent down closer to John. "Did you trip or lose your balance?"

"I felt a little dizzy is all, and I missed when I tried to grab the rail. It's no big deal," John groused.

"Had you eaten anything before the fall?"

Her mom walked next to her dad, clutching her purse. "Yes, I took a bowl of oatmeal up to him earlier."

Blake smiled at her, displaying his dimples, but then asked John, "Did you eat the oatmeal?"

"I didn't feel like oatmeal. I was on my way down to get some bacon and eggs."

"So, you ate nothing before you fell?" Blake clarified. John grumbled something to himself, and Blake spoke to the nurse who met them inside the doors. "We need to test Mr. Reed's blood glucose level, right away." The nurse nodded and left.

"First, we need to attend to your injury, John, but then I'm going to give you a full exam. I think it's reasonable to conclude that your blood-sugar levels are way off."

Caitlyn's mom reached for her arm, and Caitlyn placed her hand reassuringly over the top of her mom's. "Don't worry. Blake will take good care of Dad."

"What if they find out it's cancer?"

"Mom. Blake said nothing about cancer. Why would you jump to that conclusion?"

"I'm just scared. I don't know what I'd do without your father." Watery blue eyes peered up at Caitlyn.

She stopped and faced her mom, gently gripping her shoulders. "Mom don't borrow trouble. Let's wait and see what Blake learns from the tests. Then we'll deal with whatever it is when we know. Okay?"

Her mom lowered herself into a chair in the waiting room, and Caitlyn sat next to her, holding her hand. Colt took a seat on the other side of Caitlyn's mom. He slid his arm around her shoulders. "Whatever it is, we'll deal with it together. You and John are not alone."

It was a full hour before Blake returned to speak with them. He took her mother's hand. "Stella, John's blood-sugar levels are high, and he has been experiencing dizziness and blurred vision. You've told me he's exceedingly thirsty and hasn't had much of an appetite. Well, his test results show that he has Type I diabetes. I've given John an initial dose of insulin, but I'd like him to stay here overnight so we can stabilize his system and get him started on his new regimen."

Stella's grip tightened on Caitlyn's fingers. "Is he going to be okay?"

Blake squatted down before her and took her free hand in his. "Yes. It will probably be necessary for him to take insulin, but although this is serious, I want to encourage you. Diabetes is a manageable disease, and we will have him feeling better soon. The good news is his wrist is not broken. He gave it a good wrench and I've wrapped the sprained joint for support. Ice and rest should take care of things. It will be sore for a couple of weeks but should be fine after that."

"Thank you, Blake."

"Of course. Now, I need to get back to the clinic, but as soon as they set John up in a room, you'll be able to see him." Blake patted her hand and stood. "Don't worry, Stella. We'll take excellent care of him."

Colt rose to his feet and held his hand out to Blake. "Thanks, Doc."

Blake shook his hand. "We'll take excellent care of him."

"We're counting on it."

The young doctor nodded and glanced at Caitlyn with a reassuring smile.

16

Colt stayed with Caitlyn and Stella until the nurses settled John in his hospital room for the night. As soon as Dylan and McKenzie got there, Colt went back to his office. It was nice to have a new deputy to man the office when he was away, but they were currently in the middle of a robbery, rape, and murder investigation and he needed to get to work.

He spent the afternoon on the phone with the crime lab, trying to speed them up. If they could link their local case to the fugitives the Marshals were after, it would elevate their priority and they'd have help bringing the violent criminals to justice.

It was after 8:00 p.m. when Colt finally left the office. He called Caitlyn on the way to his car. "How's your dad?"

"He was sleeping peacefully when we left for home. I'm spending the night here with my mom."

"Will he have to be on insulin every day?"

"Yes. Blake said he'd go over everything in detail tomorrow when we meet with him again."

"I'm sorry, Catie."

"Thanks. But honestly, I'm thankful that's what it is. My mom was sure it was cancer."

"It's good to know what it is, and that it's manageable." Colt rubbed the back of his neck, easing the tension in his muscles. "Call me when you're headed into town tomorrow. I'll meet you at the hospital—if you want."

"That would be great. Have sweet dreams."

Colt grinned to himself, knowing he'd fall asleep thinking about her. "You, too."

When he got home, Colt made himself a ham sandwich, snagged a bottle of beer, and flopped onto the couch to watch the tail-end of the Chicago Bulls game. After the ten o'clock news, he clicked off the TV and went to bed. It was difficult to sleep with the details of the convenience store robbery zipping around in his brain, not to mention the brutal image of Cherylynn's abused body that he couldn't shake.

Colt finally drifted, but at 2:00 a.m. his phone rang. He reached for the device, fumbling to answer it. "Branson, here."

"Sheriff, this is Tammy over at dispatch. We've received an emergency call from Elaine Woodrow up at the Woodrow ranch. She said someone broke in. They shot her husband, Paul, and now there's a gunfight going on between her son and the shooter."

Colt already had his jeans on and was attempting to button his shirt one-handed. "Tammy, call Deputy Cooper. Have him meet me at the ranch. Be sure he knows it is an active shooting. Alert the ambulance but tell them to wait until they hear from me. I don't want them arriving there in the middle of a gun battle." Colt ended the call and strapped on his holster. After checking his Glock's magazine, he grabbed his Remington 870 shotgun and raced to his Jeep.

Colt coordinated with his deputy, and they arrived at the

Woodrow ranch with lights and sirens blaring. Elaine ran out of the house in frantic tears. "Get back inside!" Colt yelled.

"They're gone! Oh, God, Sheriff! They shot Paul and Tom, and they took Tracy! Help us!" she screamed.

Colt dashed across the grass to front steps where Elaine Woodrow collapsed into his arms. Two rifle shots echoed in the darkness, and bullets splintered the wooden column on the porch. Deputy Cooper fired his weapon into the pitch darkness of the forest where the shots originated, and Colt shoved Elaine back into the house.

"Cease fire, Cooper! The shooters have Tracy with them!" Colt pushed Elaine down to the floor. Paul lay face down, sprawled out in a puddle of blood. He had a gunshot wound to the head. Confirming what he already knew, Colt pressed his fingers against the man's carotid artery, searching for a pulse and found none. "Mrs. Woodrow, where is Tom?"

The woman moaned incomprehensible words and pointed toward the back of the house. Colt helped her to sit against the wall in the hallway. "Stay down." He commanded before bending low and running into the kitchen.

Freezing wind blew in through shattered windows, and splintered glass crunched under his boots. He found Tom slumped against a cabinet, clutching his chest. Dark, almost black blood oozed between his fingers. "Tom! Help is on the way. Were you hit anywhere else besides your chest?" Colt knelt next to the teenager and assessed his condition.

Tom squeezed his eyes shut and tears seeped out. "I—I don't—," he coughed out a fine red mist.

"Okay, try to take it easy. Paramedics are on the way." Colt unsnapped the boy's shirt to see the wound. The bullet entrance was on the right side of his chest, but without causing Tom more pain, Colt couldn't tell if there was an exit wound. He snatched a towel from a hook by the sink and pressed it against the hole in the boy's flesh. He reached up and turned off the lights before clicking on his radio transmitter. "Cooper, any more signs of the shooter?"

"No, sir."

"We can't let the ambulance drive into an active situation. I have one victim with a gunshot wound to the chest, and he's losing a lot of blood. He needs immediate attention." Colt lowered his voice. "The other victim was DOA." He peered out the kitchen window, his eyes adjusting to the darkness. "I'm going to bring Tom out to your car. Cover us."

"I got you."

Colt pulled Tom's good arm over his shoulder and helped the teen to stand. Tom cried out, and Colt stilled. "Can you make it?"

Tom gritted his teeth together. "I think… so. What about… my… mom?"

"She's okay, and I won't leave her. The ambulance is waiting at the bottom of your drive. I'll have my deputy drive you to them." Colt was torn between having the boy lie still and getting him to someone who could help save his life. The blood in the boy's cough was alarming and didn't bode well.

Together, they stumbled to the front door, but when they opened it, another barrage of bullets assailed them. Colt slammed the door and laid Tom on the floor. Outside, Wes answered the firestorm with his shotgun. "Elaine, come and keep pressure on Tom's wound!"

Elaine crawled across the wooden floor toward her son. "This should have never happened!"

"I know," Colt consoled her as she took his position over Tom. "But right now, we need to focus on getting you both out of here alive. Do you know who is shooting at us?" Silently, he cursed himself for leaving his rifle in his Jeep. Elaine was sobbing and making little sense, but at least she was applying pressure to Tom's chest. "Where are your rifles?"

"The den." Tom choked out.

Colt followed the boy's gaze and low-crawled across the room. A hunter-green gun-safe stood open in the corner of Paul's office. Colt grabbed a Mossberg 350 Legend and stuffed handfuls of ammunition into his pockets. He loaded the rifle and crawled back to the front room. When he got to the window, he smashed through one of the panes. More shots answered the shattering sound. Splinters of windowsill brushed across his face. Colt determined the general direction the blasts came from. He braced himself against the window frame and fired high into the trees. A bullet split the wood inches from Colt's head, but this time, the blast gave away the shooter's precise location. Colt aimed and fired.

Silence followed.

It was impossible to know if he had tagged the shooter or not. Moving out into the open was too risky, so he fired the rifle, still aiming high to avoid hitting the innocent girl. Again—no response.

Wes's voice cracked over the radio. "Did you get him, Sheriff?"

"Don't know for sure. Stay put." It was an impossible situation. Tom desperately needed emergency assistance but taking him out could easily cost his life... both of their lives. "On my count, let's both lay down a round of fire. Aim above the trees. Maybe we can flush him out. One, two, THREE!"

Rounds flew through the night sky into the tops of black pines, but the bombardment received no response. "Hold your fire!" Colt ordered, and silence reigned once again. He waited for a five-minute lifetime and still nothing. "I'm bringing Tom out to you, now."

Colt went to Tom but found the boy much weaker than before. There was no way he could walk, so Colt lifted him in a fireman's hold, helpless to staunch the bleeding but desperate to get him to the paramedics. He opened the door. "Cover me!" he yelled, as he ran to the deputy's car. Colt rolled him off his shoulders and onto the rear seat as gently as he could. "Go!"

Wes jumped into the car. He spit dirt and rocks, flooring it down the drive toward the ambulance. Colt dove to the ground in case the shooter was waiting to catch him without cover. No shots came, so Colt, sticking to the edge of the trees, ducked low and ran back to the house. He put his arm around Elaine and then, covering her with his own body, rushed her to his Jeep. He pushed her into the backseat before he climbed into the driver's seat and raced after Wes.

"They have Tracy! We can't leave without her!" Elaine cried.

"Tracy is your daughter?" Colt stared at her in the rearview mirror.

Elaine nodded and covered her face with her hands. "Why? Why did they take her? Why did they shoot—," she broke into sobs as Colt sailed down the drive.

Colt skidded to a stop next to Wes's squad car. "Elaine, I'm sending you with Deputy Cooper. He'll drive you to the hospital to be with Tom."

"What about Tracy?"

"Her abductors might call your house hoping for a ransom. If so, I'll be there. Meanwhile, I will search the area for evidence." Elaine nodded and let Colt help her out of the Jeep and into Wes's car. After he closed the door, he spoke quietly to the deputy. "When you get to the hospital, send Jeff and Dave back out here in the ambulance to pick up Paul's body. I'm going to stay at the crime scene."

The Woodrow's' ranch was eerily quiet in the blue-violet pre-dawn of the morning. Bullet holes scarred the logs on the front of the ranch home, and the broken windows on the lower floor made the house look like a jagged-toothed jack-o'-lantern. Colt peered into the trees. He couldn't see anyone, but the hairs on his neck stood at attention and he had the sick sense he was being watched. In case there was someone out there, he popped the empty magazine from his .45, and reloaded the weapon with his spare. He double checked his rifle as well and carried both guns with him into the house.

Colt cleared the entire house before calling Wes on the radio and asking him to escort the ambulance back up to the ranch. When they arrived, Wes stood guard over Jeff and Dave, but they entered the home without incident. The EMTs bagged Paul's body and left to take him to the morgue. Together, Colt and Wes gathered all the rounds they could find before hiking up the mountain to search for the position of last night's shooter.

"Wes, look at this." Colt pointed to the ground next to a great pine. "There must be thirty spent shell casings here. Guess we found the shooter's perch." After taking several photos, Colt squatted down and, with a gloved hand, gathered all the brass shells. Scuffed up pine-mulch was trampled down under the snow in several spots. Frozen in ice, Colt discovered a small piece of waxed paper with pink writing. It might be nothing; after all, two kids lived on the ranch and either of them could have dropped the candy wrapper, but just in case, Colt bagged the crumpled paper along with the rest of the evidence.

By the time Colt and Wes returned to the house, the sun was finally lending warmth to the frosty spring morning. Colt leaned against his Jeep and called Caitlyn.

17

Caitlyn's phone buzzed and buzzed on the nightstand in her childhood bedroom where she had spent the night. Worry kept her mom from sleeping until the early morning hours, and Caitlyn had sat up with her. Without opening her eyes, Caitlyn reached for her cell and answered the call. "Deputy Marshal Reed."

"Good morning."

"Hey." She smiled and rubbed her sleep away. "You're calling early. Everything okay?"

"Actually, no. I'm up at the Woodrow place. There was a break-in last night." Colt hesitated and lowered his voice. "Paul was killed."

Caitlyn bolted upright, instantly awake. "What? Do you know who attacked them? Is everyone else alright?"

"Their son, Tom, was shot in the chest. Kennedy is with him at the hospital now. Elaine is okay, but the intruders kidnapped her daughter, Tracy. I have little to go on. Wes and I have collected all the bullets we could find. There were a ton of spent shell casings on the ground where the shooter who pinned us down last night was firing from. Hopefully, we'll get some prints from those. I'd love it if you would bring Renegade up. Maybe he could help locate Tracy."

Caitlyn clicked her phone to speaker and pulled on her jeans. "I'm on my way." She tied her hair back into a thick ponytail. "Colt, do you think these are the same guys who killed Cherylynn?"

"I don't know. I don't even know how many of them there were. As far as I could tell, there was only one shooter by the time we arrived on scene. I still need to interview Elaine. She was too distraught for questioning."

"Where is she now? At the hospital?"

"Yes."

"Okay, well, we can talk to her later. Ren and I are on our way to you."

"Thanks, Catie."

WHEN SHE GOT THERE, Colt and Wes were talking on the porch. Colt's hazel eyes glowed from the shadow of his hat's brim when he turned to watch her drive up. Her breath caught at the sight of him, and a rush of love and contentment washed over her. Colt had become her entire world. Caitlyn hopped down from her truck and Renegade followed, wagging his tail.

Colt raised his hand in greeting and came down the steps toward her. "Thanks for coming out, Catie." He bent down and kissed her cheek, lingering long enough to send sparks down her spine. "I just got off the phone with Elaine Woodrow. I wanted to know if any of the intruders pressed further into their house than the doorway last night. She said three men came to the door and knocked. When she answered it, one of them aimed a rifle at her and they pushed their way inside. At that point her daughter, Tracy, screamed."

Caitlyn and Renegade followed Colt into the home. He pointed to the pool of blood. "Elaine said Paul came out of the den with his gun, and they shot him where he stood."

"How awful." Caitlyn pictured the scene in her mind. "Did they take anything?"

"According to Elaine, the only thing they took was Tracy. Wes and I searched the house. There are two pieces of expensive looking jewelry on the dresser in the master bedroom. If the men were here to steal something, I'd think they would have taken those."

"Maybe their main purpose was to abduct Tracy?"

"I thought that at first, but then why would they hang around to shoot at us? If they just wanted the girl, wouldn't they have split after they got her?"

"At what point was Tom shot?"

"Elaine said he tried to go out the kitchen door after the men. That's when he was shot and fell backward into the house."

"Before you got here?"

"Yes. She called 911 shortly after they shot Tom."

"Then, I agree with you. It doesn't make sense that they continued to shoot at the house, unless they wanted to make sure Tom was dead." Something in the scenario didn't line up, and she paced the room, trying to figure out what bothered her. "Strange they didn't shoot Elaine."

"I bet they didn't want Tom to follow them and didn't see Elaine as a threat."

"Maybe." Caitlyn chewed on the corner of her lip. Deep in thought, she stared blankly at the bags of evidence Wes had logged in. "Wait! What is this?" She picked up the thick plastic evidence bag holding the candy wrapper.

Colt moved to her side. "I found that by all the shell casings on the mountainside. Why?"

"Ren found a similar wrapper in Sheridan." She stared up at Colt to see if he thought there was a relevant connection.

He narrowed his eyes and cocked his head. "So, this might be the men the marshals are hunting in connection to the jewelry store and bank robbery?"

"A candy wrapper is a long, thin shot, but…"

GLAD TO HAVE Caitlyn studying the crime scene with him, Colt stared over her shoulder at the wrapper. "I've never seen that brand of candy."

"No… but there is something familiar about it."

"Hopefully, the lab can find some prints on it."

"Yeah… Colt, show me the jewelry."

Colt led the way to the main-floor master bedroom and pointed to the dresser. "It's laying right here, out in the open."

"Did you get pictures?"

"Yes. Do you think it's evidence?" He took several more shots of the room at large and then more of the jewelry, close-up.

"I'm not sure yet, but why don't you bag up both pieces—on the outside chance…"

"Why would the shooters leave it here, then?" Colt wasn't convinced the gems had anything to do with the shooting, but Colt had learned to trust Caitlyn's instincts, so he bagged them and gave them to Wes to add to the evidence log.

Caitlyn leaned against the doorjamb. "I don't think the Woodrows were in the financial position to own those kinds of gems. That jewelry has to be worth a hundred thousand dollars, or more."

"You're kidding me." *Who would spend that kind of cash on a necklace?* "Maybe Elaine inherited it?"

"That's possible… but to just leave it out like cheap

costume jewelry…" Caitlyn scraped her lip with her teeth, as was her habit when her mind dove deep into solving a puzzle. "Anyway, for now, why don't you take me and Ren to where the shooter was? We'll see if we can catch a scent to track."

Colt led the way outside and up the hill. White puffs billowed with their breath in the cold, pine-scented air. On their way up the mountain, Colt called the hospital and spoke with the nurse watching over Elaine. Mid-stride, he stopped in his tracks. His back stiffened slightly before his shoulders fell. "That's awful news." He glanced at her, and bleakness washed over his face. "How is Elaine?" He closed his eyes and pressed against the lids with his thumb and forefinger. "Okay. I'll stop by later." He ended the call and stared at her.

"What is it? What happened?" Even as the words left her mouth, she knew. Renegade sensed Colt's anxiety and rubbed his body against his leg.

"Tom. He didn't make it." The muscles in Colt's jaw flexed, and he dropped his chin to his chest. Caitlyn wrapped her arms around his shoulders but said nothing because no words could make it better. Colt let out a deep sigh. "They've given Elaine a sedative."

"Good. Now, let's find her daughter. Maybe by the time she wakes, we can bring her some positive news."

"God, I hope so. She's already lost a husband and a son." He turned to lead Caitlyn and Renegade the rest of the way to the shooter's post. Boot prints trampled the snow and scuffed the ground, making it obvious someone had been standing there.

Caitlyn had Renegade sniff the area. "Okay, Ren, *such*! Find 'em, boy!" Renegade glanced up at her, his tail waving in the cool air. He smelled the fresh ground again and then moved beyond the immediate spot, sifting his nose through the pine-mulch on the forest floor. Suddenly, he trotted off—first to the left, and then he bounded up a steep incline.

"Let's go, Colt!" Caitlyn shouted as she took off after her dog.

They followed Renegade a little over a mile before Caitlyn called him back. "It's not a good idea to chase after this guy on our own much farther away from the house. We don't know how many miles they traveled in the last hours. Not to mention, they could draw us into an ambush, and we'd have no backup."

"I can radio for Wes to meet us."

"Actually, I'm thinking of getting some horses up here. Also, I want to call Chief Spencer and tell him about everything you've found. If he thinks we're on to something, we could merit a federal task force for backup. It will take a little while to get everything in place, but in the end, I think it's the wisest course."

"I agree. Let's head back for now."

With Renegade clicked to his lead for their return hike, Caitlyn phoned her new boss. After explaining their current situation and the possible link between the two cases, Chief Spencer told Caitlyn to call Sterling and Dillinger in, since they were closer to Moose Creek than the Casper team was.

"Meanwhile," Spencer continued, "I'll contact ATF and get a helicopter on standby. We'll coordinate with more local LEOs and get a team headed your way."

"Thanks, Chief."

"Stay safe and keep me updated."

COLT HATED the idea of waiting for the team, but honestly, he was happy to share the strain of searching for the missing teenaged girl. He filled his deputy in while Caitlyn spoke with the Wyoming Region US Marshal's office and then called the field office in Billings. She let Colt know Deputy US Marshals Sterling and Dillinger were on their way before she made her last call to her brother.

"Dylan, I need you to bring some horses up to the Woodrow ranch. There was a shooting last night, and some men abducted the Woodrow's teenaged daughter. Ren found their scent, but the terrain is rough, and the kidnappers have a good twelve hours' head start. Our best chance to track them is on horseback."

Colt helped Wes load the evidence bags into his trunk. An hour later, Dylan pulled up the gravel drive towing a horse trailer, and Caitlyn ran out to meet him.

"I brought three horses. I figured I could join you and Colt."

"Thanks, Dylan. I appreciate you wanting to help, but I think I'll ride out with the two deputy marshals from Billings. They'll be here soon, and Colt needs to man the fort at the ranch house to coordinate members of the federal task force as they arrive. You should head home. Mom will want to go to the hospital to see Dad and you should be with her."

"Are you sure? I could help."

"And you'd be great, but yeah, I'm sure." Caitlyn opened the back of the trailer and helped Dylan unload the already saddled horses. "Thanks again for bringing them up. I'll call you when it's all over."

Dylan released a sigh and spoke to Colt. "Watch her back."

"I always do."

"Be careful—both of you," Dylan said. He unhitched the horse trailer, climbed into his truck, and waved as he drove off.

Finally, Sterling and Dillinger arrived, and Colt and Caitlyn briefed them on the current situation. She sorted through the evidence in Wes's trunk and pulled out two clear bags. "Here's the jewelry Colt discovered on the dresser. Does this look familiar at all?"

Dirk Sterling peered through the plastic. "I'd have to compare it to the photos we have on file, but I think you may have found some of the missing gems, Sheriff."

"This thing just keeps expanding." Colt's gut knotted at the thought of Caitlyn heading into the backcountry to track dangerous fugitives without him by her side, but this was the life they both chose, and she was gifted at her work. He'd have to trust that.

The three deputy marshals mounted their horses, and Caitlyn reached out to Colt. He squeezed her fingers as they spoke volumes without using words. She pulled her hand away from his and touched her lips with her fingertips. "We'll be back soon." She shouted for Renegade, "Find 'em, Ren! *Such,* boy!"

Like a kid forced to wait to open his birthday gifts until the next day, Renegade bolted up the mountainside with the riders tearing up the moist turf behind them to keep up.

"Be careful!" Colt shouted after them.

DILLINGER SLIPPED in his saddle when his horse bolted, and he gripped the saddle horn. "Is there a trick to staying on this thing?"

If they weren't in a deadly situation, Caitlyn would have teased him for being a greenhorn, but they needed him on the chase. "You're strong and athletic, so you won't have a problem if you focus the center of balance in your core rather than in your chest. Hold on to the horn, but don't lean forward. Stretch your legs long—don't draw them up."

Caitlyn followed Renegade, and keeping Dillinger in the middle, Sterling brought up the end. "We're always asked where our horses are—now you can say you've hunted fugitives on horseback like a real Deputy Marshal."

"Great." Dillinger grumbled as he sat back against the cantle and pushed his feet down in his stirrups.

Sterling called to Caitlyn. "Does the snow make it harder for Renegade to track?"

"It shouldn't. And it's easier for us because the men we're chasing can't help but leave visible tracks. Snow makes it tougher for the horses, though, so let's slow down." The higher the altitude, the deeper the drifts became.

Renegade bounded in and out of the woods, following the boot prints until the scent led him under a bower of branches where the snow was scant, and the footfalls disappeared. With his nose to the ground, Renegade searched for the trail. Caitlyn studied the trees and pointed to a broken branch deeper in the thicket. "Look there! Renegade, *kemne!*"

Renegade looked like a fox darting in and out of the white drifts with his auburn coat and black legs. He appeared at Whiskey's side in a flash and aimed his muzzle in the direction Caitlyn indicated. After a few sniffs, he took off again, and after several strides, he leapt straight up a steep rocky embankment.

Caitlyn followed but stopped to study the broken limb. Several strands of long blonde hair hung from the tree at the break, and below it, sharp skids marred the snowy ground. "Looks like Tracy slipped and caught her hair or hit her head on this branch. Let's go slow." Caitlyn called out as Renegade bounded up a jagged rock outcropping. "We might need to dismount to follow Renegade up. Take it easy!"

Her dog waited at the crest of the hill for them, looking down from above. "Good, boy, Ren! We're coming." Whiskey's hooves slipped on the wet rocks, and Caitlyn stopped him. She swung her leg over and hopped to the ground. Sterling and Dillinger followed suit. At a much slower pace than Renegade's, they picked their way around the boulders and found a safer path to the top.

"There!" Sterling pointed with his chin. "I can see where they treaded through the snow."

"They probably climbed the rocks to lose anyone following them," Dillinger said as he hoisted himself back into his saddle.

Caitlyn led Whiskey to where the prints left the stones. "They might have a twelve-hour lead, but they're on foot wrestling with an unwilling captive, and they didn't count on Renegade."

18

Renegade ran ahead, stopping to see if they were still following him. Fifteen feet before the forest grew dense with trees again, Renegade stopped, sniffed the ground, barked excitedly, and sat down. He barked continually at Caitlyn as if to hurry her. "I'm almost there, Ren. Good boy!"

She led Whiskey by his reins and trudged through the deep drifts on foot. Renegade sat at the edge of a ten-foot section of the trampled snow. It appeared there had been a scuffle of some kind. Bright red drops and smudges of blood-soaked slush stood in stark contrast to the virgin white.

Caitlyn knelt down to study the spot and then followed the tracks that plodded toward the trees. "They were walking side-by-side here instead of in a line. But there are only three sets of prints." She turned to face the others. "They must have started carrying Tracy. The good thing about that is, it will slow them down."

Sterling took photos of the bloody scene on his phone

from the back of his horse. Dillinger hopped down to get a closer look. "It appears the girl is still alive and well enough to give them a fight."

"Yeah, but if they're carrying her now, it's possible she is seriously injured." Caitlyn studied the footprints. "Come on. We're gaining on them."

Dillinger peered over her shoulder. "How can you tell?"

Caitlyn pointed to one footprint. "See the rim of this print? The snow is still soft. If they were still twelve hours ahead of us, the edge of the print would have a crisper, icy edge."

Sterling slid his phone into an inside pocket of his coat. "Were there four sets of tracks before?"

"I couldn't tell. They walked single file until here." Caitlyn mounted her horse and peered into the trees. A muted pop echoed through the forest, and she spun around at the sound of the distant gunfire. "Did you guys hear that?"

More shots blasted from the direction they had recently come, and Caitlyn pressed Colt's number on her speed dial, but nothing happened. "Damn it—there's no cell coverage." She tried three more times in vain before shoving her phone into her coat pocket. "Should we go back?"

"No." Sterling took charge. "We don't know if the gunfire came from the ranch. It could simply be someone out target shooting. It's impossible to tell exactly where the shots came from, and our mission is to find Tracy Woodrow and hunt down the men who took her. We're her only hope."

Caitlyn swallowed her alarm. Sterling was right. "Okay, then let's go." She turned Whiskey toward the tree line and called Renegade. "*Such*, Ren." At first, Renegade stared back the way they had come, and Caitlyn briefly wondered if he knew something she didn't, but when she asked him to seek, he obeyed immediately and ran ahead of them, darting into the trees.

A muted ringing sounded from one of Sterling's saddle bags. He reached for the strap to unbuckle it and retrieved a satellite phone. "Deputy Marshal Sterling," he barked into the receiver. He listened and nodded before his gaze sought Caitlyn's. The look in his eyes caused her muscles to seize with dread.

"What? What's happened?" Caitlyn swallowed against the panic rising in her voice.

Sterling ended his call and stared at her. "Sheriff Branson was shot. An ambulance is on the way to him now."

"What?" Her mind fought off the words as she tried to make sense of them. "Shot where? How?" Whiskey pranced under her anxiety.

"There must be another shooter in the woods. We are likely between the men that have Tracy and whoever shot the sheriff."

Fear for Colt threatened to overwhelm her control, and Caitlyn bit down hard on the inside of her cheeks. "Is he alive? How bad is it, Dirk?"

Sterling shrugged. "They didn't know. They called to warn us of another shooter on our flank and to let us know ATF is sending backup."

Caitlyn turned Whiskey back toward the ranch. Her breath rushed in and out rapidly, and she felt as though she were underwater. Her tension had Whiskey tossing his head.

Sterling moved his horse to her side, and he gripped her rein. Leaning into her ear, he spoke in a low, serious tone. "Deputy Marshal Reed, pull it together. I know you're worried about Colt, but he's in the best hands and you can't help him right now. Shove that emotion into a box and focus. We have a young woman we must rescue. Copy?"

Her chest ached, but she answered him with a single nod. "Copy." It took every ounce of will that she possessed to turn her horse back toward the trees. "Let's find these bastards."

Caitlyn urged Whiskey into a trot to catch up with Renegade. The terror she forced down was sharp and fierce and sliced at her heart. How could she keep going, not knowing if Colt was dead or alive? She couldn't live without him. But on the other hand, she couldn't handle the constant fear of living with a man whose job put his life in danger all the time. *I can't handle that. There's no way.*

Caitlyn breathed in through her nose and forced her fear into a locked cupboard deep inside her brain. She couldn't see Renegade, but the trail was easy enough to follow. The three marshals' rode through the trees, bending low on their horses so low-hanging branches wouldn't knock them off.

It started snowing again, making visibility difficult. "If this snow keeps up, we could lose their trail," Caitlyn called over her shoulder.

"Will Renegade still be able to track their scent?" Dillinger blew warm air into his gloved hands. The temperature was dropping fast.

"Snow coverage may make it more difficult, but he should be able to. I haven't seen him for a while, though." Caitlyn wasn't comfortable with Renegade so far in front of them, so she blew on the dog whistle she carried around her neck. The tone wasn't discernable to the human ear, but dogs' hearing was far more sensitive. Before long, she saw his burnt-orange coat bright against the white drifts. When he came into view, he stopped and barked. He turned back the way he came, took two strides, and then stopped and barked again.

"We're coming!" Caitlyn turned in her saddle to face the men. "Keep your horses at a walk now, since we can't see the footing, we have to be more cautious."

Flakes stuck together, making the snow fall in fluffy clumps. A deep, soulful silence pressed heavily down on the forest. They plodded forward to where Renegade waited. As soon as they got there, he took off toward what looked like a rockslide. Caitlyn led the riders to the base of the loose cascade of stones and stopped even though Renegade bolted upward.

Sterling halted next to her. "What now?"

"We'll have to find another path up. We can try going around." Caitlyn steered her horse to the left and looked for a way. She started up a less rocky hill when a rifle shot broke through the stillness. Whiskey reared up, catching Caitlyn off guard. With a squealing equine-scream, his eyes rolled back in his head, and he fell. Caitlyn scrambled to dive from the saddle before he landed on her. Whiskey's hind feet slipped on the rocks, and he crashed down on his side with a groan. With only a second to spare, Caitlyn pulled her leg free, falling hard on the loose snow-covered rocks. Searing pain ricocheted up her right arm, and she clenched her teeth, refusing to release the scream that charged up her throat and filled her mouth.

"Caitlyn!" one of the men yelled.

With her good hand, she pushed herself to her knees and tried to breathe. "I'm fine." She coughed as cold air rushed back into her lungs and she crawled toward her horse. "Whiskey!"

Dillinger had taken up a defensive position behind a boulder and aimed his rifle up the mountain where the shot came from. Sterling slid from his horse and rushed to Caitlyn, who had yanked off the glove on her left hand with her teeth. She ran bare fingers over her horse's head and neck and gasped when she held up her blood-smeared palm.

"Oh, Whiskey!" Caitlyn didn't even try to hide the tears in her voice.

Dirk gripped her shoulders. "How badly is he hurt?"

Whiskey grunted and rolled. Sterling pulled her back as her horse rocked his weight, struggling to stand. With a mighty effort, Whiskey clambered to his feet. Caitlyn shrugged out of Dirk's grip moved to check the wound on her horse's neck.

She reached up, but a stabbing pain forced her to tuck her arm tight into her chest. When she caught her breath, she reached out to Whiskey's neck with her uninjured arm. "It's just a slight gash." Tears of relief mingled with those of pain and dripped from her eyes. "I think he'll be okay as long as he didn't hurt himself in the fall." She ran her hand down all four of his legs before she asked him to walk a few steps.

"What about you? You hurt your arm." Sterling reached for her, but she turned away.

"I said I was fine." She glanced around. "Where's Renegade?"

Sterling shrugged, but Dillinger pointed up the hill. "He ran after the shooter."

"Renegade!" Caitlyn screamed. She gripped her saddle horn with her left hand and swung herself onto Whiskey's back. After a few erratic prancing test steps on her frightened horse, she squeezed her legs against his sides and they took off up the side of the mountain, leaving the other two marshals to chase after her.

Whiskey refused to run straight into danger, and he was difficult for Caitlyn to manage one-handed, as he shied and tossed his head. But Renegade was somewhere in the distance, barking like crazy. Caitlyn guessed he was about fifty yards further up the hill through a dense thicket of pines. Another gunshot echoed down the hill, and the barking stopped.

Caitlyn's heart jolted to a halt. Was Renegade shot? Hot adrenaline spiked her bloodstream, and she kicked Whiskey's sides. He bolted wildly up the mountain into uncertainty.

"Reed!" Sterling yelled from somewhere below, but Caitlyn had no intention of slowing down. She did not know what she was riding into. All she was certain of was both Ren and Colt might be dead, and she was powerless to help either of them.

19

Seconds ago, Caitlyn had convinced herself she couldn't handle a life with Colt and his dangerous job. Now as she charged up the mountain not sure if she'd ever have the chance, she begged God to let her try. She couldn't live without Colt—didn't want to imagine it. Sure, his job put him at risk, but so did hers. The truth was that any one of the people she loved could be taken from her at any minute. The image of her dad's gentle smile popped into her mind. "Please let me have the chance to tell my dad and Colt that I love them at least one more time." Her prayer wafted into the trees on a steamy cloud of breath crystalizing in the frigid air.

Caitlyn's arm throbbed—the swelling limb pressed tight inside her coat sleeve. She was certain that she broke her radius, but she couldn't let Sterling and Dillinger know or they'd force her to stand down. As it was, her fingers were numb and there was no way she could shoot right-handed. She and her brothers used to practice left-handed shooting for fun, but only Logan was any good at it.

As she reached the top of the ridge, the ground flattened

out and the trees thinned into a clearing on the mesa. She brought Whiskey to a halt and peered through the pine-needle veil. A small, broken-down shed-looking structure covered in snow stood on the right side of the glade. Caitlyn wanted to take a closer look but wandering out in the open without tree cover would make her an easy target. Glancing over her shoulder, she searched for the other two marshals. She couldn't see them, but she heard their horses off to the left.

Rustling from the same direction shook the bushes. Certainly, Sterling and Dillinger weren't riding through the hedge. Maybe it was her dog. "Ren? Renegade?" Caitlyn rode toward the sound. Maybe he was caught in the brambles or a trap of some kind. She swung her leg over the saddle and slid off her horse. The jolt from landing on her feet sent splintered heat through her broken bone, and she sucked air in through her teeth. She held on to the pommel and waited for a wave a dizziness to subside before she stepped off. In the last second, she reached for the shotgun clipped inside the leather scabbard attached to her saddle and looped Whiskey's reins over a branch.

The rustling developed into a grunting noise, and a man cried out. Caitlyn ran toward the sound. Bursting through the trees, she came face to face with a terrifying sight. An enormous brown bear was ambling toward Dillinger who stood frozen in fear against the trunk of a great pine. Caitlyn's sudden appearance caused the bear to pause. It rose to its hind feet and let loose a tooth-rattling roar that displayed ferocious fangs.

Time slowed. Her brain flushed with icy hyper awareness. Instinctively, Caitlyn gripped the stock of her gun and, with a mighty jerk, she cocked it one-handed. She drew in a great breath and yelled, "Sam! Make yourself as big as possible. Scream and holler as loud as you can. Wave your arms—but don't look the bear in the eye." As she called out the instructions, a movement on the hillside behind Dillinger caught her eye. Squinting, she focused on the dark round shape bobbing in the scrub, and prickles shot up her spine through her scalp. "Somehow, you got yourself between that mama bear and her cub."

"Shoot the bear!" Dillinger yelled as he waved his arms. The mama roared at him again, swiping a giant paw with four-inch claws through the air. Sterling, who stood opposite Caitlyn, cocked his rifle, and took aim.

Caitlyn shouted, "Wait!" Without moving, Sterling shifted his gaze to her. He kept his gun level, pointed directly at the bear. "You can't just kill a mama bear. Her cub won't survive."

"I'm the one who wants to survive!" Dillinger cried. "Shoot!"

"You will survive, Sam. We can always shoot her if we must, but let's try not to. Okay? Listen. The bear is upset because you're standing between her and her cub. So, keep waving your arms and be as obnoxious as you can, while slowly moving toward Dirk. If she makes a move toward you, I'll shoot in her direction and try to ward her off. Sterling, if she turns toward Sam and starts running toward him, take your shot."

Dillinger looked like a lunatic waving his arms and dancing around as he moved toward Sterling, and Caitlyn tamped down an inappropriate urge to giggle at the silliness of it all. The enormous bear watched his movement and lowered herself down to all fours. She took one step toward him, and Caitlyn raised her gun. Bracing it against her left shoulder, she aimed clumsily at the ground fifteen feet in front of the bear and fired. Unable to hold the weapon correctly, it kicked back and bruised her shoulder. Caitlyn grunted in pain.

The slug hit the ground in front of the bear and combined

with the spray of rock and dirt startled the giant animal and distracted her from Dillinger. But in the end, it was the cub that saved Sam's life. The adorable little bundle of fur cried out for his mother, and she trundled off toward him.

The three marshals came together behind the bears and watched them disappear into the woods. Caitlyn nudged Dillinger, "Bears are at their most dangerous this time of year. They're coming out of hibernation and many, like that one, are hungry new mamas."

Still breathing heavily, Dillinger smirked. "Well, if that bear is anything like my wife was after she had our son, a hungry new mom is a scary creature."

"That's right," Caitlyn chuffed. "Your wife's probably a mama bear, too. My dad always said that God made mamas to protect their babies, and that He made daddies to protect the world from protective mamas." She smiled, but her heart ached at the thought of her dad. Images of Colt as a dad pressed at the edge of her mind too, but she firmly shoved them aside.

Sterling shook his head but flashed her a smile. "Let's get a move on. We have some bad guys to catch and a girl to rescue."

"And I have to find Renegade. There's a clearing back the way I came. I saw a lean-to shack there that looks like the opening to an old mine shaft or something. They could be hiding in there. Ren might be there, too."

Sterling gathered his and Dillinger's horses, and they followed Caitlyn to where she left Whiskey. He clapped Sam's shoulder. "How'd you end up on the ground against that tree? You didn't fall off your horse, did you?" A snort escaped his nose.

"The crazy nag took off when he saw the bear. I suppose I should've taken off with him." He reached up and gave his horse a friendly pat.

The marshals walked their horses to the edge of the mesa clearing, and Caitlyn pointed out the broken down building she'd seen earlier. Sterling lifted his field binoculars to his eyes and scanned the entire area. "It looks like there's also a small cabin on the opposite side of the clearing. It's hard to see it under all the snow." He handed the scopes to Caitlyn. "Let's split up. I'll head toward the cabin and check it out. You two make your way over to the shack. We'll meet back here in fifteen minutes."

Caitlyn checked to make sure the horses were safe and secured to trees before gesturing for Dillinger to follow her. She slung the strap of her shotgun over her shoulder and held her Glock in her left hand.

"Hey—are you sure your arm is okay? You fired your shotgun at the bear left-handed. Ballsy move, but no way you can be accurate."

"I can manage. Besides, I've got you to cover me."

They crept toward the small, dilapidated building that appeared ready to fall with the next stiff breeze. A thin stream of smoke floated up into the air out of a vent on the roof. She signaled Dillinger, and he nodded as he unclipped a taser from his utility belt. It would be best if they could take down any guards without making a noise. He led the way.

The heavy blanket of snow muffled sound, while at the same time the silent forest magnified it. Fortunately, their footsteps couldn't be heard as they snuck up to the edge of the building. Dillinger peered around the corner and then held up one finger, indicating there was only one man standing guard. Sam sprang like a cat toward the man and tased him in the chest where his coat was open. A strangled noise gurgled from the man's throat, and it seemed as loud as thunder to Caitlyn. They waited and listened for a reaction from the man's partners, but none came. Quickly, they bound the man's hands and feet with zip ties and gagged him with a wad of fabric. Sam dragged the man behind a truck-sized boulder to hide him from view.

Caitlyn moved back to the lean-to and nudged the crooked door with the barrel of her gun. Rusty hinges groaned as she pulled it open. The interior space was dark and a roughhewn path with stone steps carved into it led down to the unknown. Caitlyn shuddered involuntarily. A soft whimper echoed against the rock walls from deep inside. The sound was human and came from approximately thirty to forty feet in front of her. With her back against the wall, Caitlyn clicked on her flashlight and aimed it into the abyss.

A young woman held up her forearm to block her eyes from the bright light. Next to her on the floor lay the crumpled-up, rust-colored form of Renegade.

Caitlyn gasped as abject fear squeezed her chest. Every fiber of her body surged to run to Renegade and scoop him into her arms, but before she could, men's voices screamed outside, yelling threats at each other. It was imperative the team secure the camp before she checked on Renegade or the girl. Tracy and her dog, if he was alive, were safe for the time being, down below ground.

"I'll be back," she whispered to them.

"Help me, please!" The girl cried out.

"I will. You're safe here for now, but we have to apprehend the men who took you." She stared down the path into the girl's eyes. "I promise I'll be back." She nodded and closed the door, willing her mind away from the image of Renegade's lifeless form. It took every ounce of grit and willpower not to run to him, but it was critical—they must secure the scene first or the fugitives could kill them all.

20

Dylan rode back toward the ranch for lunch, with Larry happily jogging alongside him. As soon as they reached the barnyard, McKenzie ran out through the back door to meet them. "Dylan, hurry and put Sampson up." She called to him as he trotted toward her. "We've got to get to town." Her belly tightened like it held a bucket of lead and she twisted the kitchen towel she carried in her hands.

"What's wrong?" Dylan's brows crunched together over worried eyes. "Is it Caitlyn?"

"No. It's Colt. He was shot."

Dylan reined Sampson to a halt. He jumped to the ground and ran to her. "What happened? Where? Where is he?"

McKenzie gripped his arms. "Deputy Cooper just called. He said Colt was shot when the two of them were up at the Woodrow ranch. The ambulance is taking Colt to the hospital, now."

Icy terror filled Dylan's eyes. "Grab your coat and meet me at the truck." He rushed to untack Sampson and put him in his stall.

Stella was standing at the back gate when Dylan ran out of the barn. "Call me as soon as you know anything," she cried.

"I will. Mom, can you take Larry inside?" Dylan opened the gate for his dog and then sprinted to join McKenzie at his truck.

She sat close to him in the middle of the bench seat and clutched his knee. "He'll be okay. He's in good hands."

He gave her a grim look. "Did Cooper tell you how bad it was? Where was Colt shot?"

"No. Wes sounded panicked, and he was driving, so I didn't keep him on the phone. I told him we'd meet him at the clinic."

"I should have insisted on riding out with Caitlyn this morning. Damn it!" Dylan pounded his fist against the steering wheel. "I could have been there to help Colt. And now my sister's up in the hills chasing the shooters!"

"Try not to worry. She's there with two other Deputy Marshals, and they all know what they're doing."

"Colt knew what he was doing, too, and he was still shot."

McKenzie squeezed his knee tighter but said nothing. There was nothing she could say that would help alleviate his worry over his baby sister or his best friend.

"I wonder if Caitlyn knows about Colt. If so, she'll be distracted."

"No one has more focus and determination than your sister. One of the things that drives me crazy about her is her ability to compartmentalize. And in this case, that trait will serve her well. Try not to worry. It doesn't do any good."

"I know you're right, but I feel so helpless."

Dylan's tires squealed as he turned into the clinic parking lot. He screeched to a stop in front of the sliding doors and, leaving his truck in the middle of the drive, they jumped out and ran inside.

The reception nurse stood as they rushed to her desk. "Doctor Kennedy is waiting for you. I'll let him know you've arrived. Why don't you take a seat in the waiting room?"

Dylan gripped the edge of her desk. "Can we see Sheriff Branson?"

"No… he's… It would be best if Doctor Kennedy speaks with you. I'll go get him."

A sledgehammer to the chest would have felt better. Dylan swung around to face her, and she tried to gauge his reaction to the nurse's cryptic words.

Dylan's face was drawn, and he pressed white lips together. "What do I do, Kenz? How will I ever tell Caitlyn?"

THE ECHO of a rifle shot bounced off the trees and surrounding rocks. A man screamed, and Caitlyn's blood froze in her veins.

"Dillinger's down! Reed—take cover!" Sterling shouted.

Caitlyn crouched down and slid out the door. She peered around the side of the shack but saw no one. It was impossible to determine where the last gunshot came from. Holding her shotgun out in front of her, she low-crawled, pulling herself across the snow with her left arm, to a more defendable location behind a small rock outcropping. Again, she jerked the cocking mechanism with her left hand to seat the round before propping the barrel of her gun on a makeshift stone shelf. She edged herself up until she could focus down the site.

More gunfire erupted. Sterling, hiding behind a huge pine tree, used the trunk as a body shield against the fusillade of bullets. He exchanged shots with someone behind the tiny cabin on the other side of the clearing. Chunks of pine bark flew off the tree with each bullet fired. The shooter had Sterling pinned in place.

Caitlyn breathed in through her nose, and when she spotted the shooter peering around the outside corner of the log wall, she placed the bead of her sight on his chest. Releasing half the air from her lungs, she paused and squeezed the trigger with her left index finger, hoping the rocks would stabilize the gun in the absence of her other hand. The shotgun blast rammed the butt of her weapon into her already bruised shoulder and her body absorbed the brutal force. She grunted in pain, and her vision blurred as the slug hit his chest and the man she targeted fell to the ground.

Caitlyn had never shot a person before. Her throat closed and alarm bells rang between her ears as she stared at the lifeless body collapsed on the carpet of snow. A red stain saturated and spread into the pure whiteness surrounding him. Caitlyn inhaled the smokey gunpowder hanging in the air, and she coughed at the burning metallic taste in the back of her throat.

"Reed! You got him," Sterling yelled. "I'll check on Dillinger and clear the cabin. You get the girl."

Caitlyn took a firm mental grip on her emotions. She would deal with the reality of what she had done later. Right now, Tracy needed her... and Ren. Poor Renegade. He'd never been anything but the best and most loyal friend she'd ever had. A sob tore from her throat.

Focus, Caitlyn!

Her shoulder throbbed when she slung her gun's strap over it. She ignored the ache and darted back to the mine shaft. She kicked open the wooden door, and called out, "Tracy, how many men are there up here in the camp?"

The girl rocked back and forth, hugging her knees. She wore no coat. Instead, Tracy had wrapped an old, thin blanket around her shoulders for warmth. She had on only jeans and a flannel shirt. "Three. There are three, but one of them went back down to the ranch to get my mom. Did you see her? Is she okay?" Tracy's voice trembled with fear.

That must be the son of a bitch who shot Colt. Caitlyn swallowed hard. "She's fine," Caitlyn said, though she didn't really know. It wouldn't do any good to upset the girl before they got her to safety. "What about my dog? Is he—"

Something cold and hard jabbed Caitlyn between her shoulder blades. "Drop your weapons, Marshal." A deep, male voice accompanied a second prod from his rifle and a freezing wash of adrenaline spiked her brain.

Caitlyn's heart pounded in her ears as she slowly raised her hands. A low growl vibrated from somewhere in the dark shadows of the shaft and sent her heart racing.

"Slowly, take your pistol out of its holster and toss it to the side." The man shoved his rifle barrel harder into her back, causing her to stumble forward. "And do it very carefully, or I'll blow your spine in two."

Caitlyn sucked in a deep breath. "I broke my right arm, and I can't grip the gun with that hand. I'll have to cross over my body with my left."

The man grunted and reached for her pistol himself, snatching it out of its holster. He tucked it somewhere inside his clothing, then patting her back, found her secondary handgun. "Now, slide that shotgun off your shoulder. Real easy like."

Inch by inch, she lowered the strap down her arm. When the butt of the gun hit the ground, she let it fall the rest of the way. The clatter echoed down the shaft, and helplessness draped over Caitlyn's shoulders.

"Now, get down there with the rest of them. We'll be back to take our revenge on you for shooting Reggie. You'll pay for that in ways you don't want to imagine." The man shoved

Caitlyn with great force, and she stumbled on the incline, falling to her knees. She rolled to avoid landing on her broken bone.

In response to the violent action against Caitlyn, Renegade roused himself. He sprang up the shaft toward the man. Surprised, their captor aimed his rifle at the dog's flying form. Aware of the man's intention, Caitlyn ignored the shooting pain in her arm and pushed herself off the rock floor. She jumped to her feet and swept her leg around in mid-air, and with all her might, she kicked the side of the man's knee. A sickening crack echoed through the mine seconds before the man's gut-wrenching scream echoed off the walls.

The powerful dog rammed into the man's chest, knocking him the rest of the way to the ground. The man's rifle clattered across the stone floor, and he lay clutching his malformed joint as the dog viciously barked and snapped, his fangs inches from the man's face.

Caitlyn scurried over to the weapon he'd dropped and snatched it up. She fell back against the wall and aimed the weapon at the man's head. "Renegade!" she cried. "You're alive!"

After catching her breath, Caitlyn crawled over to the man Renegade held pinned to the floor and retrieved her own guns. She checked their captive for other weapons, but all he carried was the rifle he had pushed her with. When she was certain the fugitive was unarmed, she fumbled to cuff his hands behind his back and then called Renegade off.

Kneeling next to her beloved partner, Caitlyn ran her good hand all over his body. Her fingertips raked over what felt like a spot of dry matted blood, but when she pulled her hand away, it was covered with a fresh coat of red. Renegade's sudden lunge must have caused his previous wound to bleed again. Caitlyn squeezed her eyes closed and swallowed a sob.

"They shot your dog when he tried to keep the men away from me. He saved me." Tracy's frightened voice quavered from her spot deep in the shaft. "He's been unconscious ever since… until now."

Caitlyn's heart thudded against her ribs. *Poor Ren.* "He saved us both this time." Caitlyn staggered to the door and called to Sterling for help.

21

With his arms held out in front of him and his gun in firing position, Sterling swung low around the doorframe. Caitlyn caught her breath while he absorbed the scene before him. Finally, his eyes settled on the cuffed man writhing in pain on the floor. "Took out his knee?"

"Yeah."

"Atta girl." Sterling lowered his weapon and knelt before Caitlyn. "Dillinger suffered a gunshot wound to his thigh, but it looks like it missed the bone and there's a clear entrance and exit wound. No arterial bleeding. I bound the wound for now. He'll survive."

Caitlyn felt for the guy. "He's had a hell of a day. First a near bear attack and then a gunshot wound? Getting him and Tracy out of the mountains on horseback will be a challenge. Sam will be in agony, and the girl has no coat. Not to mention, there's no way my dog can make that long trek."

"No worries. ATF's chopper is on the way."

"Yeah, too little—too late. So much for backup." Caitlyn

sat against the cold stone wall of the mine shaft, holding Renegade's head in her lap. She peeled back her sleeve and prodded her throbbing arm.

"Good God, Caitlyn," Sterling reached for her. "That arm is broken. Did that happen when your horse fell?"

She shrugged. "Renegade is the one who needs immediate medical attention. He was shot. I think the bullet side-swiped him, but the wound is fairly deep, and I think he might have a couple of broken ribs."

"And he charged this asshole anyway?"

Caitlyn's throat ached, and her pain seeped out through hot tears. She nodded. "Best damn partner in the world."

"No argument there."

The deafening sound of helicopter rotors drowned out their words, and Sterling darted out to the clearing to wave them in.

"Come on, Tracy." Caitlyn held her hand out and helped the girl to her feet. "Your knights in their shining helicopter are here. Let's get you home."

"Home." Her fingers were icicles when Caitlyn helped her to her feet. "Is my dad—is he?"

"He didn't make it, sweetheart. I'm sorry."

Tracy dropped her chin to her chest. "And Tom?" she asked in a weak whisper.

"I don't know. He was alive when the sheriff found him, but he was hurt pretty bad. I know they rushed him to the hospital." Caitlyn waited for her to ask about her mother, but she never did.

The ATF S.W.A.T. team ran inside through the broken door in a well-rehearsed maneuver while the two exhausted women sat waiting. After clearing the small space, they helped Caitlyn and Tracy to the chopper. Two men carried Renegade on a canvas stretcher, and Caitlyn gripped one of them by the arm. "Have you heard anything about the local sheriff who was shot this morning?"

"No, ma'am. I haven't heard anything."

Caitlyn closed her eyes against the ache of not knowing before she continued. "Listen, Renegade is a Deputy US Marshal K9. He needs immediate emergency veterinary care. His vet is in Moose Creek, and there's a helipad at the local clinic."

"Roger that, but you're coming with him, aren't you?"

"No." She bit down on her lower lip. "You're taking Deputy Marshal Dillinger and Tracy Woodrow to the clinic though. Have the vet meet you there. I need to ride the horses down the mountain with Sterling."

"Like hell you do!" Sterling stomped across the trampled snow toward her. "You've got a broken arm!"

The ATF agent stared at her purple hand. "Why didn't you say something?" He turned and yelled out the door, "Medic!" A young man carrying a medical kit ran toward them. "This Deputy Marshal needs medical attention immediately."

The medic assessed her wounds and splinted her arm. He also gave her some extra-strength pain relievers to take the edge off until she could get to the hospital. Caitlyn swallowed two of the bitter pills dry and then scooped a handful of snow into her mouth to help them go down. She waited with Renegade while the ATF team loaded the helicopter with the dead and injured.

"Hey—where's the guy Dillinger and I tazed and tied up? I didn't see them load him on the helicopter." Caitlyn pushed herself to her feet, her heart in her throat. She jogged to the spot where they'd left him. "Sterling!"

Dirk caught up with her. "I never saw him. I thought there were only two. Didn't you say the third guy was back at the Woodrow place?"

"Yeah, but he must have followed us up, because he's the guy with the busted knee."

"And the dead guy is on the chopper…"

"The third man got away!" Caitlyn kicked a loose rock. If he wasn't injured, Renegade could have tracked the man down. "Damn it!" Her frustration throbbed with fury in her swollen arm, and she pulled her wrist into her chest. Caitlyn studied the flattened spot in the snow where they had left the man. It looked as though he rolled over to a rock protruding from the ground and rubbed the zip-tie they'd cuffed him with across its jagged edge until it broke. The plastic pieces lay in pink-tinged snow. "Once his hands were loose, he was free."

"Do you see any tracks?" Sterling's eyes darted in several directions.

"Too many people have been running around over here. Without a dog, we'll never find him."

"Oh, we'll find him. Just not today. He can't come back here, and he's on his own." Sterling patted her shoulder. "Don't worry, Reed. We'll get him."

A deep sigh deflated Caitlyn's lungs. "Let me say goodbye to Ren, and then let's get these horses down the hill." She reached Renegade's side just as they were loading his cot into the chopper. She stroked his face, and he tried to lift his head. "Lie still, boy." She bent over and kissed his muzzle. "You're my hero, you know that? I'll come to you as fast as I can. Okay?"

Renegade's pink tongue slid out and swiped her face. His tail thumped lethargically two times on the canvas. "You're the best dog ever, Renegade." Caitlyn blinked back her tears and scowled. "You guys take good care of him."

"We will, Deputy Marshal. Like he was one of our own. We're leaving an investigative team up here while we make the emergency medical run."

"Good. Have them keep an eye out for the third fugitive," Caitlyn said. The ATF agent gave her a nod and pulled the door closed. As soon as Caitlyn was clear, the helicopter took off and headed straight to town.

Sterling waited for her at the edge of the clearing with the three horses. "Let's go."

Caitlyn ponied Whiskey behind her as she rode Dillinger's horse down the mountain. Her horse's neck was raw and sore, but he was going to be fine. At least physically. He was likely to have issues with the sound of gunfire, but Caitlyn trusted Dylan's ability to help sort him out.

She and Sterling didn't speak much on their way down the mountains back to the Woodrow ranch. Caitlyn did her best to ignore her pain as she grappled with the events of the day. She prayed silently for Colt. They hadn't heard anything, and she tried to believe that no news was good news, even though there was no way to get any information—good or bad.

Images of the man she had shot falling dead to the ground attempted to force their way to the front of her mind, but she diligently resisted them, over and over again. At least Renegade was alive and, though he'd be out of commission for a while, he would make a full recovery. Thank God for that. Once again, her heroic dog saved her life.

Caitlyn pushed the horses faster than she normally would have traveling down the snowy hillsides. Fortunately, Sterling managed his mount well. "You sit that horse like you know what you're doing. You must have experience?"

"At one time, I thought I wanted to be a rodeo cowboy." He flashed her a rare grin.

"Really? What changed your mind?"

"A broken shoulder, a punctured lung, and a couple of concussions. Eventually, I got smart enough to change career paths."

Caitlyn chuffed. "Because being a US Deputy Marshal is so much safer?"

Sterling sent her a wry glance. "Speaking of safe, I know you want to get to the emergency room as soon as possible, but can we try not to kill ourselves, or the horses, on the way down?"

"You're doing fine. Besides, we're almost there."

When they finally arrived at the Woodrow ranch, Wes was the only one there. They found him blocking the front door with yellow crime-scene tape. At the sound of the horses' hooves on the drive, he spun to face them, his hand flying to his holster.

"It's just us, Deputy Cooper," Sterling called out.

Wes relaxed and jogged down the porch steps. "Where's the other marshal?"

Sterling swung his leg over the cantle of his saddle and hopped down. "He was shot in the leg and is flying to the clinic in the ATF chopper."

"How's Colt?" Caitlyn asked. "Have you heard anything?"

Wes's shoulders deflated. "The doc had him flown to Rapid City for emergency surgery. I haven't heard anything since."

"What? Wes—how bad was he hurt? Where was he shot?" She fired questions at him as she yanked her phone out of her pocket. Poking buttons on the screen, she dialed Blake's personal cell number. Her gut sank like she'd swallowed rocks.

"Caitlyn?" Blake's deep voice came through the speaker.

"What's going on with Colt? Wes said you sent him to Rapid City. Was it that bad?"

"Caitlyn, where are you? Are you with anyone?"

"I'm at the Woodrow ranch. Wes Cooper and Dirk Stirling are here with me. Why? What is going on?"

"Colt was shot two times. Once in the chest and once in

his upper arm. The bullet entered in his chest right at the edge of the armhole in his Kevlar vest. It's lodged up against his scapula. The bullet must come out as soon as possible, and I didn't feel I had the necessary equipment to do the surgery here. He's in excellent hands."

"But is he going to be all right?" Exhaustion and pain were winning, and hysteria wound its way into Caitlyn's voice.

"You need to get to the clinic right away. The ATF agents that brought Renegade and the others down in the helicopter told me you have a broken arm. You should have flown down with them."

"Answer me, Blake!"

"I'll call the hospital in Rapid City and get an update. I'll share it with you as soon as you get here. Can someone drive you?"

Tension was thick, and her head swam. Caitlyn's stomach rebelled, and she bent over to heave. Bile burned her esophagus. Sterling handed his reins to Wes and dashed over to support her. She leaned into him, and he helped her sit. He took her phone and moved the horses away.

"Doctor? This is Deputy Marshal Sterling. We have horses that need to be trailered back home to the Reed Ranch. As soon as I get them loaded, I'll drive Caitlyn to the clinic." He listened to the voice on the other end. "On our way."

Caitlyn peered up at Wes. "Where's Dylan?"

"He drove to the clinic, but he left the horse trailer here."

"Okay." She rummaged in her coat for her keys and tossed them to Sterling. "Hook the trailer to my truck. Wes, help Dirk load the horses, will you?"

As Sterling ran toward her truck, he yelled over his shoulder. "First, let's get you inside the cab to warm up. I promised the doctor I'd get you down there fast and in one piece."

"I need to get to Rapid City. I can always have them fix my arm there."

"Absolutely not."

22

McKenzie and Dylan were at the hospital debating whether they should drive to Rapid City to be with Colt now, or wait for Caitlyn, when the ATF helicopter landed on the helipad behind the clinic. Agents ran from the chopper with three stretchers.

"Dylan, look!" A cold lump formed behind McKenzie's sternum as she pointed at one of the canvas stretchers. "That's Renegade!" She hurried toward the men. "Wait! I know this K9. What happened?"

The agents carrying Renegade stopped while the other two stretchers were rushed to the emergency room. "He was grazed by a bullet. He'll need stitches, and his handler thinks he might have broken ribs. Do you know his vet?"

McKenzie's fingers were already flying across her phone screen. She nodded as she held her phone to her ear. While she waited for the vet to answer, she ran her fingers over the soft fur on Renegade's nose. "Doctor Moore? This is McKenzie Torrington. Renegade has a gunshot wound. Looks like it just grazed him, but he might have broken ribs and he's lost some blood."

"Can you bring him here? I'll prepare for the surgery."

"On our way." She hung up and directed the agents to take Renegade to the bed of Dylan's truck. "The vet clinic is only a few blocks away. We'll drive him."

Dylan gripped one of the agent's shoulders. "His handler —Caitlyn Reed—where is she? Is she okay?" McKenzie was concerned, too. Why hadn't Caitlyn accompanied her injured partner?

"We tried to get her on the helicopter, but she refused. She said she had to get some horses down the mountain, and that she'd meet us here. It may take her awhile though—she has a broken arm."

Dylan closed his eyes and tossed his chin upward. "She is so damn stubborn."

"Our medic splinted her break, but that's all she'd let us do."

McKenzie slid her arm around Dylan's waist. "Come on. Let's get Ren to the vet. You can yell at your sister later. At least we know she's safe."

CAITLYN HELD her good hand up to the heat vent in her truck. She had cranked the temperature up in the cab while Dirk drove them back to town. Still, she couldn't seem to warm up, and she shivered inside her coat. "We can drop the horses off at our ranch on our way to town."

"Stop talking, Reed. You're not making any sense. I'm driving you straight to the clinic." Dirk's grip on the steering wheel whitened his scuffed knuckles. "The horses will be fine in the trailer a little longer. Besides, we can have the vet look at Whiskey's neck while we're in Moose Creek."

The truck slammed into a rut in the road. Caitlyn groaned and bit her lip so she wouldn't scream out from the blinding pain caused by the jolt. She didn't have the energy to argue with Dirk, and besides, she wanted to see Renegade. As soon as the vet had him bandaged up, he could sleep in her truck while she drove to Rapid City. "Okay, I'll have my brother pull the trailer home from town."

Sterling stopped, trailer and all, in front of the double glass doors of the emergency room entrance and honked. A nurse pushing a wheelchair ran out the door with Blake on her heels.

Blake yanked open her door. "Caitlyn Reed, is there any trouble you're not smack in the middle of?" he admonished as he gently inspected her splinted arm. "Let's get you inside. Nurse, please get a couple of heated blankets for Ms. Reed. Her body temperature is low. She's in shock." Blake lifted Caitlyn from the truck and set her in the wheelchair. Glancing up at Sterling, he said, "Why didn't you force her to fly down here in the helicopter?"

"I don't know how well you know Deputy Marshal Reed, Doctor, but have you ever tried to force her to do something she doesn't want to do?" Sterling glowered at her. "I'll go park this rig, then I'll be right in."

Caitlyn gripped the sleeve of Blake's lab coat. "How is Colt?"

"I haven't heard anything yet. I called over for a report, but he's in surgery now. I'll let you know when I hear." Blake wheeled her inside and straight to imaging for an x-ray. "How long ago did this break happen?"

"I don't know, around noon I'd guess."

Blake helped her onto the exam table before covering her legs with a heated blanket. "You should have come down in the med-evac. Not tending to a break right away can be serious, Caitlyn. You might have nerve damage."

"It was far more important to save Tracy Woodrow from a fate worse than a simple broken bone. Don't you think?"

He shook his head and sighed. "We need to cut off this coat."

"No way. I love this coat."

"Caitlyn, for God's sake! You can get another coat." He undid the splint.

"Let me just slide my arm out." She tugged on the sleeve, and searing pain caused pricks of light to swim in her vision."

"That's enough." Blake pressed her back onto the table, and with a large pair of shears, he cut the sleeve away from her arm. The nurse helped him remove the coat, and they tucked more warm blankets around her. "From now on, you are going to do as you're told."

"You promised you'd get an update on Colt."

"I'll call while they're getting your x-rays." Blake brushed a loose strand of hair out of her face. "You stay still and behave."

When the imaging was complete, the nurse reloaded Caitlyn into the wheelchair and took her back to the emergency room. Blake met them in the hallway. He looked directly into her eyes and gripped her good shoulder. "Colt is still in surgery. They'll call me as soon as they have an update."

Caitlyn closed her eyes. She was cold and tired, in terrible pain, and scared. "And Renegade?"

"He's at the vet with McKenzie and Dylan. McKenzie called when she couldn't reach you on your phone. She asked me to tell you that Renegade is fine. Doctor Moore says he needs to rest until his ribs heal, but he expects Ren to be back to normal before long."

A sigh of relief escaped her lungs. *Please, God. Please, let Colt be okay.*

. . .

Several hours later, Caitlyn's arm was casted, and after doping up on medication, she felt no more pain. Blake had wanted to admit her to the hospital overnight, but she refused. "It's just a broken bone. I'm fine. Have you heard from Colt's doctors yet?"

"Yes. The surgery was delicate, but it went well. Colt is currently in recovery. He's stable and resting."

An aching sob wrenched from Caitlyn's chest, and she covered her mouth with her fingers. "Thank God."

The pale-yellow curtain draped around her exam room slid back, and Dylan and McKenzie entered her space. Dylan stared at her before glaring at Blake. "What's wrong? Why's my sister crying?"

Blake grinned, his dimples cutting into his cheeks. "Actually, the tears are because Colt is going to be all right. I just heard from his surgeon."

"That's great news!" McKenzie rushed to Caitlyn's side and gave her good shoulder a gentle squeeze. "Renegade is doing well, too. He's resting in Dylan's truck." She looked up at Blake. "Can we take Caitlyn home now?"

"No!" Caitlyn pulled away from her. "I have to go to Colt."

"Caitlyn..." Dylan took a step toward her.

"If you won't drive me, I'll drive myself." She tried to stand, but her head was heavy, and dizziness forced her back down to the bed.

Blake steadied her. "You absolutely cannot drive while on the medication I gave you."

McKenzie flung her purse over her shoulder. "I'll drive you, Caitlyn. But we should wait until tomorrow. It's too late to go tonight."

"McKenzie is right. They won't let you see him tonight anyway," Blake reasoned.

"But what if he wakes up and I'm not there?" Caitlyn

knew she sounded whiny. Her eyelids drooped, and she couldn't find the energy to argue any further.

"We'll go there first thing in the morning. But tonight, we're taking both you and Renegade home to rest." Dylan helped Caitlyn into a wheelchair, and McKenzie held the curtain back for Dylan to push the chair through.

"Dylan?" Caitlyn's voice came out sing-songy. "Whiskey was grazed with a bullet across his neck. He's okay, but will you check him out for me?"

He ruffled the hair on the top of her head. "I'm going to tell dad to ground you for not taking better care of your animals."

"He won't do it, though." Caitlyn gave her brother a big, cheesy grin.

He rolled his eyes. "True, you always get away with murder."

Caitlyn knew Dylan was teasing, but the image of the man she shot earlier splashed in vivid color across her mind's eye. Her ears grew hot, but the rest of her body turned to ice.

23

The first thing that sifted through Colt's mind was that he must have fallen asleep sitting up again. But when he tried to move, a red-hot pinching prevented him. His eyelids were weighted by a groggy sleep, and he struggled to blink them open. A seam of angry light forced his eyes closed again, and he tried to cover them with the back of his wrist, but something held his arm down.

"Colt? Are you awake?"

His eyes snapped open. *Catie?* A brilliant stream of light stabbed into his brain. His lips moved to say her name, but his dry mouth stuck to itself. Colt ran his tongue over his lips, though it didn't help.

"McKenzie, call the nurse and tell her Colt is waking up." Caitlyn sat on the side of his bed and lifted his hand onto her leg. She leaned toward him. "Good morning." She smelled like lilacs and rain.

He let his eyes remain closed as he breathed her in. Someone entered the room with McKenzie. "Waking up, are we?" the unfamiliar voice sang. "Are you thirsty, Sheriff Branson? I'll bring you some water."

When the nurse returned, Colt opened his eyes again—this time with less pain. He sipped the cold drink, and with each swallow, he became more alert and aware. Caitlyn had a blue cast on her arm. "What happened?" His throat scraped like he had gravel coating it, and he coughed, causing an acetylene flame to flare in his chest and shoulder.

"You were shot." Her eyes grew moist, and she kissed his forehead. "Thank God you're going to be okay."

"No—I mean, what happened to your arm?"

"This?" She sat back and held up her cast. "Nothing. I just fell off my horse."

He shook his head, instantly regretting the movement. "You've been riding since you were a kid. You never fall off your horse." He sucked in a breath. "Tell me what happened."

She scooted closer to him on the bed and caressed the side of his face with her good hand. "We have plenty of time for stories. Right now, I want to tell you the most important things."

He scrunched his brows. "Where's Ren?"

"He's at home."

"Then what's wrong?"

She sighed dramatically. "For one thing… I have realized I can't live without you. So, you can't ever get shot again. Period."

McKenzie smiled and slipped quietly out of the room.

"Yeah?" A warm glow spread across his chest.

Caitlyn smiled and kissed him softly. "Yeah."

"Does this mean you want to marry me?" Mischief sparked in his blue-green eyes.

"Should I get down on one knee?

Colt's heart rate ramped up, and his shoulder throbbed. It was probably time for more pain medication, but he wasn't about to interrupt what was happening. "Actually, *I* want to do that, but…"

"We can wait."

"No." He held up his right hand and looked at his fingers. "Where's the ring that was on my pinkie finger?"

Caitlyn lifted a manilla envelope from his nightstand. "It's probably in here." She opened it, reached inside, and pulled out the ring.

He took her hand in his and nodded. "This was my mom's wedding band. Will you wear it until I can talk to your dad and do this the right way?"

Tears filled her eyes and danced down her cheeks. She lifted his hand to her lips and kissed his palm. Caitlyn never cried, and Colt held his breath. He wiped her face with his thumb. "Catie, what's wrong?"

Colt tried to sit up, and the machines monitoring his stats blared with alarms. Caitlyn shook her head and gently pushed him back against his pillow. Had he said the wrong thing? Gone too fast? "You don't have to wear her ring if you don't want." Pain, confusion, and the spike in his blood pressure caused his breath to stutter.

Two nurses rushed into the room and pushed Caitlyn away from his bed. He reached for her, but the nurse tucked his arm under his blanket. "You need to take it easy. Lie back, now."

"Catie?" He searched her face. Her eyes were filled with tears, and now also held fear. He lay back against his pillows and willed his heart to slow down. He'd do anything to get the nurses to leave. "I'm fine. I just moved too fast."

"Maybe it's too soon for visitors." The older nurse glowered at Caitlyn, and Colt wanted to shove them out of the room.

"I'm fine. Really."

Once the nurses were satisfied he wasn't crashing, they lectured both Colt and Caitlyn about him staying calm and the importance of resting. Finally, they left.

"Tell me what's wrong, Catie. What did I say?"

"Nothing's wrong. Well... there's a lot wrong, but nothing you did, or said." She approached his bed and lifted his hand again. "I'm sorry I upset you. The truth is, I'd be honored to wear your mom's ring. Forever. I don't want diamonds. I'd just lose them, anyway. A simple band is perfect, and the fact that it was your mother's means everything to me."

Pure, exhilarating joy flooded his heart and expanded his chest. "If I weren't stuck in this bed, I'd show you how happy you've made me."

"It can only be a fraction of how happy I am." She squeezed his fingers.

"Then why the tears?"

"I've been through a lot the last couple of days, and I think it's all coming to a head. I'm sorry for crying." She rubbed her damp cheeks on her sleeve. "Truly, Colt, I'm the happiest woman in the world."

"Take the ring."

Caitlyn rolled her lips between her teeth and bit down. She slid it onto her finger and smiled, but there was something lurking in Caitlyn's eyes. Something she wasn't telling him.

"I love you, Catie."

"Oh, Colt. I love you too."

The nurse came in with a little paper cup and interrupted their moment. "Time for your pain meds." She handed him the cup and then offered Caitlyn a brief smile before plumping his pillow. "He'll be drifting off here shortly, and he needs the rest."

"Of course." Caitlyn brought his hand to her cheek. "I have to drive down to Casper today to file my reports, and the chief wants to talk to me. I'll probably have to stay down there a couple of days."

Colt nodded. "With any luck, I'll be home by the time you get back."

"If so, have Dylan pick you up and take you to my place. I'll come home as soon as I can." Colt's eyelids closed against his will, and he stretched them open again. Caitlyn laughed. "Get some rest."

"We have plans to make." He gave up and let his eyes close, but he smiled.

"There's plenty of time for all that. You focus on getting back on your feet." Caitlyn kissed him, but he was already drifting, looking forward to her kiss being the last thing he knew every night before he fell asleep. *She said yes.*

24

Caitlyn left to find McKenzie in the solarium. She was taking a quiz in an outdated magazine while she waited. "Ready to go?"

McKenzie held her finger up, asking Caitlyn to wait for a minute while she tallied her score. "Looks like Dylan and I stand a seventy-five percent chance of living happily ever after."

"According to some random magazine?" Caitlyn rolled her eyes. "I'd give you two at least a ninety percent chance, and I know you."

A worried frown settled on McKenzie's face. "Why not one-hundred percent?"

"Oh, brother. I'll give you the hundred percent as soon as my brother gets around to asking you to marry him." Caitlyn reached down to tug McKenzie to her feet.

McKenzie's eyes widened. "What happened with Colt?" She blinked up at Caitlyn, who couldn't help grinning like a kid at Christmas. "You weren't wearing that ring when you went into his room."

"Nope, I wasn't." She held out her hand to show her friend. "This ring was Colt's mother's."

"So… you're engaged?" McKenzie stood and hugged Caitlyn.

"Well, engaged to be engaged. He still wants to talk to my dad."

"That's so old-fashioned… and sweet." McKenzie's eyes were teary when she drew back.

"Yeah." Caitlyn squeezed McKenzie's hand. She changed the subject before her emotions could well up in the middle of a public waiting room. "Come on. I need you to drive me to the Moose Creek Clinic on our way home."

McKenzie dropped Caitlyn at the doors of the clinic. "I'll wait for you in the lobby. Take your time."

Voices and toddler noises sounded from behind Sam's hospital room door, so she knocked before entering.

"Yes?" a woman's voice called out.

"It's just me, Caitlyn Reed," she said as she opened the oversized door.

"Reed. Come on in." Sam pushed himself up on the bed. "This is my wife, Laurie, and my little man, Caleb." He grinned with pride.

Caitlyn shook Laurie's hand and waved at the busy little blond-headed boy who drove his toy truck across the floor. "I'm on my way to talk to Tracy Woodrow, but I thought I'd stop by and see how the leg is doing?"

"Hurts like hell, but I'm alive." Sam chuckled. "Better than being mauled by a bear. Hell of a day, right?"

She glanced at Sam's wife to gauge her reaction to his bravado. Laurie's mouth pursed, but her eyes held humor and Caitlyn relaxed a little. "You were lucky all around, I'd say."

"Yep. And now I get a couple of months off to recuperate. It's like a paid vacation. I'll watch TV all day and Laurie can wait on me, hand and foot. I'm looking forward to it."

Laurie scoffed. "In your dreams. I'll be the one with the cattle prod, making sure you do your physical therapy."

Caleb ran his truck over the toes of Caitlyn's boots. Laughing, she said, "Well, it looks like you're in good hands and you'll survive. What's Sterling up to?"

"Paperwork." Sam laughed.

"I need to do my reports, too. Any word on Jason Palmer?"

"Thanks to your Karate Kid kick, he had to have knee surgery. But as soon as he's well enough to travel, Sterling will escort him to Denver to face his first set of charges." He rubbed his chin. "I heard the Woodrow boy didn't make it. Sterling told me he died in the OR."

Caitlyn closed her eyes as she absorbed the sad news about Tom again. He was so young. "I was sorry to hear that. I guess I better go see Tracy. She might be able to give us more information on her abductors. She might have heard something. Maybe a clue as to where Raymond Burroughs might be hiding."

Caitlyn said goodbye to Sam and his family and then walked down to Tracy's room. She pressed on the door and called. "Hello?" The hospital rooms were identical, and she stepped to the bottom of the bed.

Tracy appeared physically well, beyond a few bruises and abrasions, but Caitlyn knew it would take the girl a long time before she'd heal emotionally. Tracy faced the loss of her father and her brother, not to mention the terror of being kidnapped by their killers.

"Hi, Marshal Reed. Come on in." The girl's voice sounded weak and resigned.

Caitlyn entered the room and nodded to Elaine, who sat in the visitor's chair. "How are you feeling?"

Tracy shrugged and laid back against her pillow. "Okay, I guess. I just want to go home."

"I know, but it'll be better if you wait until the investigation team is through and the cleaning company gets everything back in order." Caitlyn swallowed against the ache in her throat. "I'm terribly sorry about Tom."

Fat tears spilled from Tracy's eyes, and Elaine wiped her own away with a tissue, though she didn't move to comfort her daughter, so Caitlyn reached for Tracy's hand. Elaine shifted her red-rimmed eyes to Caitlyn. "I heard one of the men who kidnapped Tracy is in a hospital in South Dakota and another one was killed."

A high-pitched ring blared inside Caitlyn's head. She squeezed her eyes shut against the persistent image of the man she shot falling to the ground and the white snow underneath him growing crimson. Bitter bile edged its way up her throat, and she let her breath out slowly. "Yes. But the third man escaped. Tracy, do you remember hearing the men talk about anywhere they were headed? Was there any talk about their plans?"

Elaine sat up and moved to the edge of the chair. Tracy wiped her face on the bedsheet and shook her head. "No. They didn't talk very much. The one man went back to the ranch. The other two took me up to the mine. And besides ordering me around, they didn't say much of anything. When they shoved me inside the mine shaft, I could hear them talking to each other outside, but it was too garbled to understand." The girl twisted her blanket in her hands. "How's your dog? No one has told me anything about him since they took him off the helicopter."

Caitlyn touched the girl's shoulder comfortingly. "Renegade had to have a few stitches and he has a couple of broken ribs, but he's going to be okay. He's at home resting."

"He was so brave."

Caitlyn smiled. "Yeah, he's amazing, but you are awfully brave yourself."

Elaine cocked her head. "Did you say one of the men escaped?"

"Yes, but you have nothing to worry about. He's probably long gone by now, and besides, Deputy Cooper will keep an eye on you and your ranch," Caitlyn reassured her.

"He doesn't need to do that." Elaine reached for her purse and stood. "In fact, I'm going to head home and start cleaning things up, myself." She walked toward the door, and as though suddenly remembering Tracy, she crossed back to the bed to embrace her daughter.

Tracy sat still and unresponsive. Elaine shrugged, nodded at Caitlyn, and left the room.

"Are you okay?" Caitlyn asked Tracy.

"Fine," the girl murmured and slid down under her covers.

A niggling sensation poked at Caitlyn's gut. She pulled out her phone and called Deputy Cooper. "Wes, it's Deputy US Marshal Reed. Will you drive up to the Woodrow ranch? Elaine Woodrow is on her way there now, and I don't think she should be there alone."

"Yes, ma'am. I'm on my way."

"Thanks, Wes." Caitlyn clicked off.

Tracy watched her. "My mom will be fine."

"I'm sure she will. I just want her to have some support. That's all."

"I mean, even if that man is there—she'll be fine."

Caitlyn didn't know where this line of conversation was going, but the niggling turned into a hard knot. "Why do you say that?"

Tracy shrugged. "I'm tired. I'd like to take a nap."

"Tracy, if you know something, you need to tell me. I can help."

"You can't bring my dad and brother back."

Breath rushed from Caitlyn's lungs, and her shoulders drooped. "No. I can't."

Blake entered the room. "Caitlyn, what a nice surprise. I didn't expect to see you here. How's your arm feeling?

"I've got good meds."

Blake's mouth curled into a half grin. "How is Colt?"

"He's going to be okay. The surgery went well, but he's exhausted. I think they want to keep him for four or five days. He fell asleep while I was there." She twisted Colt's ring around her finger with her thumb. "Thanks for sending him to Rapid City. It was a good decision."

"I know my limitations." Blake gave her a bashful grin. "Exhaustion is normal after that type of surgery. Is that a new ring?" Blake stared at her hand before his gaze darted to her face.

"Yes. Well, it's old, but new to me."

Blake's brows arched in question.

"It was Colt's mother's."

His bright blue eyes studied her long enough to make her squirm. "Does this mean congratulations are in order?"

Caitlyn bit her lip before grinning. "Not yet, but soon."

Blake nodded. "I'm happy for you."

"Thanks."

He turned his focus to his patient and asked how she was feeling.

Tracy folded her sheet back. "I'm fine, and I want to go home."

Blake patted the back of her hand. "Physically, you'll be fine in a few days. Nothing some rest and good home cooking won't cure, but I would like you to see a therapist. You've suffered tremendous loss and survived a traumatic situation. Trouble sleeping, anxiety, and feelings of depression are to be expected, but I'd like you to have help coping with them."

Tracy stared up at him, her eyes wide and filled with fear, but when Blake gave her his reassuring, dimpled smile, she relaxed. "If you think I should..."

Caitlyn stifled a smirk. *I guess when solid reasoning doesn't work for him, his good looks and charm do.* She had been on the other side of that powerful gaze often enough, so she understood Tracy's response.

Blake nodded. "I'll write a few recommendations in your discharge paperwork. There's no reason you can't go home whenever you're ready. Where is your mom?"

"She left." Tracy looked away and pulled her blanket up to her chin. Blake glanced at Caitlyn.

"Elaine went home. Deputy Cooper is going to meet her there. I can have him bring her back here to get Tracy."

Blake nodded and spoke to the girl. "Tracy, will you have her page me when she gets here? I have a few things to go over with her before I release you." He turned to Caitlyn and lifted her cast. After pinching each finger, he asked, "Any numbness or tingling?"

"I'm fine."

He met her eye and worked his lips into a smile. "Congratulations, again." He bent down and kissed her cheek. "Take care of that arm."

Caitlyn bobbed her head, and he left. Her phone buzzed. "Reed, here."

"This is Deputy Cooper. I'm up here at the Woodrow ranch, but no one is here."

"Okay, well, maybe Elaine stopped off at the store or something."

"No, I mean, someone *was* here, but now they're gone.

When I pulled up, the front door was wide open, so I called out and went inside. No one was anywhere, but there were some open drawers in the master bedroom."

"Stay there. I'm on my way. And, Wes, be careful." Caitlyn schooled her expression so she wouldn't alarm Tracy. "I've got to go, but I'll be back in a little bit."

"My mom left town, didn't she?"

"I don't know. Why do you say that?"

"She was in on it.

Caitlyn's body stilled. What was Tracy saying? "In on what?"

"The shooting."

Caitlyn held her breath for a few seconds before slowly sitting on the edge of the bed. "Why don't you tell me what happened."

"Everything happened the way you were told, only before the men showed up at our house, my mom and dad were fighting. Something about some guy giving my mom something expensive. I don't know. But when the men showed up at the door, the older one—the one who got away—shot..." Anguish flowed through her words, and Caitlyn put her arms around the girl, pulling her into her chest. "He killed my dad! But Mom... she didn't do anything. She didn't say *anything*! Not until Tom..." Tracy's words and tears tumbled onto Caitlyn's shoulder.

"Okay. Shh." Caitlyn rocked Tracy in her arms until the tears stopped flowing. Eventually, she sat back and handed the girl a tissue. "I'm going to drive up to your place and see what's going on. I'll tell Doctor Kennedy to keep an eye on you until I get back. Okay?"

Tracy blew her nose and nodded. "She didn't care. Not until they shot Tom."

Caitlyn pressed the nurse's call button. When the nurse

came in, Caitlyn asked her to page Blake. Within minutes, he rushed through the door. "Is everything alright?"

"I need to go up to the Woodrow place, but I don't think Tracy should be alone."

His eyes searched hers, and his voice dropped. "What happened?"

"Tracy has implicated her mother. I'll be back as soon as I can, but will you make sure she isn't alone?"

Blake gripped her arm. "Be careful."

Caitlyn nodded and left to find McKenzie. She needed a ride to her truck. Now.

25

McKenzie drove Caitlyn to her cabin, where Caitlyn spent a few minutes with Renegade. He was doped up on pain medication. The only way to keep him calm enough to heal was to make him continually drowsy. He woke when she stroked his silky black face, and his tail flopped lazily, letting her know he was happy to see her.

Caitlyn's insides turned warm and gooey, and she kissed Ren's cold, wet nose. The glazed look in Renegade's eyes was the same one that Colt had when he had drifted off earlier. Both her guys needed rest to heal, but she had a job to do. She swept the smooth spot between Renegade's closed eyes with her thumb, and she pushed herself to her feet.

"Thanks for keeping an eye on him, Kenz. I should only be a couple of hours, and then I'll come back to pack a bag before I head out."

"Can't you do your paperwork remotely? Seems like a waste to make you drive three hours down to Casper just for that. You could email your report in." McKenzie opened the refrigerator and stared at the shelves of leftovers. "You want something to eat before you go?"

"I'll grab an apple." Caitlyn flipped her back holster around on her belt, so the tooled leather pocket canted to the left. It would be a little uncomfortable, but if she needed her secondary gun, she'd have to access it with her left hand. "Normally, they'd allow me to file reports remotely, but a few things happened in the mountains that the chief deputy wants to talk with me about in person."

Caitlyn's chest tightened at the thought of lining out the details of her shooting. Both Dirk and Sam assured her that her action had been necessary—a clear and legal use of deadly force against a man actively firing a weapon at another law enforcement officer. Still, she couldn't shake the heavy darkness that came with the crushing finality of taking a life. No matter what the justification was. Worse, she knew that was exactly what her boss wanted to talk to her about. They'd make her see a therapist and keep her off active duty until she did. *Damn.*

"I don't know how long I'll have to stay in Casper, but it shouldn't be more than a few days. Do you mind staying here at my place with Renegade? I'd rather not move him."

"It's not a problem at all. That's the norm for us, anyway."

"I don't think you should bring Larry over here while Renegade is recovering. Ren would only want to play and could pop his stitches." Caitlyn flung her jacket over her shoulders and slid her left arm in the sleeve. "I can't wait to get this stupid cast off."

"Patience." McKenzie brought her an apple and helped pull Caitlyn's coat the rest of the way over her right shoulder. "You've only had that cast on for one day."

. . .

Caitlyn hopped out of her truck in front of the Woodrows' house. Wes walked out the front door and down the steps. "Thanks for coming. I left everything like I found it."

"Good. So, the front door was open?"

"Yeah. Worried me at first. I thought maybe the missing fugitive came back for revenge or something. But no one was in the house—dead or otherwise."

"You said some drawers were left open too?" Caitlyn climbed the porch steps and went inside. Wes followed.

"Yes. But only in the master bedroom. I'll show you." He led the way down the hall. When she passed the office, Caitlyn noticed the gun safe door was ajar, and she stopped.

"Wes, do you have an inventory of the guns left in the safe after the CSIs finished their investigation?"

"Back at the office. Why?"

"I know there were more rifles in that safe than there are now. I'd like to know exactly which guns are missing."

"Do you think someone broke in again?" Wes went to the safe and peered inside. "Looks like some of the ammo is missing too."

"Did you see any signs of breaking and entering?"

"Not other than the door hanging open. But that isn't really a sign, is it?"

"No. I think it was probably Elaine Woodrow who left it open. It looks to me like she came home from the hospital, packed some clothes, grabbed several rifles, and left in such a hurry she didn't bother to close the door."

"But why? Where would she go with her daughter in the hospital and all?"

Caitlyn rolled her lower lip between her teeth. "She didn't leave a note or anything?" Wes shook his head, and Caitlyn looked through the few papers on the desktop. Something in the wastebasket next to the desk caught her eye. "What's this?"

She reached for the bin and lifted it up. Inside was a wax paper wrapper with that same strange rockeT logo printed on it. Only this wrapper still held a broken-off piece of the candy inside. "These wrappers keep showing up. Do you have gloves?"

Wes pulled on a pair of latex gloves from his utility belt and reached for the wax paper. "This candy looks kind of like a Pez. Compressed powdered sugar, like a SweeTart." He sniffed at it.

"Don't sniff stuff like this, Cooper!" Caitlyn grabbed his forearm and pulled it back. "You don't know what that is. It could be some kind of drug or toxin."

His eyes grew large as he stared at her. "It's just candy."

"You don't know that. It's not worth the risk. Bag it up and take it to the evidence locker at the sheriff's office. I'll call down to the lab and see if they've studied the other candy wrappers we've found." Caitlyn pulled out her phone and found the number. While she waited for the lab to answer, she told Wes to dust the open drawers for prints. "We probably won't find anything besides family prints but do it anyway."

Caitlyn walked out onto the porch as she spoke to the lab tech and asked if they'd found anything on the wrappers associated with the case. The woman put her on hold, so she paced the plank floor, forced to listen to *Staying Alive* Muzak style.

"Deputy Marshal?" The tech's voice cut into the tinny music. "Normally, we don't have any results this quickly, but the wrappers you are asking about responded immediately to a swab test. The wax papers have residue of methamphetamine."

"You're sure?"

"Absolutely. There is no doubt. There might be other

substances as well, but we won't get to those tests for a while."

"That's okay, you've been extremely helpful. Thanks." An alarm sounded in her mind. "Wes!"

The deputy jogged outside. "Yeah?"

"That candy is crystalized and pressed methamphetamine. And now, the logo makes perfect sense."

Wes wiped his nose with the back of his hand. "Why?"

"The label says 'rockeT'. Sometimes meth is referred to as rocket fuel. I can't believe I didn't think of that before."

"I'm glad you stopped me from taking a big whiff."

"Somebody—or a gang of somebodies—is putting meth out on the street that looks like candy under that specific logo. All lower-case letters except the last capital T. Either our fugitive is hooked in with the sellers or he's a buyer. Either way, we have a whole new issue on our hands."

26

It was past time for Caitlyn to be on the road to Casper. As it was, she wouldn't get to there until well after dark. She had walked Wes through the initial steps of his investigation at the Woodrow's before she left him. What a terrible time for Colt to be out of commission.

McKenzie carried Caitlyn's bag out to the truck for her and Caitlyn hugged her friend before she opened the door. "Will you and Dylan check on Colt for me, too? I hate that he's so far away."

"Of course, we will. And Renegade will be just fine. Don't worry. We'll FaceTime you tomorrow."

Caitlyn tossed her overnight bag on the seat, then glanced wistfully back at her cabin. She hated leaving Renegade behind. Again.

By the time she merged onto the highway, she knew she'd have to listen to something besides music to distract her mind from its constant replay of painful images. Her mental film reel insistently replayed her fall and the sick crack her arm made when it broke, the bear careening toward Dillinger, Renegade lying lifeless on the mineshaft floor, and the worst image of all—her shot blasting a man in the chest, his blood spraying across the pristine snow, and his body's collapse to the ground. She gritted her teeth and turned on a spy-novel audiobook. One with lots of action.

It was dark when Caitlyn pulled into the US Marshals parking lot in Casper. She sat in her truck for several minutes, building the courage to face the chief. Spencer wanted to talk to her about the man she had killed during the hostage rescue incident, and that was the last thing in the world Caitlyn wanted to discuss.

She sucked in a fortifying breath and opened her door. Her arm throbbed, so she popped the lid on a bottle of ibuprofen and shook a couple of pills into her mouth. Having no water, she swallowed them dry and purposefully strode into her boss's office.

"Good to see you on your feet, Reed." Chief Spencer sat back in his chair with his elbows propped on the armrests. He steepled his fingers. "How's the break?"

A woman sitting in one of the two chairs in front of Spencer's desk drew Caitlyn's attention and she nodded at her before she glanced down at her cast and shrugged. "It's fine. I have to wear the cast for six weeks."

Spencer considered Caitlyn a minute before he shifted his gaze to the other woman and gestured in her direction. "You remember Marshal Williams?"

"Yes, of course." Caitlyn held her left hand out. "Marshal."

"Reed, good to see you." Williams shook Caitlyn's uninjured hand and gestured to the chair. "Take a seat."

Spencer got up to push the other chair out from the desk for her.

Caitlyn ran her tongue across her lower lip and slid into the chair.

"How's Renegade?" The Marshal leaned against the edge

of the chief's desk. "I heard he was grazed by a bullet and has some broken ribs."

"Yes, he's home resting. The vet has his torso taped, and he's keeping Ren doped up on meds that make him sleep. He thinks Renegade will be fine in six to eight weeks."

"Good. That's about the amount of time I suspect it'll take before you're fit for duty again, too. Mentally, I mean."

Heat shot up Caitlyn's neck. "I'm fine to work, and as soon as this cast comes off, I'll be ready to go back into the field."

"That's not how this is going to go, Deputy Marshall Reed. You shot a man who subsequently died. Not only is this the first person that you've killed in the line of duty, but it's the first person you've ever shot. Isn't that correct?"

Caitlyn clamped her teeth together. She stared at the desktop and took a few seconds before raising her gaze to look Marshal Williams in the eye. "Yes, ma'am. But I'm fine. And even if I can't be out in the field, I can still work."

The Marshal took her time to answer. "You're not fine, Caitlyn. Any decent LEO—any decent human being—has a hard time after they've killed someone. That's to be expected. Not only do regulations require that you see a therapist after a shooting, but I personally insist upon it. I would order therapy even if it wasn't regulation. Make an appointment with the department's therapist first thing tomorrow morning. I'll need a written statement from her, stating she believes in her professional opinion that you're mentally and emotionally ready to return to work before I'll sign off on it."

"Honestly, ma'am, I don't think I need to see anyone, but if you insist, I'd like to see someone closer to home."

"That's fine with me, as long as it's someone experienced with this type of emotional trauma in law enforcement officers. And if your therapist agrees, I don't see any problem with you doing some light desk work from home. We definitely can use the extra pair of hands."

"Thanks, Marshal." Caitlyn's muscles twitched, and she wanted to get up and move around. "Is that all?"

"Yes, for now. I'd like you to write out a full incident report covering the entire time you were involved in this case, from the moment you set foot at the Woodrow place, through the casting of your arm. Be especially detailed in your description of the man who got away. It's almost quitting time today though, so why don't you go get some dinner and rest tonight? You can start tomorrow morning."

"Yes, ma'am." Caitlyn stood and shook out the edgy muscles in her legs. "My report will also include something I ran across today." Caitlyn filled her bosses in on her visit to the Woodrow ranch and the wrapper she found there. She showed them a photo on her phone of the rockeT logo. "Looks to me like we have a new product hitting the Wyoming and Montana region. I don't know how Raymond Burroughs is involved in this yet. It's possible he's simply a user, but I suspect he's farther up the food chain than that."

"Excellent work, Reed." Chief Spencer stood and shook her left hand. "I'll give the information to local law enforcement and your fellow Deputy Marshals. They'll work the case until you come back."

She swallowed the spikey lump in her throat. "Thank you, Chief."

Caitlyn missed Colt and Renegade and felt their separation like a missing limb. Maybe after she FaceTimed with Colt, she could get McKenzie to hold her phone up so she could FaceTime with Renegade too.

Caitlyn left Chief Spencer's office and was walking toward her desk when Dirk Sterling entered the door. "Hey, Reed. Good to see you back at work."

"Sterling. Fancy seeing you here."

"How's Dillinger doing?"

"Hanging in there. He's got a long recovery ahead of him, but I think he's happy to be stuck at home with his wife and little boy."

He chuckled. "How's the sheriff?"

"He's going to make it. He was hit two times in the chest, but thankfully, one of the rounds hit his Kevlar vest. It bruised him badly and broke a rib, but the second round hit him right at the edge of the vest's armhole. It penetrated and lodged against his scapula. He had to have surgery to remove the bullet, but it went well, and he should heal up just fine."

"Lucky guy."

"I guess," Caitlyn laughed. "If you call getting shot lucky."

Sterling smirked. "I call getting shot and living lucky. Are you working down here for a couple of days?"

"Yeah. I have to file my report and some other paperwork, then I have to have my head shrunk for a couple weeks before they'll let me come back to work."

Sterling perched on the edge of Caitlyn's desk and peered up at her. "I know you don't want to, but it's a good thing to talk through everything that happened. Besides, it'll give your arm a chance to heal. When you're ready, we can go to the range together and reestablish your aim."

"That'd be great."

"By the way, do you remember the crime family that was involved in the case a year ago, back when we first met?"

Caitlyn pulled out her chair and sat down. "Yeah. The Trova Crime Syndicate, headed up by Anthony Trova from New York. What about them?"

"I got a report of some drug running going on up in Billings, and a few of the names from the previous case have been mentioned. I'm thinking Trova is still trying to get his fat fingers into the market in Montana even though Russo testified about the crime family's drug running intentions in the area."

"Interesting..." Caitlyn chewed the corner of her lip as she pulled out her phone and brought up the photo of the waxed paper wrapper. "The lab told me today that these wrappers contain methamphetamine residue. Look at the logo. Rocket with a capital T."

"T for Trova, you think?"

Caitlyn shrugged. "It's a good possibility. He's absolutely that arrogant. How is Russo doing in witness protection?"

"He's still serving some time at Rikers before he gets to disappear, but his WITSEC contact tells me he'll be settling into suburbia."

"I wonder how his neighbors would feel if they knew the new guy on the block was once a hitman for the mob?"

Sterling chuffed. "He's requested you to be part of the team that escorts him to his new location. Says he trusts you."

"Maybe he knows more information about the drug trafficking than he's told us. I'll hit him up."

"Good idea. You need to get your psych write-off done ASAP. I could use your help on this one."

"I'll make an appointment first thing."

27

Colt sat on the couch in Caitlyn's cabin with his feet propped up on the coffee table, enjoying the warm and mesmerizing effect of the fire that McKenzie lit before she drove over to Reed Ranch. Caitlyn was due home, and he couldn't wait to see her. Renegade lay on his cushion before the fireplace. McKenzie had given the dog his pain medication before she left, and he was sound asleep, snoring soft puppy rumbles. Colt shifted and sucked air in through his teeth and grunted at the sharp jab in his side. At times, the broken rib hurt worse than the bullet wound.

The clock on the mantle ticked like a metronome, emphasizing the slowness of the passing seconds. It seemed forever before the front door of the cabin opened and a cold breeze brought Caitlyn through the door.

"Look at you two, all cozy before the fire." Caitlyn closed the door and dropped her bag at her feet. She slid the left side of her jacket off and wriggled her right arm through the other sleeve. She tossed her coat on a nearby chair and bolted across the room to him.

Her lips and the tip of her nose were cold when she

kissed him, and Colt cupped his hand to warm her petal-soft cheek. "Welcome home."

She gave him another quick peck before she moved to Renegade's bed. Caitlyn stroked her dog's face, and he groaned, drunkenly licking at her fingers, and thumping his tail. Her usually exuberant dog remained lying on his pallet. "Has he been doped up like this the whole time?"

The fire cast golden highlights through Caitlyn's dark hair and sparked a glittery reflection in her amber eyes. Colt had a hard time focusing on the topic of conversation. "Pretty much. McKenzie takes him out and feeds him whenever the medication starts to wear off, but I think Doctor Moore wants to keep him as still as possible for a while longer."

"It's weird to see him so sleepy. Poor guy." She gave him a final stroke and stood. "What is that delicious smell? It's making me hungry."

"McKenzie made chili in the crock-pot."

"Yum. Can I get you anything?"

"Yeah—you. Come sit by me." Colt opened his arm, and Caitlyn snuggled against his chest, resting her head on his good shoulder.

"How are you feeling?"

He pulled her close. "Better now that you're home."

"Mmm, me too." She brushed his jaw with her lips. "Is McKenzie at the ranch?"

"Yeah. She feeds Renegade and me in the morning, spends all day with your mom and helps take care of your dad, then she and Dylan come back here for dinner. Those two seem to be getting pretty cozy." He felt her cheek bunch in a smile against his chest.

"I know, isn't it great?"

"Speaking of getting cozy... kiss me again."

Caitlyn pushed herself up and leaned toward him. She

reached for his face with the fingers poking out from her cast. She kissed him, and her lips tasted like spring. When she lowered her heavy brace, it bumped his sling. Colt winced and bit back a yelp.

"I'm so sorry. Are you okay?"

"Fine." He eased in a breath and waited for the pain to subside. "Looks like we're going to have to figure out how to manage our injuries." He winked at her worried expression. "But I still want that kiss."

She laughed and kneeling beside him on the couch, leaned over and pressed her mouth against his. His body, forgetting its broken state, responded, and he pulled her onto his lap. Her cast and his sling made their movements stilted and awkward.

Caitlyn giggled. "My mom wants us to come for dinner tomorrow night. I was thinking it would be the perfect time to tell them we want to get married."

Colt pulled her in tight to his chest, and even though the embrace caused painful flames to lick the inside of his ribcage, he nibbled her lip. "I can't wait."

"Any news on Cherylynn's homicide case?"

"Yes. In fact, Blake called me this afternoon. He's been in contact with the crime lab and the DNA from the tissue samples scraped from underneath Cherylynn's fingernails is an exact match to the DNA from the guy you shot."

Caitlyn's muscles tensed, causing Colt to peer at her. "How are you doing with that, by the way?"

She sighed. "Mostly fine. Sometimes I can't shake the image of him falling or his blood coloring the snow." Colt tightened his hold on her and rubbed her arm with his hand. Caitlyn smiled at him. "I have to see a therapist before they'll let me go back to work."

"That's a good thing." He brushed his lips across her hair.

"It might help to know for certain that he was the one who raped and murdered Cherylynn."

"It does."

"Jason Palmer, the guy with the busted knee, came through surgery fine and is now recuperating in a jail cell. He's not talking yet, but I imagine he might loosen up when he learns he is now facing accessory to murder charges because he was with Reginald Burroughs when he brutalized Cherylynn."

"Reginald? The guy who escaped was Raymond Burroughs. Are they brothers?"

"I think so."

Caitlyn rolled her lower lip inward and watched the flames lick at the logs in the fireplace while she thought. "Tracy Woodrow said her mother, Elaine, was somehow involved with the men who killed her father and brother."

"You're kidding?"

"That's what she said, and when I met Wes up at their ranch, it looked like Elaine had gone through her drawers, packed a bag, and left so fast she didn't even bother to close the front door."

"You think she ran to meet up with Ray Burroughs?"

"I do."

"What is Tracy going to do? She's the only one left at the ranch?"

"Hm," Caitlyn murmured. Her mind busy with the facts of the case. "She's seventeen, so I don't think she'll have any legal issues with being on her own. I'll check in on her and see if she has any relatives to lean on." She sat up and faced Colt. "Ray and Elaine think they got away, but we'll find them. Sooner or later."

CAITLYN'S DAD sat at the head of the table gazing proudly at his family. Caitlyn sat next to Colt across from Dylan. Her mother bustled out of the kitchen with the last dish, setting it on the hot pad in the center. She was followed by McKenzie who carried a basket of freshly baked rolls. They took their seats, and her mother reached her hands out, signaling the time for grace. Everyone held hands, and her dad bowed his head.

"God, thanks for each one at this table, that they are safe and well—or at least healing." He opened one eye to look at Caitlyn. She smirked. He always caught her with her eyes open. "We're grateful for this house and the food before us. Thank you for my beautiful wife; for Dylan and McKenzie's hard work; for sparing both Caitlyn and Colt's lives last week, and for keeping Logan and Addison safe. Amen." Everyone responded with an amen and promptly dug into the hearty meal.

Caitlyn's mother thoughtfully served both her and Colt plates of food that had already been cut into bite-sized pieces. "This reminds me of being a little kid." Caitlyn grinned and picked up her fork.

Her mother reached for her hand and gave her a squeeze. "You'll always be my little girl, Caitlyn." They shared a loving look that wove warm tendrils of belonging around Caitlyn's heart.

Colt pushed back his chair back and, reaching for his wineglass, stood. "John, I'd like to ask you something."

Her dad reached for his glass, and, joining Colt, rose to his feet. "It's about damn time." He chuckled.

Caitlyn grinned as Colt continued. "I couldn't agree with you more, sir." His Adam's apple bobbed. "I would formally like to ask you for your daughter's hand." Her dad stretched his wineglass across the corner of the table and tapped it against Colt's. "Colt, I've always thought of you as a third son. I'm proud of you and couldn't be more pleased that you and Caitlyn have finally decided to make official what we've all known since you were children. You two are meant to be together, and it's my honor to welcome you officially into this family."

Caitlyn's chest expanded and her heart stirred at the ruddy color creeping up Colt's neck and into his cheeks. She blinked as tears of joy filled her eyes. She knew how much her father's words meant to Colt.

Dylan shoved his chair back and hopped to his feet. He thrust his glass into the air. "Congratulations, you two!"

The table erupted in chatter and laughter, and within minutes, Caitlyn's mom was making plans for the wedding.

"*Mom*," Caitlyn laughed. "We haven't even picked a date yet."

Her mom held her hand. "How about getting married here on the ranch this summer? It's beautiful here in July."

"Mom!" Caitlyn laughed and shook her head. She'd have to be careful, or her mother would take over. A ringtone chimed from her pocket, and Caitlyn looked at the screen. "Excuse me." She glanced at Colt. "I've gotta take this." When she stood, her brain instantly shifted to work mode. Caitlyn crossed the room, away from the noisy celebration. "Deputy US Marshal Reed, here."

"How's that arm feeling?" Dirk Sterling's voice came over the line.

"Still throbs but it's getting better."

"How about Renegade?"

Caitlyn ground her teeth. "It'll be a few weeks."

"Well, hurry up and heal. I got another lead on that drug case. We're meeting with the sheriff in Billings along with representatives from the FBI and ATF tomorrow morning to begin organizing a task force."

"No reason I can't sit in a meeting. I'll be there first thing."

EPILOGUE

Ray stared at the cream swirling around in his coffee. He gripped the warm pottery mug and swallowed resolutely against the grief threatening his resolve. It was bad enough that his partner, Jason, was now in jail, but that bitch marshal killed his baby brother. He'd make her pay for what she did. Ray slammed the mug on the table, and the hot brown liquid sloshed out and splashed over his hand. Recoiling, he stood and knocked his chair over behind him.

"Ray! Are you okay?" Elaine reached for him, but he turned away and stomped out of the dining room at the bed-and-breakfast they were hiding out in.

Ray stalked out the front door and paced the planks of the wooden porch. He lit a cigarette, took one puff, and then squeezed his temples between his thumb and middle finger. How did he get to this place in his life? His little brother was dead, his partner was in lock-up, and the woman he did it all for was making noises about going back home for her daughter. Didn't she understand? Choosing him meant leaving everything behind, including her family. She couldn't have both lives. He had been clear about that but then her son had been killed. That hadn't been part of the plan, and now they were both reeling with grief that made the tough decisions even more difficult to make.

His dreams of starting his own drug empire and living the high life with Elaine by his side were crumbling at the edges. Ray slapped his hand against the porch rail. A curled up tabby cat that had been snoozing on a chair cushion startled awake from Ray's abrupt movements.

"What are you looking at?" Ray scooped the cat up with one hand and threw it over the porch rail. Yowling in loud complaint, the tabby darted for cover under a nearby chokecherry bush.

The door to the house opened, and Elaine stepped out. "Ray, I know you're upset, but you don't have to take it out on the poor cat."

His eyes clashed with hers. "I have a lot on my mind. I thought you understood you were leaving your family behind."

"I did, but then your brother killed my Tom!" she cried. "So much has changed from our original plan. Like Jason kidnapping Tracy. Why did he do that? How could you let those things happen?" Tears streamed down her face as she glared at him.

Ray pulled Elaine into his arms. "I didn't mean for any of that to happen, and I'm sorry. But when your son started shooting, Reggie fired back. What else was he supposed to do?"

"But he was my baby… my only son…" Elaine sobbed into Ray's chest.

"We've both lost loved ones in this mess. It's bad, Elaine. I know. But we have to stick to the rest of the plan. You must choose. It's either Tracy or me. You can't have both. Besides, your daughter will be fine. She's got the ranch. You and me—

we've got our own plans. And we have to be careful. Trova is pissed that the marshals are involved, and we need to lie low till this all cools down."

Elaine blotted her face with a crumpled used tissue. Nodding, she looked up at him with watery eyes. "Where will we go?"

Ray's shoulders relaxed. Maybe she was going to cooperate after all. "Without the jewelry, we don't have much money. I still have my bag of rockeT samples. I need most of it to create a demand, but I suppose I can sell enough to make do. I have kin up in North Dakota we can stay with until we figure out our next step."

"Does Jason know about them? What if he tells the cops where you are?"

"Jason is loyal. He'll never say anything. Not if he wants back in after he does his time." Heat climbed his neck. His anger at the marshal who broke Jason's knee resurfacing. She had a lot to answer for and he relished the thought of making that happen.

"We'll be fine for a month or so." Elaine broke into his thoughts. "I cleaned out my checking account this morning when I left the hospital to come find you, so we have some cash." She reached up and trailed her fingers over his new beard growth. He'd shaven his head and face clean after the jewelry heist, but now, after the mess in Wyoming, he was growing it back.

"You'll need to change your look." He twirled a lock of her naturally blonde hair around his finger and tugged suggestively. "Would you rather be a brunette or a redhead?"

Elaine's eyes sparked. "Which do *you* prefer?"

The energy from his anger and frustration redirected itself into a lustful flame, and he yanked Elaine against his body. "Go with red." He grabbed a handful of hair and pulled her head back so he could kiss her neck. He made his way to her ear and murmured, "They say sex is good for the grieving soul."

She breathed, "Let's go upstairs."

His burner phone buzzed in his pocket. Only one person had this new number. "Go on up and get ready for me. I'll be right there."

Elaine sent him a sad but sultry smile and slid back inside, blowing him a kiss through the screen before she closed the door.

"What?" Ray answered.

"You're in deep shit, asshole. The boss is pissed. He wants you at a meeting in Billings tomorrow morning at nine o'clock sharp."

"I can't go to Billings. US Marshals are crawling all over the place there."

"You'd better figure it out. I wouldn't try to argue with Trova right now. Dealers are a dime a dozen, and you've already screwed up."

"Trova shouldn't show up in Billings either. They'll be watching the airports. See if he'd agree to meet in Missoula or Spokane."

"Listen, Burroughs. Be at the estate outside of Billings tomorrow morning at 9:00 a.m. Make it happen. He's already at the estate, so he doesn't have to worry about airports. I suggest you go up to a town called Roundup and drive down from there. Skip going into the town altogether."

Ray sighed. "Fine. I'll be there." The worst that could happen was he'd get caught and go to prison. But arguing with Trova would get him killed.

Thank you for reading Marshal. I hope you had fun chasing fugitives with United States Deputy Marshal Caitlyn

Reed and Renegade. The next book in the Tin Star K9 Series continues their story as they fight for Justice, Integrity, and Service with the US Marshals Service.

Order Justice Now!

If you enjoyed reading Marshal ~ Book 3 in the Tin Star K9 Series, I would be most honored if you would please write a quick review.

Review Marshal

Thank you!

ALSO BY JODI BURNETT

Flint River Series

Run For The Hills

Hidden In The Hills

Danger In The Hills

A Flint River Christmas (Free Epilogue)

A Flint River Cookbook (Free Book)

FBI-K9 Thriller Series

Baxter K9 Hero (Free Prequel)

Avenging Adam

Body Count

Concealed Cargo

Mile High Mayhem

Tin Star K9 Series

RENEGADE

MAVERICK

MARSHAL

JUSTICE

ACKNOWLEDGMENTS

I was blessed beyond measure during the writing of Marshal to meet some fantastic people at a conference I attended this fall. These people helped inform my final thoughts on the pages of Marshal and gave me much needed encouragement and friendship. Thank you to Lolo Simenson for her energetic friendship and for introducing me to Marc Cameron, author of the Tom Clancy – Jack Ryan novels. As a retired US Deputy Marshal, Marc was beyond generous and kind enough to give me an insider's view of the US Marshals training and graduation ceremony. Thanks also to Patrick O'Donnell of The Cops and Writers Podcast and book series, who invited me to be a guest on his wonderful podcast, and to Adam Richardson of The Writers Detective Bureau Podcast for answering questions regarding correct police procedure. Finally, I must thank my beta-readers all of whom gave invaluable feedback to help shape the final version of this book. That being said, any and all errors in my work come from the use of literary license and are solely mine.

ABOUT THE AUTHOR

Jodi Burnett is a Colorado native and a mountain girl at heart. She loves writing Mystery and Suspense Thrillers from her small ranch southeast of Denver, where she lives with her husband and their two big dogs. There she dotes on her horses, complains about her cows, and writes to create a home for her nefarious imaginings. Burnett is a member of Sisters in Crime and Rocky Mountain Fiction Writers. Connect with Jodi at Jodi-Burnett.com, on Facebook @ Jodi-BurnettAuthor, on Instagram @ JodiBurnettAuthor, or on Twitter @ Jodi_writes. Get free books by Burnett on her website.

Made in United States
Orlando, FL
25 July 2022